# Twilight

by
Nicholas S. Stember

PublishAmerica
Baltimore

© 2003 by Nicholas S. Stember.
All rights reserved. No part of this book may be reproduced, stored in a retrieval system, or transmitted in any form or by any means without the prior written permission of the publishers, except by a reviewer who may quote brief passages in a review to be printed in a newspaper, magazine, or journal.

First printing

ISBN: 1-59286-868-1
PUBLISHED BY PUBLISHAMERICA, LLLP
www.publishamerica.com
Baltimore

Printed in the United States of America

For my wife,
*Eileen*,
who breathed life back into my muse,
and gave me faith in what I create.

## *Prologue*
# Twilight

    The rush of adrenaline was something that always happened to her before an assignment, but even as she darted out of her room and turned towards the main facility, she knew in her heart that this time it was different. Not that it could be explained, but it was there none the less. She ran the mental checklist that would prepare her for any mission, but finding it hard to concentrate she settled for quickening her pace.
    The cool white hallways of the center gleamed around her as she hurried along, bustling past others like her, and their families.
    Many bystanders waved their respective race's greeting as she past them…she was well known in this place, a person of some regard, though she acknowledged that most were only recognizing the armored uniform she wore. A quick smile curved the corners of her full lips as she hurried past the guards, finally entering the Departure Nucleus.
    The chamber's many symmetrical walls formed a vast polyhedron, covered in flashing lights and laser images. She was taken aback by its sheer elegance, a reaction she always had, despite her many years in this place.
    "It took you long enough," came from the lead of two men that stood behind the monitoring station.
    "We're all set here," the other man informed her, as he cheerfully walked up to meet her.
    A wave of warmth filled her as she watched his lithe form approach, and hold out the mission docket. The neon lights reflected softly off his ebony and scarlet body armor, as he waited, standing an easy half foot taller than her.
    "What's the gig?" she asked, trying to conceal the slight trembling in her voice. Then she chastised herself silently, suddenly embarrassed by her fear.

"I'm not sure why, but we're each flying solo this time," he responded carefully, trying to read the tension in her eyes, eyes that he had gazed deeply into on many a happy night. "Mine's a minor situation with some kids…nothing serious, I can see why they only need one of us for it."

She glanced down at the small clear plastic card that he had handed her, and inserted it into the thin slot on the Wrist Control Device on her left arm. Her WCD's screen lit up, revealing to her the orders that she was to follow that day. A cold bead of perspiration formed on her stress-creased forehead; today was the day. But somehow, she'd known it all along, felt it in her guts.

"You okay?" he asked as he placed a firm gauntleted hand on her armored shoulder, his deep blue eyes wrought with concern.

She tentatively bit her bottom lip as she tucked a loose locket of her long hair back into her helmet, then smiled up to him, trying to conceal her apprehension. "Yeah…yeah, I'm fine." The two of them stepped up on the wide, raised pad, and activated their WCDs.

"Take care, guys," the one at the monitoring station said, a look of earnestness replacing the annoyance that had been there earlier. "And Starfox," he added, looking sharply at her as he warmed up the unit, causing the floor beneath them to glow an iridescent blue, "stay alert, you're going right into the heat of it."

"Gotcha, Sender," she responded with a quirky grin on her ruby lips. Then she glanced over at the man standing next to her and winked, trying to ease the obvious concern he was feeling for her. "Ease up, old man," she laughed, "you'll upset yourself."

He laughed in return, feeling a weight lift at the lilting sound of her soft laughter. "Look who you're calling 'old,' you old woman."

"True," she agreed, preferring not to think of her age, which was not as young as she would have liked to remember. "You just stay on your toes, and so will I."

He flashed his own wide grin in return, relaxing slightly at her show of confidence.

"Ready, folks?" the monitor asked again, then threw the power switch when they both nodded their readiness, bathing them in the rising cobalt glow.

Simultaneously, they both touched the flashing emerald buttons on their WCDs, adding their own light to the floor's, instantly turning the chamber into a sparkling melody of brilliant azure illumination.

## Chapter 1
# Phantom

Major Fletcher A. Taylor took in a deep breath as he pulled back on the flight stick of his F15-E Strike Eagle, causing the sleek craft to climb even higher into the crystal blue sky. For a moment it hung there, suspended, a rampant steel god floating in the heavens. The lone star on its wing, in a small field of sapphire, briefly dreamed of joining its cousins out in space. Then the Air Force jet drifted back down, slicing through the clouds like a saber through cotton.

"Come back down to Earth, Phantom," came the annoyed yet cheerful voice behind him, from his co-pilot and best friend. "We still have a job to do."

Grudgingly agreeing, Fletcher continued his descent until they were back at twenty thousand feet, smoothly cruising at slightly over Mach one.

"Hey, Phantom, Jackal," came a much relieved voice over the mike in his helmet, "nice of you guys to rejoin us down here. It's not like you're our wingleader or anything important like that."

"Smart ass," burned the voice from behind.

But all Fletcher allowed himself was a slow grin, as he swallowed most of what his hot headed co-pilot could never let pass.

"Temper, temper," returned the playful voice from the sister F-15E that rose from below them, to match their altitude and speed.

"You know what you can do with your temper?"

"Cool it, Con," Fletcher instructed his co-pilot as he deactivated his mike with a flick of his finger. "Just let it ride."

"Fine," Captain Conrad Striker grumbled in congruence. "But I just hope that they need our help today. If there's a God in heaven…they'll need our help."

*I know you don't mean that, buddy,* Fletcher thought as his smile turned into a grin. *If it really came down to a dogfight out here, you'd give the very blood out of your body to save a fellow pilot's life. I should know, you once did that for me, and we had been little better than strangers back then, on our first mission together as co-pilots.*

The Air Force major shook his head, as he returned his concentration fully to the mission at hand, his fiery blue eyes studying the electronic readouts. *Enough of the past, time to take care of our futures.* "How far to primary target?"

Con's anger faded like a fog bank in a strong gale, as he flipped some switches, zeroing in on the mobile scud platform that they were to take out today. "Um, we're just over two hundred out, and behind schedule. We might want to step it up to Mach two."

Fletcher nodded and turned on his mike again, as he glanced over at his two companions in the jet that was hovering off his left wing. "This is Phantom calling Warlock. You think you can stir us up some magic to get us to our targets on time?"

He watched as the lead pilot of the sister plane shook his head and gave the thumbs down gesture.

"Sorry, Phantom," came the saddened response. "I'm totally dry on magic resources today."

"He didn't get a balanced breakfast this morning," added Warlock's co-pilot with a laugh.

"Then I suggest we get a move on it," Con advised.

"Sounds good to me," confirmed Warlock. "Stepping up to Mach two."

"We're with you," Fletcher assured, as he nudged the accelerator.

The twin F110 engines of both aircraft flared a sun yellow as the jets surged forward, adamantly continuing on their mission. Long trails of cable thin smoke were left behind, the only marker to a ground observer that these twin arrows of death raced overhead.

"So far, so good," Con spoke confidently into his mike. "We still haven't been tracked by any SAMs yet."

"Let's just keep it that way," Fletcher responded earnestly. "I have no desire for any Surface to Air Missile gift packages to come our way today."

"Hear, hear," came from their sister jet.

"Let's cool it on the radio talk," Fletcher suggested. "Were leaving Saudi air space now, and are well within tracking range."

"Gotcha, Phantom," Warlock accented. "We're following your lead…just don't take us on another sightseeing tour again."

Despite the situation, Fletcher found it hard not to chuckle. These were good men, all of them, especially his co-pilot and best friend. He sighed internally as the thought forced him to the gravity of the situation at hand. *Damn,* his mind raced sardonically, *two years ago, the only combat missions I had to worry about were my weekly Jujitsu matches on the air base back in the States. But now, only a month into this war...no, strike that, 'political situation' is what they're still calling it, we've flown in over eighteen combat missions. Lacing napalm and dropping Mavericks on targets that two years ago I barely knew existed.*

"Hey, Fletcher," came a concerned voice from behind, "you all right?"

"Sure," he responded, quickly forcing the cheerless thoughts out of his head, "why?"

"You're not usually this quiet on a mission," his friend laughed, trying to lighten the obviously dark mood that surrounded his co-pilot. "How about some tunes?"

"Do you ever think about it?" Fletcher asked pensively, suddenly wondering if his thoughts were reflected in the man behind him.

"About what?"

"The people down there."

"The Saudis?"

"No," he responded curtly, wondering if his partner was purposely being dense, "the people that we're going to waste today."

A long moment of silence hung in the small cockpit, disturbed only by the roar of the twin General Electric engines that filled their ears.

Suddenly, a warning beep shattered their thoughts as the radar tracking system informed them of two incoming projectiles.

"What the hell?" shouted Con as he tried to pinpoint their location. "We've got two bogeys coming in, but my system is all fouled up, I can't get a bearing. Some sort of jammer."

"Talk to me, Jackal," Fletcher called back, as he pulled sharply on the flight stick, going into evasive maneuvers. Then he tapped his mike. "Warlock, we've got—"

"I know, I know," came the frantic voice back over the line. "But where are they?"

"I don't know," Fletcher admitted as he banked back the other way, pulling the sleek F-15E into a counter spin. "Engage defensive devices: drop Chaffs and Flares," he ordered his wingman. "Let's see if we can throw these bastards off."

"Gotcha—"

An explosion cut off the end trail of Warlock's response as the unseen missile sliced his jet in half.

"*Warlock,*" Fletcher called despondently, as he pulled the F-15E into a vertical climb, hoping to out distance what ever had taken out his wingman. The steady drone of the alert warnings continued to harass his ears with its persistent wail.

"What the hell was that?" Con yelled frantically. "Where did it come from?"

"Shut up, Captain," Fletcher ordered harshly, "and get me a fix on that missile." He dropped another decoy, hoping to foul up whatever tracking method the lethal seeker was using on them.

"I still can't see it," Con responded, as he abandoned the nonsensical readings on his radar and went for a visual attempt, but the skies seemed clear. Then he saw it behind, a bright, white hot point of light trailing a long stream of smoke. "Right behind us," he yelled.

Not waiting to think, Fletcher pulled the flight stick to the side, dropping another flare as he did so; hoping that since Chaffs weren't disrupting any radar tracking the missile used, the flare should kill its heat seeking abilities, if that's what it used.

The silver jet banked sharply to the right, pulling out of the vertical climb...but not fast enough, as the projectile finally found its target and clipped the F-15E's left wing, slicing it off in a shower of sparks. The explosion rocked the cockpit as fires erupted and smoke filled the confined area.

The Air Force major pulled his oxygen mask off and called behind him, as he pounded on the button that was no longer working. "Con," he called, desperately, "can you reach the manual eject? Mine's busted."

No answer came from behind as he fought the nausea that threatened to consume him, as the fatally wounded craft spun wildly out of control, plummeting downward.

"*Con!*"

He struggled against the pounding inertia as he forced himself to look behind him to see why Con wasn't responding. He finally caught a glimpse of his friend, leaning against the cockpit canopy as blood poured out of a crack in his helmet.

Fletcher sank back into his chair and fought back the sudden sting in his eyes, as he called out again, knowing this time that there wasn't going to be an answer. "*Con!*"

Then he took a deep breath, they were already closing on ten thousand feet and he realized that in another few seconds it wouldn't make any difference if he ejected or not. Gathering up the last of his strength, he pulled at his harness and turned around, determined to reach the manual eject on his own—and froze in astonishment. There was someone else in the cockpit with them, a person crouched over Con, checking his pulse. The intruder was dressed in black, with a flight style helmet and visor on, similar to his.

Then the stranger turned to him, and he gazed into her eyes, impossibly magnificent jade green eyes that pierced from under the few strands of red hair that hung out from her ebony helmet.

"He's dead," she called, her calm voice slicing through the howl of wind that whistled between cracks in the canopy, and the roar of the dying engines.

Finally finding his voice, all he could do was look back at the man who had been the only person he'd ever called best friend. "I know."

"We've got to go now," she urged as she took his hand, her black gauntlet grabbing his flight suit.

"Go?" he yelled through the noise, his faculties slowly returning. "Go where? Who the *hell* are you?"

"No time to explain," she informed him as an adorable quirky smile flashed across her lips, "just hold on tight."

Falling into the softness of those words, Fletcher had to fight for consciousness, as the pain in his head hammered away. "I don't understand."

"You will," she responded, her voice calming him like a cool breeze on a hot summer day. "Just hold on to me."

He grabbed her arm, as she touched a few buttons on some device on her left wrist, then glanced back up, her eyes suddenly sparkling shyly at him, touching him deeply inside. "Here we go."

He wanted to ask her just where she thought that she was going again, but his words were killed by an impossibly blinding azure light that filled the small cockpit, and surrounded him like tingling electrical sparks.

All he could do was close his eyes, and keep thinking to himself, *I've got to hold on*…as he finally slipped into blackness.

## Chapter 2
# Arrival

There were long moments when Fletcher thought he was awake, followed by more moments when he was sure he was still sleeping, followed by the inevitable moments when he knew he was dead. Light finally pierced into his darkened world, forcing a sense of reality into his turbulent dreams. His eyes fluttered open as the brightness caused him to wince.

"He's awake, Doctor," a disembodied man's voice proclaimed.

"Prepare twelve CCs of stimulant," a woman responded in a stark, professional voice.

Fletcher was finally able to focus, as the doctor and her assistant were accepted into his reality. Running his hand through his short blonde hair, he tried to ignore the pounding headache that was thundering inside his head. He glanced around slowly, as his muscles tightened in painful spasms. The room was lit by blue neon filaments that encircled the edges where stark white wall met even starker white ceiling, and a bright white glow that emanated from the luminous floor. "If this is heaven," he half groaned, "it must be run by George Lucas."

The doctor appraised her new patient with her gentle mahogany eyes and smiled, admiring his tight, muscular frame. "This must seem strange to you, Major Taylor. But let me assure you that you are in no danger." Then she let out a soft laugh. "And this isn't heaven."

Fletcher studied the doctor for a moment, relaxing at her gentle manner and seemingly forthright attitude. "All that we see or seem, is but a dream within a dream."

"What?" the assistant asked.

"Edgar Allen Poe," the Air Force pilot laughed. "I guess it seemed appropriate to the setting."

"I think we gave him too much stimulant," the assistant said with a look of concern.

"Can you sit up?" the doctor asked.

He slowly sat up, wincing at the strain in his muscles. "I haven't felt this stiff since the Air Force Academy."

"A natural reaction to the skimming," she explained. "That's why no one ever does it without wearing the body armor."

"The what?"

"Skimming," she replied. "That's how you got here."

"Which brings me back to a really important question," he said with a half smile. "Where's here?"

The doctor looked over at her assistant, who shook his head thoughtfully. Then she went to a tray and brought back a glass of blue liquid. "Drink this; it will make you feel better."

Fletcher stared at the fluid with mild distaste. "It looks like Kool-Aid."

"Is that a medical drink?" the doctor asked.

The major glanced up at her, trying to judge if she was teasing him or not and quickly read the sincerity in her eyes. "What did you say your name was?"

"I'm Doctor Paula Kesseler," she said then motioned to her assistant. "And this is Skimmer Med Tech Eric Van Winder."

Eric gave a curt smile with a nod.

"Charmed," Fletcher responded with a grin. "Since you already seem to know *who* I am, maybe you can answer my question of *where* I am?"

"That's up to Justin," the doctor informed him, as she offered the blue drink again.

"And when do I meet this Justin person?" he said as he took a sip. Instantly he felt the liquid surge through his system like a bolt of electricity. His aches and pains faded in a flash, leaving his headache a mere memory. "Fantastic!"

"It does the job," Eric commented stoically, as he took the glass from the major.

"As for when you meet Justin," Paula informed him, "he's most anxious to do that. If you're ready, Eric will take you there now."

Fletcher took in a deep breath. "I'm ready now."

The two of them left the medical section and entered a wide hallway, lit like the room that they had left behind. Fletcher could not help but gaze about in wonder at the splendor of the complex that he was in. They left the hallway behind, which opened out into a giant multilevel enclosed gallery.

All around him were people milling about, dressed in exotic clothes that put old B-movies to shame. The large hall was easily two football stadiums across, opening up to many levels above which circled the gallery in tiers.

"Does this place have a name?" Fletcher asked, hoping to gain some information from the quiet medical technician.

Eric nodded silently as he continued to lead his guest across the arcade, through the throng of people.

The major stared at the med tech for an instant, realizing that getting a straight answer from him was like trying to siphon a gas tank with a straw. "And that name is?"

Eric glanced over at Fletcher and seemed to study him judgmentally for a moment. "It's called *Twilight*."

"That's a strange name."

"*Twilight* is a strange place." Eric gazed across the roof of the main room, easily thirty stories above them, seemingly satisfied that he had given all the information that was necessary.

The major glanced over at a group talking nearby, suddenly realizing that they were not at all human. Their tall feline ears and fur coats of varying colors struck his mind as surely as did their long swaying tails. A wide sweep of the gallery exposed the fact that there were more than a few people there that were not human, of so many varieties that his head swam. He tugged at Eric's sleeve as they walked along, trying to decide how to ask a question that any sane man would consider verging on insanity. "They aren't human," he finally asked as he pointed at the felinoids, "are they?"

The med tech stared at Fletcher for a moment, then nodded thoughtfully. "You're from pre twenty-second century Earth, right," he commented rhetorically. "Yes, they're not human. Don't be so small minded, *Twilight* isn't just here for us humans."

Fletcher remained silent, suddenly deciding to hold any other questions until he had met this Justin person, as he continued to gape at the many different people that swarmed throughout the busy complex.

"Welcome to *Twilight*," the thin, auburn-haired man said with a warm smile that lit up his soft hazel eyes.

Fletcher walked into the lush office cautiously as he glanced around at the luxurious accommodations. Then his attention returned to the man that had been introduced to him as Justin, who although lacking in physical stature, more than made up for that in sheer presence. "Thanks, I think." Then he took in a deep breath, deciding it was time to stop playing games. "Look, I want a few questions answered—"

"I understand," Justin cut in softly. "If I was in your situation I'm sure I would feel the same. Let's handle this in the proper order though. Your name is Fletcher A. Taylor, a major in the United States Air Force. Your age is thirty-five, you are five foot eleven inches tall, you weigh—"

"Thanks for the short biography," Fletcher cut in, annoyance creeping into his voice. "It's plain that everyone here knows everything about me."

"Including that you died in a plane explosion, five thousand feet over the Middle Eastern dessert sands."

"So now you're telling me that I'm dead?" Fletcher asked, his confusion compounding.

"Do you feel dead?" Justin asked, his smile never wavering.

The major shook his head slowly.

"Then most likely you aren't. You were pulled out mere seconds before your death by one of our specialists and brought here."

For an instant Fletcher found himself thinking about his savior, and momentarily forgot himself in the memory of her jade eyes.

"So here you are," Justin continued. "And as I said before, welcome to *Twilight*."

"Just what the hell is *Twilight*?" the major asked, snapping back to reality.

Justin seemed to contemplate the question for an instant as he sat down and motioned for Fletcher to do the same. Once the major had taken a seat opposite the desk, he let out a soft breath that turned into a thoughtful grin. "That's a very good question, Major," he admitted, "one that I've never really found an answer to. It's here, and it's nowhere...lost somewhere between fantasy and reality."

"That makes no sense."

Justin laughed, a short chuckle that set the room at ease with its earnest warmth. "To tell the truth, neither does *Twilight*. But you are here, as are we all."

Suddenly Fletcher remembered the aliens in the gallery. "Are we on Earth?"

"Another good question," Justin said with a smile. "Again, though, there is no set answer for that." He nodded at the med tech, who quietly walked out the door. "I call it *nowhen*."

"Nowhen?"

"As apposed to nowhere." The *Twilight* leader chuckled sympathetically at the puzzled expression on the major's face. "I know it sounds confusing. When I discovered what we refer to as *Twilight Space*, and realized that I could build a hidden complex within that strange dimension, I didn't ask too many questions; too many questions can spoil the dream."

"You discovered this place? How?"

"The idea of time travel has always been a favorite subject of many races throughout the galaxy. I suppose that it simply occurred to me that there must be somewhere that people go when traveling through time, on their way from point A to point B…and this is it. We don't exist in any time frame here, since there really isn't any around us. We experience time passage within the *Twilight* complex because of its powerful shielding, but outside these walls lies a void where time doesn't exist. Like I said…nowhen."

"And I'm supposed to believe that?" Fletcher asked with a forced laugh.

"Believe what you want to, Major," Justin responded. "However, there's no denying that you are here."

Fletcher rubbed his face in his hands and took in a deep breath. "So I'm here, now what?"

"That's mostly up to you," Justin said lightly, the cheer returning to his voice. "We do important work here, and I'm hoping that you'll want to join the team."

"What about all those people out there," Fletcher asked, his thoughts suddenly straying. "Who are they all?"

"A small number of them are just like you," Justin's voice grew serious. "People who were at the wrong place at the wrong time: a train before a crash, a burning building, a starship collision, all brought here to live out their lives. The rest are made up of their families, and the families of the many technicians and workers who keep this place running."

"Brought here by those people in black armor?"

"What you're referring to are our Twilight Skimmers," Justin responded, his voice full of cheer again. "They're the elite that I told you about, the team that I want you to join."

Fletcher gazed intently at the thinly built man, trying to judge his sanity. "So these Twilight Skimmers run around saving people that were supposed to die?"

"No, not really," Justin admitted. "Saving the doomed from their fate is a tricky thing…we've made many mistakes in the past, and now we only do it when we're absolutely certain, and need to recruit more Twilight Skimmers. Mostly what our Skimmers do is prevent injustices that don't have a great historical impact, but will significantly help a life out. Such as stopping a mugging from happening, or rescuing a woman from a would-be rapist."

Fletcher glared at him flatly. "Doesn't that make you the time police?"

Justin let out another laugh. "I suppose you could look at it that way."

"But I still don't understand," Fletcher's voice rose a bit. "Why save me and let Con die, or even my wingmen? Why didn't you save them all? You knew that they were going to die."

"As I told you, time skimming is a dangerous thing," Justin tried to explain. "The past is not as concrete, black and white, as most people think. Every event in your life, every decision that you make, creates a multitude of possible realities that could affect any given action we thought would happen. So in truth, we didn't know for sure that you were going to die until the missile hit your jet. Unfortunately, by then your friends were already dead."

Fletcher shook his head in disbelief. "So how can you prevent a crime before it happens in that case?"

"We don't," Justin admitted. "What we do is predict how an event will turn out and have our Twilight Skimmers standing ready to act." Justin's smile faded again. "I won't kid you, it's a very dangerous job, and we *have* lost Skimmers once or twice before. But every piece of injustice that we prevent helps a little, sometimes far more than we could ever imagine."

Fletcher caught himself dwelling on his best friend, Con. *How he would have loved all this,* he thought with a silent laugh. "What if I say no? What if I want to leave?"

Justin shook his head. "You can live out your life here in *Twilight* as a civilian or a tech if you wish, but you can never leave."

"But what's to stop me from training to be one of these Skimmers and then staying somewhere in the past?"

"Everyone needs a home, Fletcher," Justin tried to explain. "You don't belong back there, and you'll understand that better later on. There have been Skimmers who wanted to stay in the past, but they've always come back home." Justin let his smile return, then stood up. "What do you say, Major? Have I got myself a new Skimmer?"

Fletcher remained silent for what seemed to him to be an eternity. He still felt that he had no idea of where he was, but there was something fantastic about this place, and he knew that he needed to learn more. But there was more, he felt an affinity towards the *Twilight* leader that he couldn't explain, and he knew that he trusted him. Underneath it all, was his plain stubbornness which refused to be beaten by this strange turn in events. "Fine, you've got yourself a new Skimmer."

"Great," Justin beamed. "You'll start your training tomorrow, right now I'm sure that you could use some rest. The Skimmers all go by call signs, but I'm sure that you're familiar with that since you were a fighter pilot."

Fletcher found himself recalling the woman that had pulled him out of the cockpit again, as a smile came to his lips. "Phantom," he finally said in a soft but firm voice, "my call sign was Phantom."

"Very well, Phantom," Justin laughed. "You don't know how pleased I am that you decided to join the team."

"You're right," Fletcher agreed carefully, as he got up from the chair, "I don't. But I'm damn well sure that I will know that someday."

As is by some unseen signal, Eric walked back into the room and waited patiently by the doorway.

"Major Taylor has decided to join us, Eric," Justin informed the med tech. "I'm logging him into classes for tomorrow as Twilight Skimmer Phantom. Please show him his new accommodations and help him get settled."

"Yes, sir," Eric responded as he motioned for Fletcher to follow him. "This way, Phantom."

Fletcher glanced back at Justin, who gave him a parting smile and returned to work. Then he shrugged his shoulders and followed the med tech out the door back into the hallway.

"I'm pleased that you're part of the team now," Eric told him with a smile, as they reentered the large gallery area and crossed to another section of the huge complex. "I'm one of the main techies that help keep you Skimmers going."

Surprised at the show of emotion from this before hand stoic young man, Fletcher studied him as the walked along. "You didn't seem to give a squat about me before, why do you care now?"

"Because you're one of us now," he responded with a boyish grin. "You don't know how many come to us and freak out, or shrink into a hole, or plain refuse to accept what happened to them. I try not to care about any new arrivals until I know how it's going to go down."

Fletcher nodded thoughtfully, noting the young man's language usage. "I suppose that makes sense." Then he glanced around at the new hallway that they were in, still awed by the grandeur of the complex. "So the Skimmers go by call signs, huh?"

Eric nodded. "The Twilight Skimmers ride the time waves even harder than you flew your jet back in your time. The call signs keep them all together, kind of like a family."

"What about that red head that brought me here," Fletcher suddenly asked, hoping to learn more of her. "What's her call sign?"

A slightly confused look crossed Eric's face, then he shook his head. "I didn't recognize her when she brought you in, but since she Skimmed right back out again I would guess that she's from a different time."

"I don't understand."

"Sometimes Skimmers are told to bring people to a different time in *Twilight's* history, especially if there was a big need, and there was."

"What do you mean?"

"We lost three Skimmers last month due to a horrible accident in the past. It doesn't happen often, but it happens. We were starting to do research to find some replacements when you arrived. It's possible that a future Justin sent a Skimmer to get you and drop you off here where you're needed more."

The ideas that were being presented to him seemed mind boggling, so Fletcher decided to concentrate on assimilating for now, and hope to meet the red-haired woman with the fantastic jade eyes another time. They walked along in silence for awhile, as he absorbed the surroundings. Then they entered a section that was labeled *Time Skimmer Control*. This section seemed even more high tech and fantastic than what they had left behind. They passed by a large room with many controls and a flat platform in the center that was illuminated from the floor in bright neon blue.

"What's that?" Fletcher asked as they paused at the room.

"That's the Twilight Skimmer's launching pad," Eric informed him. "It's from here that they travel to the past. We call it the Departure Nucleus."

"You say past," the major asked, "but I thought that *Twilight* was timeless."

"Technically it is," Eric admitted. "But we in *Twilight* judge time by the farthest along in time that any of our citizens came from. And we have people here that date from Earth's twenty-fourth century."

"I see." Fletcher shook his head in wonder as he gazed at the luminous platform. Then he turned back to the med tech, indicating his readiness to move on.

They walked on in silence as they left the section that they were in, passing a few people in black and red armor that milled about their business. Fletcher studied them, remembering the one that brought him here.

"So those are the Twilight Skimmers," he commented half to himself as they entered a long corridor flanked by many numbered doors.

Eric nodded as they came to a doorway and paused in front of it. "These are your quarters, Phantom," he told him while opening the door.

Fletcher looked inside, instantly pleased by the luxury of what he would have called a condo back home. It had a large bedroom, as well as a lounging area and a private bath. He scoped it out from wall to wall, then turned back to the med tech. "Do all the Skimmers live like this?"

Eric nodded. "One of the privileges of the elite, I guess. There is a cafeteria down the hall, and a bar lounge up on the observation level, and if you're worrying about money, don't, everything here is on a work-for-your-food basis."

Suddenly Fletcher realized that it had been hours since he last ate. "Well, that seems like a fair system," he said with a grin. "Show me the way."

## Chapter 3
# Tactics

It was early the next day when Eric dragged Fletcher out of bed to attend his first Skimmer training class.

"Don't Skimmers need to get their rest?" he groaned while stumbling towards the shower and stepping in.

"*Skimmers*, yes," Eric responded with a grin, "trainees, no." He tossed a fresh towel into the bathroom as the major pulled himself out of the refreshing water. "Come on, you don't want to be late your first day, do you?"

Fletcher glared at the young med tech under his eyebrows as he pulled on the ebony trainees' jumpsuit. "It's been years since I was in the academy. And I was glad to put all that behind me."

"Haven't you ever trained for a new type of jet that has been released?"

"I trained for months on the space shuttle," Fletcher admitted, "but the mission got scrubbed due to budget cuts."

"Well," Eric said thoughtfully, "this is sort of like that, only more relaxed."

The two of them walked past the cafeteria, where they retrieved some coffee and rolls. Then they arrived at a small lecture hall, set up in semi circles of chairs around a podium.

Fletcher glanced at the others who were dressed in their black jumpers, all younger than himself, and let out an audible sigh. "I always hated school," he commented under his breath.

"You probably never gave it a proper chance," came the soft and sunny voice from behind him.

The major turned to find himself lost in those magnificent jade green eyes, causing his breath to fade from his mind. His lips hung open as he held her glance, caught in a numbing trance that he prayed would never be broken.

"You're standing in the doorway," the young woman said with a lovely smile as she turned her head to the side, allowing her long silken hair to cascade down her shoulders in waves of sunlit fire. She glanced deeply into his blue eyes and smiled again, seemingly amused. "The doorway," she reminded him, "you're blocking it."

When he had been told that the angel who had brought him here was not known, he had been devastated. Yet as he beheld her once again, he knew the reason that he had cast away all sanity and had placed his trust in her back in the crippled jet. "You're the one," he finally found his voice, though it was hoarse from lack of breathing.

"The one?" she asked, her delicate russet eyebrows lifting in surprise.

"The one who brought me here," he persisted, wondering how she could have forgotten so soon.

Her soft green eyes searched his face silently for a moment, as she cocked her oval face to the side in concentration. "There *is* something familiar about you," she admitted, "but I certainly didn't bring you here."

Eric's own eyes widened at the conversation as he reached over and grabbed the major's arm, pulling him away from the doorway. The lithe woman gave Fletcher another puzzled smile, then moved to a chair near the front and sat down, seeming to recognize some of the other students.

"What do think you were doing?" he demanded while shaking off Eric's grasp.

"Keeping you from making a fool of yourself," the med tech informed him in a sotto voice. "She obviously doesn't know you."

"But how's that possible?" Fletcher asked as his eyes never left the silken ivory skin that gently flowed like milk from under her deep red waves. "She's the one who saved me, I'm positive of it."

"Are you?" Eric asked, hoping to quiet the major. "Are you really?"

Doubt crossed Fletcher's mind briefly, and he wondered if he was seeing things. "I...I guess so. I don't really know. The Skimmer who brought me here...well, her eyes seemed less...naïve...older, I guess."

Eric shook his head, as if dealing with a child learning to walk. "These things clear themselves up with time. Now take a seat and learn something."

Fletcher nodded absently as he chose a seat near the exit, never taking his eyes off the young woman. Then the general talk in the classroom died as Justin entered the room and approached the podium. The major searched for Eric, but the med tech had already left the room.

"I want to welcome you all to Twilight Skimmer training," Justin began in his usual light tone. "Although some of you started here yesterday, there are a few new faces that should be pointed out."

Fletcher lost Justin's voice as his attention returned to the red-haired beauty six rows in front of him. Why would he look familiar to her, he wondered, if she wasn't the one who rescued him? Every little move she made entranced him, even though he could not explain why. From the tiny twist of her smooth shoulders to the light spring in her sunfire red hair as she gently pulled at one of the waves. So absorbed was he that he barely heard his name called the second time.

"*Phantom*," Justin raised his voice a bit to draw the attention he desired. When Fletcher's head snapped in his direction he let out an almost knowing smile. "Fletcher Taylor is another recent comer to *Twilight*, and has joined our team. His call sign is Phantom." He gave the major a reassuring nod then turned to the center of Fletcher's preoccupation. "Carridan Whitney has been here for quite some time, but is beginning her Skimmer training today. Her call sign is Starfox."

Fletcher smiled at the sound of her name, and felt his grin grow at the light flush that came to her ears at the mentioning of her name. He somehow felt closer to her now, even thought they still had not really met.

"Please make our new students feel welcome," Justin continued. "After all, they could be the ones that save your life one day."

One of the problems that Fletcher knew he had in life was the all too easy way he could fixate on something, shutting everything else out. Such was the case with Carridan Whitney. As his eyes drifted over the contours of her neck, he vaguely realized that Justin was continuing with the introductions. It was only when he heard mention of *Twilight's* creation that he managed to snap himself back to hear what was going on.

"So then," one of the trainees asked, "*Twilight* is just floating here? But isn't that impossible?"

Justin smiled the smile of a teacher who has had to explain the impossible many times. "No, not really. I had the entire *Twilight* complex built on Earth in the late twenty-fourth century, then propelled it into Twilight Space with huge time traveling generators."

"Is time travel that common there?"

An almost sad look covered his face for a moment, then he shook his head. "No, we are the only users of time travel that I know of. That is why I placed *Twilight* here, so no one could ever get hold of its massive power."

Fletcher nodded silently, for what he said made sense, but that didn't explain the hows or whys to him in the least.

"I always feel that the best place to start is here," Justin said, as he turned to a screen behind him, where an image appeared of the main control center of *Twilight*. "It is here that the Omni computer works twenty-four hours a day, using its three hundred micro-Cray chips to calculate all the time streams that are constantly flowing around the outside of *Twilight*. You see, outside these walls, in Twilight Space, there is no time definition at all. Outside could be Earth at fifteen hundred, or five hundred BC, or any other world at any time; it all depends on which time stream you travel along. The Omni computer's entire function all day is to scan these time waves, computing all the odds and probabilities as the various time streams flow past *Twilight*. What you think is a clear cut event in history is, in fact, happening right this moment outside this complex, and the computer lets us know when an opportunity is arising to correct a 'situation'."

Carridan raised her hand.

"Yes, Starfox?"

"If the time streams are flying past *Twilight*, and the computer doesn't realize a 'situation' is happening until it sees this time stream, how does a Skimmer have time…?" She lost her question as the right words failed her.

"Time to get to that moment in time?" Justin finished for her.

She nodded gratefully.

"The actual time to affect any moment in history is only a fifteen minute window. If the window is missed, so is the opportunity to help that 'situation'. And the opportunity may never come by again."

All the students seemed amazed, and a low murmur sifted through the trainees.

"So how can you decide what to help with and what not to?" another student asked.

"That's another function of the Omni computer," Justin informed him. "The computer also runs each world's history constantly through its data bases, and informs us of moments when time anomalies seem to have occurred which would bear investigation, if we get the opportunity. It's not that we have no control of our time travel, we do. There are so many time streams going past this place at once, that we can almost always choose roughly where and when we want to go somewhere. It's those special 'situations', those specific time anomalies that we want to fix, that are fleeting and we must catch when we have the opportunity."

"So you had no choice of when to come and get me?" Fletcher asked without waiting to be called upon.

Everyone looked back at him, and he felt her eyes on him. A tingling sensation crept through his gut, and for a moment he feared that he was actually blushing.

"Actually," Justin answered with a smile, drawing the students' attention back to him. "We have not gotten that opportunity yet. A Skimmer from the future of *Twilight* had, or should I say, will have, that opportunity, and brought you here instead, where you were obviously needed more. But even now, we knew that your jet was destroyed, and were planning for a moment when you might be retrieved."

"How long from now was, or will be, the opportunity to get me?"

"If I knew that," Justin said with a glint in his soft hazel eyes, "I could tell the future."

A warm laughter flowed through the trainees, and even Fletcher chuckled at the almost absurdity of the situation. His admiration grew for the *Twilight* founder, to manage all this must be an amazing thing, and he barely looked ten years older than himself. It was then that he took a long look at the other students and shook his head, realizing that he was more than ten years older than all of them as well. How Justin intended to turn these kids into skilled time travelers was beyond him. But then again, he reminded himself, was he any different when he came out of the academy? Then his gaze returned to the object of his earlier attention, and he really looked at her. She was magnificent, but clearly only in her mid-twenties. Was it possible that she wasn't the one who rescued him? Or was it as simple as that she hadn't rescued him yet? He tried to comprehend the complexities of considering the future the past, especially where his rescue was concerned, and found the mixture of tenses baffling to the point of giving him a headache, so he turned his attention back to the *Twilight* founder to find him answering another question.

"Actually, Tsunami," he said to a young Asian woman in her late teens, early twenties, "I've lived both here and the late twenty-fourth century. It was there that this station was built."

"But that isn't possible," she countered. "How would you know where this station was even going to be located?"

He smiled knowingly, then laughed a soft chuckle that set the whole room at ease, as his presence covered them like a blanket. "I told myself. Actually the old me who was running *Twilight* told the younger me all I needed to know."

This caused more than a few gaping mouths, including Fletcher's.

"As a matter of fact, don't ever be too surprised to see yourself here in

*Twilight*. Although quite rare, sometimes Skimmers have to travel to different times here in the complex itself." Then his face grew dark, as if a shadow had crossed into the room. "But you must *never* meet yourself outside the protective walls of *Twilight*. This is why you will never be sent to any time or place where you might have been."

"Why?" came the inevitable question.

"Outside *Twilight*, there is no protection from time paradoxes. If two of you meet, the barriers of time that surround you will begin to collapse. After a few seconds, the younger of you will vanish into thin air."

"What about the older one?" Fletcher found himself asking. "If the younger one vanishes, then wouldn't the older one vanish as well, since he or she couldn't have gone to *Twilight*?"

"Well, yes…and no," was the slow response. "Since the younger one of you vanishes, and doesn't come here, that means that the older version would never have had the chance of going back in time in the first place. So when the younger one vanishes, leaving the older one, a lot of your life could get lost, especially if you were to meet yourself when you were five, for instance."

This caused more than a few of the students to start squirming uneasily.

"Unless you precisely repeated the steps that got you here in the first place, you will never have come. Fortunately, since *Twilight* doesn't exist in the normal time frame, it would take some time for us to lose all records of you, maybe a month or two of our time here, but eventually it would happen, and we would forget that you ever even existed with us."

"How can you just forget someone exists?" Carridan asked, her voice like a sad whisper.

"I don't know," Justin admitted, "since I don't remember it ever having happened. However, the Omni computer estimates that there is a seventeen percent likelihood that it has happened to us in the past, and we just don't remember it."

Everyone was silent for a few moments, as Justin allowed the implications of what he had said sink in. Then his face melted back into a smile, as he changed the image behind him to a list of rules and regulations.

"Just like back where you came from," the *Twilight* leader said with a firm tone that gently flowed over the students with its underlying softness, "there are rules and regulations that we have to follow here, but none are more important than the rules followed by Skimmers while on assignment. They are more of what you can't do rules, as opposed to what you can do rules."

Fletcher's eyes drifted to the screen, making mental note of the rules that seemed to make perfect sense.

"Consider these rules your prime directives when away from here," Justin said with a smile. "Just like with the crew of the *Enterprise*."

The major let out a short laugh, but noted that he was one of the few that made the connection desired.

The *Twilight* leader let out a soft sigh, then gestured to the screen.

"First of all," he started, "Skimmers can't interfere with anything that they weren't sent back to do. For example, if you are sent back to New York in twenty-twenty five to help someone, don't take it upon yourselves to get involved in the Red Monday riot that happened that year. Or if you find yourself in Florida in nineteen eighty-five, don't go trying to warn NASA about the space shuttle *Challenger* disaster."

"Why not?" Tsunami asked, reflecting the mood felt by all the trainees.

"Let me go over all the rules first," the *Twilight* leader answered, "then I'll get to questions. Second, Skimmers sent back in time can not interfere with their own lives. So no giving yourself or loved ones winning lottery numbers or anything like that. Third, and most important, Skimmers can't kill anyone, or by action cause someone to be killed. You can kill by inaction, however, because that is obeying the natural time flow."

A low murmur swept through the class like a wave washing in, and Fletcher found himself once again thinking of Con. What would the harm really be of going back to save him, or the other two pilots that died that day? He looked up to find the *Twilight* leader staring straight at him, seemingly ignoring the other students.

"You are thinking of your comrades," Justin said softly, then glanced around the room, "as is the same for many of you." He stepped out from behind the podium and sat in one of the chairs in the first row, facing the students. His face remained calm, but his eyes betrayed the concern he felt for this extended family of his. "When we send a Skimmer back in time to change history, every possible variable is checked to make sure that the time stream won't be changed for anyone but the target...However, if a Skimmer saved someone from dying and allowed them to continue their lives, the computer can't possibly predict what any future offspring might do or not do, and how it will then change the time stream."

"We could bring them here," Starfox half whispered.

Justin nodded. "Sure, that would seem the logical answer, wouldn't it?" He waited as they all glanced at each other nervously. "You all know how you got here, you all know that we didn't pull you out until your death was imminent... This is very, very hazardous to the Skimmer going in. The chance of success is not high, but the chance of the Skimmer getting injured or killed is. I won't risk one life for another except in dire need. Besides," he said with a warming laugh that eased the tension that covered the room like a burlap tarp, "we aren't that big here, and we already have to control population with the families that we have."

The trainees stopped searching the faces of their friends and began searching inside, each remembering the torrential events that led to their arrival here, and the death-defying acts the Skimmers who had saved them had performed.

Justin watched this transformation quietly with a soft smile on his face. "You're thinking about the Skimmers who risked their lives so that you could be here, and that's good. Because one day you might have to do the same. But I will never put you in that situation without imperative need, and your consent. The regular skims that you will do will be dangerous enough without tempting fate."

It was not until early evening that Fletcher finally got a chance to sit down in the cafeteria and relax. He savored the harsh aroma of the black coffee that was wafting up from his cup, as he closed his eyes and relaxed his aching muscles.

"Certainly the first day didn't get you that bad," came a lilting voice next to him. "You're not that old."

The major opened his eyes as a grin came to his lips at the sight before him. "Hi, Starfox, or do you prefer Carridan?"

"Actually," she said as she flashed a grin, "Carrie's just fine."

"Fletcher," he responded after a moment of stunned silence when his faculties seemed to be on sabbatical. "I'm Fletcher."

"Very well, Fletcher," Carrie said, "care for some company?"

Noticing the tray of food in her hand, he quickly got up and pulled the other chair out for her, as her russet eyebrows raised in amusement.

"I guess you're from a time before chivalry died," she said with a soft laugh as she sat down. "I hope you don't turn out to be a chauvinist."

The major's mouth opened quickly with a curt response, then closed again as he reconsidered his answer, settling on a question instead. "Why do you ask?"

She shrugged slightly as she started picking at her food with her fork.

"Chivalry and chauvinism often go hand in hand. When are you from, anyway?"

"Nineteen-nineties."

"Oh, I think that's after my time."

The major fought for something clever to say, but when that failed to arrive he settled for the obvious. "You think?"

"I practically grew up here in *Twilight*," she confessed as she continued to pick absently at her food, her mind far from eating, "from age five on or so."

"Who raised you?" he asked as he suddenly sensed the sadness that surrounded her mood shift.

"Everyone, sort of," she admitted. "We're a tight knit society here, we all look after each other."

"What about your parents?"

A far away look crept into her jade eyes as she shrugged her shoulders again. "They died at the same time I came here, but that was twenty years ago and I haven't thought about it in ages. Besides, I always had Justin, he really looked out for me."

Realizing that he was prodding an old wound of hers, he quickly searched for something new to talk about, fortunately she was one step ahead.

"So what did you think of training today?" she asked, her face brightening.

A smile came to his lips at the new subject. "Very interesting. I wasn't expecting the rigorous workout after class."

"What's a couple dozen laps and stuff to an ex-Air Force major?" she said as she flashed her quirky grin at him.

"Hey," he tried to defend, "I was in a war zone back home. I didn't have free time to exercise. Besides, I'm a little old for boot camp."

"Didn't I just tell you that you're not so old," she said as she finally started to eat.

"What about you?" he asked as he took a sip from his coffee, frowning as he realized that it had turned luke-warm. "If you grew up here, why wait until twenty-five to do this Skimmer thing?"

"Who told you I was twenty-five?"

"You did, a few moments ago," he responded with a laugh. "In a roundabout sort of way."

She thought about if for a moment, then laughed. "I suppose I did."

Fletcher suddenly felt taken aback as her laughter filled him with a warm glow. It was as if the change in her mood had brightened the entire room with its radiance, and he realized that he could not stop from smiling, even if he had wanted to.

Carrie's ears flushed pink as she felt his fiery blue eyes openly smiling at her. Then she cleared her throat, as she tried to sound serious.

"It wasn't the same for me here as it was for you and most of the other Skimmers," she tried to explain. "You all were pulled out of death's grasp and immediately thrust into a situation of becoming a time traveler. I was brought here as a child and grew up watching the Skimmers and other people at *Twilight*."

The major nodded thoughtfully, as he tried again to suppress his wide smile, this time having a little more success.

"As time went on, I wasn't sure if I wanted to be a Skimmer. I spent four years back on Earth in the twenty-fourth century, going to college, but that still didn't help me make up my mind."

"Justin let you live away from *Twilight* for four years?" Fletcher asked, amazed at the trust the *Twilight* leader must have had in this woman.

She nodded, then started poking at her food again. "Skimmers have a lot of responsibilities, a lot rests on what they do…or fail to do. I often think of the Skimmer who saved me back when I was a child, and I wonder if I could do what he did. So I waited, and it seemed that the longer I waited, the harder it was to make the decision."

"What finally made up your mind?" he asked as he leaned forward, uncontrollably pulled into her story.

"Justin," she replied as if were the obvious answer. "He came to me not long ago and talked to me about the day I was brought here, and what the Skimmers who had brought me here had risked to do so. After all, I'm the only person that was ever rescued from death that wasn't supposed to become a Skimmer right away. As he talked I realized that becoming a Skimmer was something that I had to do. I had known it all along, but I just needed the right push to get me there. So here I am."

His smile returned. "So here you are."

"This was a great time to start anyway," she threw in, "with the class cycle just starting again. That doesn't happen too often."

Fletcher nodded, his head filled with questions, like why save her as a child, when according to Justin's prime directives, only Skimmer prospects were saved…unless Justin knew all along she would choose to become a Skimmer. He shook his head at the complexity of taking on a responsibility like the *Twilight* leader did. A short silence lapsed as Carrie started to eat again, and he took another mouthful of his coffee, wincing at the extreme bitter taste of the now ice cold drink.

"So," he asked again as he pushed his cup far away from himself on the table, in hopes that he wouldn't forget the coffee's state and drink anymore of it, "who was the Skimmer who saved you, is he still around?"

She nodded, while swallowing her last bit of food. "You'll meet him tomorrow. He usually gives the tactical training for new Skimmers, but he was on assignment today. He's called Checkmate."

"Checkmate, huh? I guess he knows his tactics then?"

Carrie smirked, then let out a short laugh. "Yeah, he knows his stuff."

Fletcher raised an eyebrow at her tone, wondering what she was not telling him, then shrugged it off. He unconsciously reached across the table and grabbed his cup, then looked at it as he remembered why he had put it there. Suddenly, he became aware that she was staring at him with a look of amusement drifting from those jade pools.

"What?" he asked, a small defensive note invading his tone.

"I was just wondering if you were going to drink that cold coffee again."

The major's lips parted in surprise as he found himself speechless.

"You make the cutest expression every time you drink from it." She flashed him a smile again, then they both laughed.

"I haven't been called cute in some time," he admitted with a chuckle.

"Don't let it go to your head."

Fletcher studied the enigma before him for a moment. Here was someone who he had just met, yet her gentle, open frankness had swept him into her life, making him feel as if he had known her for months. He realized that his infatuation was growing, perhaps too quickly, to the point that he was forgetting the bizarre turn his life had taken yesterday.

"So," he finally asked, breaking the lull in their conversation, "what made you come over here tonight?"

"Did you mind?" she asked, her expression betraying the forced hurt in her voice as amusement.

"Not at all," he confessed, practically blurting it out. "Just wondering…there are lots of Skimmers here in the cafeteria, and I noticed that you already knew a lot of them from the class."

"Something new?" she said with a shrug that caused her russet hair to cascade across her shoulder, drawing his attention briefly to her open neckline. He squirmed in his seat for a moment, as she cocked her head to the side. "To tell the truth, Justin recommended that I get to know you."

This snapped Fletcher's attention back from the lilting fantasies that had invaded his thoughts. "Justin, really?"

"He said that you were interesting, and that I'd probably enjoy talking with you."

"Did he?" Mild suspicion crept into his voice, but he chose to file it away for later consideration as the grin returned to his face. "Was he right?"

A sparkle flashed in her eyes as she opened her mouth for her response, but was cut off by Tsunami coming over.

"Starfox," the young Asian trainee called out as she approached the table. Both of them turned towards the newcomer.

"A bunch of us are going Ring Skating," she told them. "Want to come along?"

Carrie's eyes lit up. "Cool, I'd love to." Then she reached out and lightly touched Fletcher's hand. "Kim, this is Fletcher Taylor. Fletcher, this is Kim Lee."

"Tsunami," Kim added with a smile.

"Phantom," the major said in turn, trying to ignore the tingling sensation her touch caused.

Kim bowed slightly in an Asian fashion, then put her hand on Carrie's shoulder. "We're going now."

"Can Fletcher come along?"

"Sure."

"Um, just what exactly is Ring Skating?" the major asked, suddenly feeling the ache in his muscles again as he looked past Kim at the group of young cadets waiting by the door, somehow making the differences in their ages feel more pronounced.

"It's great," Carrie exclaimed with obvious excitement. "It's kinda a virtual reality thing where you skate on the rings of Saturn with jet boots. You've gotta try it to appreciate it."

Although somewhat intrigued at just what level the virtual reality would be like on a place like *Twilight*, all he wanted at the moment was a shower and some rest, now that he thought he knew what the training days were going to be like. He glanced at Carrie and almost drowned in her jade pools as she gazed at him hopefully.

"I'm going to pass on this one, I think," he finally said, internally wincing at the disappointed look on her face.

"Well," Kim said, "we've gotta go now, before the VR center closes for the night."

Carrie let out a sigh, and gave his hand a quick squeeze. "Maybe next time?"

"Sure," he said with a nod, feeling the tingling sensation drain out of his body as she let his hand go and stood up. "I'll see you in class tomorrow."

"Looking forward to it," she said earnestly. Then the two young women went over to the other trainees and they all left together, laughing and joking as they vanished down the hall.

For a moment he stared at the empty place they had all been as he silently chastised himself for not going along with them for no good reason he could comprehend.

It wasn't until three hours later as he lay sleeplessly on his bed, staring blankly at the ceiling, that he finally realized that the only reason that he had not gone with them was that he had simply chickened out, and that realization cost him the whole night's sleep.

Fletcher could barely keep his eyes open as he stumbled into class the next day and sat in his seat, purposefully sitting in the same chair as yesterday, three rows behind where Carrie and her friends were happily chatting away.

Eric stared at him flatly as he studied the exhausted major, then let out a sigh. "Up partying all night?"

Fletcher glanced up at the med tech who was standing over him like a vulture over fresh carrion. "Not exactly."

A sly grin came over Eric's youthful face as he patted the major on the shoulder. "I know all about it. I heard how you guys were up all night Ring Skating and having a great time."

Fletcher glared at the med tech, his red-rimmed eyes fixing in annoyance. "Glad to see that you are willing to get into the swing of—"

"Look," he cut off the young tech, "I didn't go…alright?"

Eric's mouth hung open for a moment, and then he shrugged. "Why not?"

The major looked back at the new Skimmer tech manual that had been placed at all the desks, and tried to figure out how it worked, ignoring the med tech.

Eric let out a small, "Humph," then walked down to the other group of students, joining in the early morning chatter.

Fletcher glanced back up at the cadets and let out a small grumble of his own, as he questioned his feelings in the matter again. He never considered himself a "lady's man" and it had been some time since he was attracted enough to a woman to give her a second thought. Yet ever since the incident in his F-15E, he could not stop thinking about her...wondering about her...wanting to get to know her. *Damn*, he grumbled silently, *I'm acting like an adolescent here*. His thoughts briefly turned to their conversation last night, and the fact that it was Justin who had prompted her to talk with him. But before he could give it another thought, the *Twilight* leader entered the room, bringing everyone to silence.

Justin walked back up to the podium and smiled. "Good morning, trainees. I'm not going to take up much of your time, instead I'm going to introduce your technical trainer who will be your instructor for the remainder of your training, Charles Borlin, call sign Checkmate. He can teach you more about Skimming than any of us, because he's been doing it the longest.

The class' attention fell to the door in the back, as a tall lanky man in a black and scarlet jumpsuit walked past them, moving with a sureness about him that instantly convinced Fletcher that he had a soldier's background. Justin shook his hand with a warm grin, as the two met at the podium.

"Give them hell," he audibly whispered to the class trainer.

Charles Borlin nodded in return, then turned to face the class, his deep brown skin taut over the chiseled features of his stoic face as he glanced over the students with the judgmental eye of a lion studying his prey.

Minutes passed as a silence reigned over the class, as he seemed to study each and every student. When his deep chocolate eyes hit Fletcher he paused for the slightest moment, and the major was almost certain that the trainer flashed the briefest of grins.

Fletcher found himself squirming uncomfortably for a moment, emphasizing his dislike of classroom settings.

"Do you know why you are here?" Borlin finally asked in a deep voice that sang with the clear tones of a strong British accent.

For a moment the students all glanced at one another, almost afraid it was a trick question. It was Kim who first raised her hand.

"To become Skimmers," she answered.

He stared at her for a moment with an intensity that caused the young woman to shrink into her seat from the glare.

"Is there anyone else who agrees with this woman?" he demanded of the class.

Slowly the hands went up, leaving the only people not in agreement Fletcher, and a linebacker-sized youth that he had learned was called Tank.

Checkmate watched all the hands go up, then stared at the major and Tank, then cocked an eyebrow. "You have a different opinion, Phantom?"

Fletcher smiled internally at the manner and tone of the man before him, recognizing it well from his own life in the Air Force. The tall trainer was using standard "drill sergeant" mentality, to quickly draw the attention of his students. He actually had almost agreed with the other students, but the look in Borlin's face as the hands went up sent a flurry of signals to Fletcher's trained eye. Besides, he recognized the question as quite similar to one that was asked of him during his initial training in the Air Force Academy.

"We're here for the people," the major said in a moderate tone.

The smallest of smiles inched its way onto Checkmate's face. "And you, Tank," he said as he glared at the youth. "Do you agree with Phantom's assessment?"

Tank glanced about him, obvious apprehension dominating his face. Then he nodded slowly.

"I see," Borlin commented. Then he proceeded to look at his tech manual. "Please activate your Skimmer manual and set it to page five."

The students stared at him blankly for a few seconds, then began turning on their books.

"So which was right?" Carrie blurted out after it was apparent that no one else would.

Borlin glanced back up at her, his deep brown eyes sinking into her spirit. "Both are valid responses, Starfox, as are over half a dozen others. That's not why I asked the question."

More than half the class seemed on edge as the invariable question waited to be asked, but when it became apparent that no one would ask, and he was not volunteering the answer, Fletcher found that he had to force himself not to laugh, as he instantly decided that he liked the stoic trainer.

However, his pleasure was cut short as he studied the electronic book on his desk, and struggled to find a way to activate it. Before he realized it though, a deep brown hand reached across his face and touched the screen of the book, instantly starting it up. Fletcher glanced up to see Borlin standing over him with an eyebrow cocked. Then the trainer strode back to the podium.

"Now that Phantom has caught up to the rest of us," his clear British voice rang, "we can get started."

Fletcher looked up as he pursed his lips in annoyance, then froze as he realized that Carrie was staring at him. Their eyes locked for a moment and she flashed him the briefest of smiles, as he felt a pull growing within him. Even when she finally turned back to the front of the class his eyes could not seem to leave her. It was almost twenty minutes later when he started to really pay attention to what Checkmate was saying.

"It is always imperative to stay alert, and watch for your partner while on assignment."

"Partner?" Tank asked.

"Each of you will be assigned a partner," Borlin explained, "who will go on almost all of your calls with you. Skimming is a dangerous thing, which I'm sure Justin explained. Having two Skimmers there is a pure safety factor. Rarely, when the assigned Skim is exceptionally easy, a Skimmer will go alone. Also, there are some situations where only one Skimmer can go because of the specific situation."

Fletcher found himself thinking of his rescue and nodded to himself. One Skimmer had barely fit in the cockpit of his plane, two would never had made it.

"I could lecture on what it is like to Skim until the edge of night, but nothing teaches like experience. So that is exactly what you are going to get."

The major sat forward in surprise; surely they weren't going to send the cadets into the past yet.

"How many of you here have enjoyed that sport, Ring Skating, here?"

Everyone's hand shot up except for Fletcher's, leaving the major feeling out of the circle.

"Pretty realistic," Borlin said with a smile, "isn't it?"

Everyone nodded.

"As you all know, Ring Skating is done with an extremely advanced form of virtual reality. We use the same technology to perform what we call Spiral Runs. A Spiral Run is a simulation of a Time Skim in virtual reality. It will seem almost real, and with good reason. Unlike Ring Skating, where you can't be hurt, the pain controllers in Spiral Runs are not activated. You can get hurt, you can even die."

Mouths hung open in surprise.

"Or should I say you can 'virtually' die, which would send you out of the program instantly. These Spiral Runs will be executed exactly like the real thing. You will get a partner who will work with you during all your Spiral Runs. You will go on missions, and then we can discuss, one on one, what went wrong and how to not let such things happen when real lives are in the balance. There will also be some classes where we can discuss general questions. These Spiral Runs are based on real Time Skims that Skimmers have gone on in the past."

"You said that we get partners that will be with us through the training," Carrie asked. "Are these the same people that will be our partners when we graduate?"

"Excellent question," Borlin said. "The answer is…perhaps." He glanced over the questioning faces and nodded. "Being a partner is an important responsibility. You literally place your lives in each other's hands from time to time. If the partner match seems good in the Spiral Runs, then you will become permanent partners. If not, we'll set you up with another partner during the Spiral Runs. We usually catch these mismatches early on.

"Now, if you will all follow me, I'll take you to the Spiral Run chambers."

*Chapter 4*
# Inside Out

    The control center for the Spiral Runs was larger than the actual Departure Nucleus where the real Time Skims took place. Red neon filaments lined the walls like some elaborate highway seen from far above, illuminating the many computer screens that covered the work consoles, tracking all the Spiral Run chambers. Shooting off from the main room, like the tentacles of an octopus, were winding halls that ended in each of these chambers. As the cadets arrived, Checkmate pointed them towards the locker rooms.
    "You'll find your Skimmer armor waiting for you in your locker. This is not just a training suit, but this is your actual uniform for when you go on real Skims as well. Once you are suited up, then come out and I'll go over the details."
    "This is the same place were we go Ring Skating," Tsunami commented absently as she headed into the ladies' locker room, followed closely by Carrie, who flashed a nervous glance at Fletcher before heading in.
    Once in the locker room, the major quickly found the locker with his name on it. Inside he found a copy of the armor that he'd seen the other Skimmers wearing. For a moment he studied it in silence, then quickly changed into it.
    He was amazed at how perfectly it fit, as if molded to his body. It wasn't until he looked into the large mirror that covered one wall, that the reality of this sank further in. Gone was the black jumpsuit he had worn since arriving here. In its place was a flexible, latex, scarlet body suit, covered in form-fitted ebony armor plates, constructed out of some lightweight, plastic-like material. The plates covered the majority of his body, leaving only the joints free where he could still see the bright scarlet color. The black flight-style helmet had a retractable clear visor that just covered his eyes and nose bridge, leaving the lower portions of his face exposed. His lips hung open for a few

minutes in silence, as the other cadets swiftly prepared as well.

"I look like a damn Stormtrooper," he grumbled in half amazement. "All I need is R2D2 and I'd be all set. What the hell am I doing here?"

"Learning to be a time traveler, amigo," Condor, a short Hispanic cadet said with a grin as he put his own helmet on. "Pretty wild, huh?"

"Pretty wild," Fletcher said in agreement as he fastened his helmet into place and walked back out to the control center. Most of the cadets had already reassembled, and the major was struck at how this group of students suddenly seemed like some elite military force, transformed as if just emerged from a chrysalis. It reminded him of basic training in a way he'd thought he had forgotten. But he knew it took more than a new uniform to change a person, and he hoped these kids had what was needed inside them. He quickly glanced around, hoping to catch sight of Carrie. Then he saw her; she was emerging out of the ladies' locker room and was slipping her helmet on for size. As the ebony helmet settled into place, and she reached up to brush her sunfire red hair out of her eyes, a chill flushed through him like a cold sea wave, as all doubt left his mind who his guardian angel had been.

Carrie's jade pools locked onto his fiery blue eyes as they both stood there silently. The other cadets seemed to fall into the background as she stepped up to him, her eyes reflecting his own amazement. Neither spoke as they continued to gaze into each other's eyes. She slowly bit her bottom lip in confused wonder, then reached out and touched his arm.

"Suddenly you really seem so familiar," she whispered, her eyes wide, almost with a child-like amazement. "It's like deja-vu."

"*I'm* familiar?" he asked, confused, suddenly remembering the first time they met in class yesterday.

"Have we met somewhere before?" she asked, her face reflecting her need to understand.

He ached to say yes, ached deep inside to tell her about the fighter jet; yet in his heart he knew that wasn't what she was referring to, and that only made it worse. "Only in my dreams," he whispered in return as his smile deepened.

"What?" she asked, her voice like a soft breeze.

"If I can have all of your attentions, please," the trainer's voice cut in as they felt Checkmate's deep stare bore into them. "Posted on that monitor over there are your partner assignments. Find your partner and come back over here."

Carrie glanced down shyly, and then quickly ran over with the other cadets to find out her placement.

After taking a deep breath, Fletcher turned to join them and found Borlin staring at him. He cocked his head to the side, wondering what he had done to draw such attention.

"You strike me as a man caught in the middle," Checkmate said as he walked over to him, his British tones low.

"The middle of what?" the major asked.

"Good question," the trainer said with a smile, "a very good question indeed."

"I have to see who my partner is," Fletcher commented, as he noticed Justin wander into the room.

Checkmate glanced at his own electronic note pad. "I have it right here. You are partnered with Tank."

The major's head snapped back to the instructor, as he made a visible frown. "Tank?"

"That's what it says here," Borlin answered. "Do you have a problem with that?"

"No, not really…He's just not exactly my type."

"And who is?" the trainer asked with a sidelong glance that peered out from his eyes which appeared as bottomless black pools in the dim, neon-lit room. "This is not the dating game," he commented quietly, which drew a sharp glance from the major.

"What's going on here?" Justin asked as he walked over to the two men, appearing out of nowhere.

"We were discussing partner assignments," Checkmate commented stiffly. "Our newcomer here isn't fond of his."

The *Twilight* leader's eyes opened in surprise, "What's wrong with Starfox?"

"Starfox?" both echoed at the same time, trying to keep their voices down as the rest of the cadets began to pair up on the other side of the large control room.

"Phantom is paired up with Tank," the trainer stated flatly. "That's what's in the roster you set up."

"I paired Phantom with Starfox," Justin said, a note of puzzled concern coming into his voice.

Although pleased with this information, the motives behind it raised Fletcher's inner suspicions, and he recalled Carrie telling him that Justin had recommended her to get to know him. "Why Starfox?" he finally asked.

"Why not?" Justin said with an innocent smile. "I saw the two of you talking yesterday at class and it just struck me as a good match. Most of the way I pick partners is gut instinct. I have to be very careful, since so much relies on picking the right partners for each other. So I trust my guts."

Fletcher considered his words for a moment, amazed at how the *Twilight* leader could take a situation that seemed suspicious at best, and make it all seem perfectly innocent. Finally he sighed, realizing that arguing with something he agreed with would be ludicrous. "Well, Justin...you've got some pretty good guts."

"I pride myself in them," Justin said with a chuckle. "Make the roster change, Checkmate. I wanted Tank with Firestrike. I also want to talk with you later, this isn't the first time records seemed altered. Let the class know the situation if they ask."

The Brit nodded thoughtfully as he made the electronic change. Then he transmitted the change to the bulletin board that the trainees were looking at and called their attention, just as Fletcher joined the others.

"Note that Tank is now with Firestrike, and Starfox is with Phantom," Checkmate stated as he motioned for them to all come back over.

Carrie walked over to Fletcher with a shy smile on her face. Then shrugged as she reached him. "Pretty cool that we're paired up, don't you think?"

"Interesting, to say the least," the major agreed, as he watched Justin leave the control center.

"Checkmate," Kim asked, "why the change in rosters?"

The instructor seemed to consider it for a moment, then took a deep breath. "The change was to correct an error in the roster. I shan't hide the truth from you, since you will all soon be part of *Twilight's* elite. There have been a few computer intrusions. They have been minor, but we are keeping our eye on them."

"Is there a problem?" Fletcher asked.

"Although we are not sure, we think we may have a rogue Skimmer on our hands."

"How can you not be sure?" Kim asked.

"Because we have never seen him...or her, and have no positive proof that he is even out there," the trainer admitted. "However, some 'accidents' have happened to Skimmers in the past, and the evidence has pointed to the possible existence of this rogue Skimmer."

"How can such a person exist?" Carrie asked. "Doesn't he need *Twilight's* help to move from place to place?"

"He might *have* Twilight's help for all we know," Checkmate commented. "After all, we don't know what will happen to *Twilight* in the future. However, even if he doesn't, the WCDs have a half life of ten thousand years, and they can keep a Skimmer going for quite some time."

"WCDs?" Tank asked.

"Of course," Borlin said with a smile, "I'm jumping ahead of myself." He held up his left gauntlet and pointed to the micro computer screen on it and the buttons below it. "Look at the controls on your left wrist. This is the Wrist Control Device, or WCD. This is your life blood when on a Skim, so you better bloody well take good care of it. Missions are given to you on these clear plastic cards," he emphasized by holding one up. "They are inserted in the slot below the screen on the WCD like this." He demonstrated, by taking a card and inserting it in his WCD, causing it to light up and flash information across the tiny black screen in luminous emerald letters.

"The card holds a large amount of information that it gives to the micro-computer in the WCD. This information includes the details of your mission, the coordinates of where you are going so that the Time Skim will put you in the right place, and a tie-in to the Omni computer so that when the mission parameters are met this green light will light up on the screen, here."

"How does it know the mission parameters are met?" Fletcher asked.

"By the information the Omni computer fed it in the mission docket. It knows when the mission is done by recording and monitoring the events around it. Also, when the mission is completed, your return buttons will light up a bright blue." Checkmate pointed to a small blue circle to the right of the screen on the WCD. "Here in the center is a small directional arrow which will point towards the person you are there to help. Any questions?"

"This probably sounds silly," Carrie said almost too quietly to be heard, "but when we are in the past—won't we kinda stick out? We're in black and red armor."

A few chuckles sounded through the cadets, followed by a lot of head nodding. Fletcher smiled ever so slightly, glad that someone asked the obvious.

"First of all," Borlin responded, "you will almost always Skim into a deserted place so no one sees you arrive. Secondly, there is a device on your WCD that activates a crystal that refracts light all around you, making you appear practically invisible—but it only lasts for thirty seconds. It's called 'hazing'."

"Thirty seconds?" Kim remarked. "That's not a lot of time."

"No, Tsunami," Checkmate agreed, "it's not. But for the most part you shall just have to stay out of sight. Sometimes missions can be completed without contacting anyone, by just setting certain events in motion. Sometimes you may find disguises that you can borrow for a few minutes in the past. However, if you need to move in a crowd or make an escape, that's when this device comes in handy. I wish that we had ample opportunity to dress you appropriately for each mission, but there simply is not sufficient time for that. Also, you may or may not remember, but Time Skimming is an extremely disorienting experience. The armor you are wearing is specially designed to protect you during the Skim. I've never met anyone who can make it through a Skim unarmored and not pass out—"

"I did," Tank said gleefully as he struck a prideful pose.

"That is true, Tank," the Brit consented with a wry smile. "But considering that you arrived evacuating the contents of your stomach, you would hardly have been in any condition to complete a mission in a timely fashion."

Soft laughter echoed through the control room, as Tank turned a light shade of pink.

"Any other questions?"

"What if the WCD gets damaged during a mission?" Condor asked, his nervous voice breaking the humorous tone of the room.

A solemn look flushed over Checkmate's face like a grave blanket being laid. "Then, Condor, you would be in a lot of trouble. That is one of the reasons we team people up with partners most of the time. If one person can't use his WCD, the other can bring him or her back by holding on to them when they Skim back—as you were all brought here by Skimmers yourselves."

The trainees all looked at each other with apprehension, as the gravity of what was said sunk in.

"Alright," the trainer said, trying to lift his voice to break the mood, "time for your first Spiral Run." He started handing out mission dockets to each team member, explaining the rules again as he moved from person to person. "Remember, although this is just a simulation, treat it as if it were a real Time Skim. You will be graded on your success, or lack there of. You are to focus entirely on the subject of your mission and nothing else. Do not interfere with anyone's lives except the person you are there for. Remember, the Omni computer has calculated out every possible consequence for the mission. If you leave the mission parameters and either save, or harm another, the consequences to history could be devastating. Have I made myself perfectly clear?"

Various nods from the trainees were the only responses.

"I hope so, for your sakes," Checkmate commented curtly. "In the Spiral Runs, the only one you can harm is yourselves. In actual Time Skims, the repercussions are far greater."

Fletcher held the clear plastic card in his hand for a moment as he considered the situation. Then he slipped it into his WCD. Instantly the screen lit up as the mission spelled out across his screen.

> *Spiral Run Chamber 6:*
> *July 4, 1976 — New York City. Eight-year-old Brenda Sykes is in the custody of her father Carl. At 12:07 her mother, Sharon, tried to abduct her during a parade to have her live with her in Virginia...she fails and never tries again. Under the emotionless rule of her father, Brenda grows up bitter and cold and eventually continues this cycle to her children. Omni believes that life with her mother would have made her a happier child and the result will most likely prevent six generations of misery.*

He read it a second time, and then glanced over at Carrie, who had the same details on her screen, then he looked up at the trainer. "What are the time constraints, if any?"

"As soon as you Skim into your situation, your WCD chronometer will begin counting down how long it will be before the event happens that you are to fix. This is a random number based on how close to an event the time stream came...it may be minutes...it may be hours. If you miss the event, then your WCD mission indicator will turn red, and your return lights will light up for you to come back."

"What then?" Kim asked. "Do we try again?"

"Like Justin told you yesterday," Borlin explained, his British accent ringing sternly as he emphasized his point. "Although we can go to a lot of places from here, we have no control over the time streams that surround the *Twilight* complex. The opportunity to interfere with a specific situation comes and goes with a fifteen minute window. If you miss it, the opportunity to arrive at that specific time and place again may not happen for a long, long time...perhaps never. So I want you to go to the chamber indicated in your mission and wait for me there. I shall go over last minute details with each of you before you depart."

Fletcher glanced around and found the corridor that was labeled with a neon six. He reached out and lightly brushed Carrie's shoulder as he pointed out the way they had to go. Then the two of them started off down the narrow walkway, as the rest of the cadets paired up and followed suit. At the end was a small chamber with two recliner chairs in it, and a wire that was coiled up on the seat of each. Aside from this, the room was black and barren, giving the two trainees an almost empty feeling like walking into a realm of darkness.

"What do we do now?" Carrie asked quietly, as if her voice could disturb the blackness.

"I guess we wait," he said as he picked up the wire from one of the chairs. He studied it for a moment, then returned it to the cushion.

For a moment they stood there in silence, waiting, both shifting from foot to foot, each in their own thoughts.

"What were you talking to Checkmate about?" she asked as she turned her attention to him. "Back right before we were paired up."

"Nothing really," he said with a smile. "I was asking about the assignments…things like that."

"Oh," she said as that quirky grin formed on her full lips, "I thought you were trying to convince him to let you partner with me."

Fletcher's face went blank for a moment.

"Something about the 'dating game' was what I heard," her grin had formed into a full smile now.

The major slowly drifted to the far wall where he flattened himself like a cornered animal, as his skin flushed pink. Then he let out a soft laugh. "It wasn't what you thought," he said in his defense.

"No?" she asked as she moved over to him. "It sounded like it was. Especially when Justin came over."

Fletcher's lips parted and hung there in silence for a moment as his mind sought escape, but he was spared as Checkmate walked into the small chamber and cleared his throat.

"Am I interrupting something?" he asked.

"No, sir," Carrie quickly responded as they both turned to face him.

"Have you both read the mission information?"

They nodded.

"I have a question," Fletcher said as he moved from the wall. "The mission seems simple enough, however, it's the results that I have doubts with."

"What do you mean?" the Brit asked.

"Well," the major started as he glanced side longingly at Carrie, "the mission states that young Brenda turned into an all-around nasty person because she was raised by her father. But if her mother raised her, she would have been a princess or such. How can we possibly know that?"

The trainer smiled then put his electronic notepad down and leaned against the wall. "That's what the Omni computer is there for. It calculates all the possibilities to come up with the best possible scenario."

"So we're trusting a computer to predict human nature?" Fletcher asked dubiously. "For all you know, it was just in her nature to be that way, and all we're doing is messing up her life."

"But this is just a Spiral Run," Carrie reminded him. "Nothing we do today will affect Brenda one way or the other."

"That's not the point," he responded. "It may be a Spiral Run now, but one day it will be the real thing…and Checkmate said that all the Spiral Runs were based on real Skims…so a Time Skimmer had to deal with this case already." He turned to face the Brit. "True?"

Checkmate nodded. "If you want to over analyze each of these cases, you could drive yourself bugger. We have to *believe* in what we are doing here, Phantom, or there's no point to it at all. Trust Justin, he knows what he's doing."

Fletcher seemed to consider for a moment in silence. "What about the real Brenda Sykes? How did that Skim turn out?"

"I'll tell you that when the Spiral Run is over," the Trainer said with a stern face. "Now let's get down to the details. Both of you sit in the chairs and plug the wires into the jack on your WCDs." He pointed to the small hole next to the slot that had swallowed up the mission card.

Both of the trainees sat down and plugged into the system. For a moment they felt a tingling sensation and then the clear, form-fitted visors on their helmets clouded over, eventually going black, leaving them in darkness.

"This is just like the Ring Skating," Carrie said with a touch of excitement and glee in her voice.

"Quiet now, Starfox," Checkmate ordered. "I've started your countdown. In ten seconds the Spiral Run will start in full virtual reality mode. It will end when you return to the Departure Nucleus."

He paused for a moment, as they heard the computer slowly counting down in the background. Then he patted them both on the shoulder and walked to the door. "Above all else, remember that you are a team. You must work together, your lives depend on one another…and good luck."

For a few moments Fletcher felt a little dizzy, but when his vision cleared he was standing in the Departure Nucleus. At first he was shocked at the reality of what his senses were telling him. In the room with him were both Carrie and the man that had been introduced to him once before as Sender, who was in charge of operating the Time Skim controls.

"This is great," Carrie said, her excitement plain in her voice. "Absolutely fantastic."

Fletcher nodded dumbly, totally bowled over by the sense of reality he was feeling. He had half expected to be dealing with some form of computer graphics, but this seemed as if he was really there. Touch, smell, noise: everything. For a few seconds he tried to feel the chair that he knew in reality he was in, but it simply was not there. He glanced at her again, then noticed the slightest wave of distortion that was almost as if she had blurred for a second, but it was so fast that he easily could have missed it. However, with that small ounce of assurance that this was indeed reality of the virtual kind, instead of the real kind, he walked over to the raised illuminated platform and stepped up onto it.

"Isn't this fantastic?" she asked as she stepped up next to him. Her smile spread from ear to ear.

Despite his misgivings, he found himself smiling as well. She was right, this was indeed fantastic.

"Nothing to say, Major?" she asked with a teasing grin.

"It is pretty intense," he admitted.

She shook her head with a chuckle, then turned to the virtual Sender. "Let's get going."

As if activated by her voice, Sender suddenly became animate. "Ready, folks?" he asked them.

When they both nodded, he touched some of the buttons on the control panel that he stood behind, suddenly bathing them in the intensifying cobalt light.

"Anytime you're ready," Sender said, after neither of them did anything.

Fletcher looked over at her, and saw the nervousness in her eyes that reflected his own. Despite his realization that this was a simulation, he felt his heart beating faster, as if he was about to leave on a mission back home.

"Let's do it," she said suddenly, and he nodded in agreement.

Simultaneously, they both hit the flashing emerald buttons on their WCDs, causing a blue light to emit from the devices as they become bathed in a sparkling azure glow.

Then the nausea hit him as his world seemed to turn inside out. For a moment he thought he would be sick, but it faded quickly and he realized it was only a shadowy reflection of his experience when he first arrived at the *Twilight* center. Multicolored lights swirled about his body, causing him to wince from the sensation. A moment later his vision cleared again and he was in a deserted alleyway in an urban metropolis.

"I'd almost forgot what the outside world looked like," she said softly as she gazed about in wonder.

"I know what you mean," he agreed as he walked up to the edge of the alley and peered into the street that was shadowed by the late afternoon sun filtering around the behemoth towers that created the skyline of New York City.

The street was wide, but deserted, which struck him as totally bizarre. Then he heard the sounds of the parade in the distance, not more than a few blocks away, and he realized that the street was most likely blocked off from all traffic.

"What do we do first?" she asked, as she looked over the street as well.

Fletcher glanced at his WCD and noticed the change. The mission indicator was off at this point, and there was a clock that was counting down from fourteen minutes. She noticed what he was doing and looked at her own WCD.

"I guess we have fourteen minutes until the incident happens," she commented. "We'd better get going. The arrow indicator points towards the parade."

He nodded as they started to move out into the street, keeping to the sides. "Despite the fact that this is New York," he said with a grin, "we'll still stick out like sore thumbs here. Let's try to keep to the sides until we spot our target. Then we can enter hazing mode and help her get the kid."

Carrie considered it for a moment. "We only have thirty seconds of hazing. Maybe we can try to blend with the people first in some way."

The major surveyed the area for a moment, his eyes studying the surroundings like a tiger on the hunt. Then he spotted something that instantly gave him an idea.

"Look over there," he said as he pointed to an open manhole cover with red tape around it to block it off.

"So?"

"I see two utility worker's coats," he explained while starting to walk towards the manhole.

She quickly matched his stride while trying to pull on his arm. "It's not going to work."

"Sure it is. The coats will cover our armor and help us blend in."

"If the person is blind, maybe," she answered, angered that he hadn't slowed down at all. "The coats are too short, and have bright orange stripes on them. They'll attract more attention than without."

"Going in there in this armor with no cover is just plain stupid," he snapped back. "Look, leave these details to me and try not to get in the way."

The instant the words left his lips he wished his WCD could reverse time and take them back. Her face registered the shock for a moment, then her crystal clear jade eyes darkened as her brow creased in anger.

"I'm not some kid who you can bully around, *Major*," she hissed at him. "We're supposed to be partners here—a team. A team works together and doesn't order the other half around. If that doesn't work for you then perhaps we shouldn't be a team."

Fletcher took the verbal blows like a trained fighter, as his inner defenses took over his higher faculties and propelled him into Air Force officer mode. "If you can't fall into place in this team then you aren't ready to leave the base."

Once again he cringed internally as he saw the hurt in her eyes as she appeared to have been slapped across the face. For a moment they stared at each other, then she turned and started to walk away, towards the sounds of the parade, each pronounced stride emphasizing her fury.

Fletcher watched her vanish around the corner in stunned silence, as the anger flushed through his veins, then his senses returned to him as a reality check rang in his head and he brought his hand to his face in wonder.

"What the hell was I saying?" he asked himself in disbelief. For a moment he thought of running after her, but no words came to mind that could explain why his boot had become so tightly lodged in his jaw. Then he glanced down at his WCD and cringed internally. There were less than ten minutes left and he still had to find the mother and the girl. Taking in a deep breath, he broke into a run and started towards the parade sounds. The soft city breeze rushed past him as he tried to complete scenario after scenario in his head to accomplish the mission, but all that kept coming up was Carrie's hurt expression. As the first block passed by, his purposeful run became a slow jog, and as he came to a building just behind the parade he was only at a quick walk. He passed three bystanders on the sidewalk, who stared at him with curious eyes, but he barely even noticed them there. Finally, he came to a stop as he approached the throng of people from the rear.

Giant cartoon balloons filled the sky, as even larger multicolored floats drifted along Madison Avenue. American flags waved everywhere, and small fireworks sizzled and popped near the proud banners that celebrated the anniversary of independence on the country's bicentennial. There were bands waving school flags, and clowns dancing along the edge of the crowd, and everywhere there were police, mostly on horseback, to control this maintained bedlam.

So enthralled were the people by the spectacular event before them that Fletcher was able to move behind them without so much as a side-glance from the spectators. His eyes darted from area to area as he searched for his quarry. According to his directional arrow on the WCD, the mother should be dead ahead. However, when he swept the area for a third time and failed to find her, he finally accepted that it wasn't the mother he was really searching for at all, it was his partner.

He checked the chronometer again, and saw that there was only five minutes left until the event that they were here to stop, but he suddenly didn't care. Finally spotting her in a narrow alleyway just one block over, he started moving again as a smile grew on his lips, as if it was a seed being slowly coaxed to form by the persistent rays of the sun. By the time he had reached the place she was hiding, he had totally forgotten about the mission here, all that mattered to him was the person he had hurt.

So intent was she on watching the mother, Carrie practically didn't see Fletcher until he was right in front of her.

"You're in my way," she half grumbled as she pushed him aside and started to move towards their quarry.

Grabbing her arm lightly, the major pulled her back to face him, his purpose set to make things right, but as he read the annoyance in her eyes his mind went blank, as everything he had planned on saying to her drained out of his mind like a plug had opened in his brain and all his thoughts were seeping out.

"*What?*" she asked, obvious anger in her voice.

"Um…we should stay together," was what he finally managed to get out.

"I don't need or want your help, Major," she snapped back.

"Look," he responded back curtly, "I'm trying to apologize here."

"I don't want your apologies, either," she replied as she fixed her arms across her chest in a show of defiance.

"Then what do you want?" he asked, confusion fading into anger at her attitude.

She stared at him for a few moments, her eyes wavering. "You just don't get it do you, Major?" she hissed at him while pulling her arm free. "I don't give a damn about your macho style or your desire to be king of the mission. But there is one thing I do demand…"

"And what's that?" he cut back, his own arms crossing in front of him.

"I'll be damned if I'm going to tell you, flyboy. Now if you'll excuse me, I have a mission to complete." She turned away from him, as a very soft, but steady whine sounded from their WCDs. Both glanced immediately down as their indicators turned a bright red, signaling their failure.

Carrie whirled on her heels to face him again, the fury burning like fire in her jade pools.

Fletcher's mouth opened slightly but was cut off by her pointing a sharp finger at him.

"*Don't even say a word,*" was all she said. Then she stared down at the return indicator on her WCD that was flashing for attention and pressed it, bathing the area in azure fire.

Fletcher let out a soft breath between his clenched teeth. Then pushed his button as well.

Carrie refused to even look at him as she disconnected the virtual simulator from her WCD and stormed out of the Spiral Run chamber. Fletcher scrambled with the controls that tied him to the machine, fighting like a fly caught in a web as he tried to free himself. Finally escaping the tangled snare, he dove out of the room—running straight into the large figure of Checkmate, who stopped him dead in his tracks with a powerful arm and even more menacing cold glare.

Despite his veteran status as a soldier, the Air Force major suddenly felt like a five-year-old facing his father as those eyes continued to bore holes into his psyche. Borlin remained silent, as Fletcher finally stopped thinking about getting past him, his eyes straining to catch a glimpse of her as she vanished back into the main area.

"What?" he finally said in a harsh tone, as he retreated back to the two chairs in the Spiral Run chamber.

Checkmate let out a deep breath and leaned against the entranceway, blocking the major's pathway to freedom with his tall form.

"You care to explain what happened in there, Phantom?" his even tone demanded.

A dozen possible responses popped into his head, but none escaped his dried lips. He slowly ran his tongue over them, as if the action would buy him time to sort out the confusion in his brain.

"Phantom?" Checkmate persisted, his tone ringing like an old British school master.

"I don't know what happened," he finally shot back.

"Well, you'd bloody well better figure it out then."

"Look," Fletcher defended himself while flattening himself against the far wall in exasperation, "one moment we were talking about the best way to accomplish the mission, the next we were at each other's throats."

"*You* were the one who wanted the two of you to be partners."

"No," the major corrected with a sharp turn of his head to face the trainer, "it was Justin who wanted us together."

Checkmate raised a curious eyebrow as his lips curled into a knowing smirk.

"Alright," Fletcher admitted, "I didn't object."

"Then let's forget the semantics and get to the point," Borlin suggested. "You and I both have military backgrounds, and I saw what happened to you two down there. You felt totally out of your element and you panicked."

"*Of course I was out of my element*," Fletcher half yelled. "I'm an Air Force fighter pilot, not a *God damned time traveler*."

"You were also trained to handle difficult situations," Checkmate reminded him. "I know this is a tough situation to get used to—but ripping into your partner, to cover your own fears, isn't going to make it any easier."

Fletcher's blue eyes fixed coldly on the trainer as he felt his insides clench up in frustration. "You're saying I was wrong..."

"You were wrong," Borlin said in an even tone.

Seconds passed as the two men stared at each other, the only sounds the low hum of the Spiral Run equipment. The major felt his fists curl into tightened wads, as the blood drained to the center of his body, leaving his extremities with a strange tingling sensation. Then he finally let out the breath that he realized he was holding in, and sighed, then nodded.

"I was wrong..."

"I'm not the one you need to tell that to," Checkmate reminded him. "If you two are going to function as partners, then you have to work as a team. Now, she's not blameless either. She should not have run off like that, and it takes two to argue. But I want you to know that you can only have *one* failed mission during the five Spiral Runs."

"What happens if you have two?"

"You get dropped out of the program and have to wait for the next time we start up a class to begin again."

Fletcher rubbed his hands, feeling the blood returning to them with a prickly sensation. "You don't have to worry, Checkmate, we'll work out just fine."

The instructor nodded and stepped aside, giving the major room to pass.

Fletcher started to walk down the corridor then turned back. "By the way, what service and rank were you?"

A slow grin formed on Checkmate's lips. "I was a lieutenant in Her Majesty's royal forces stationed in India…long, long before your time. So if I can adjust to all this…" he gestured about, "techno-wizardry…then bugger, so can you."

Despite his feelings, Fletcher felt his own face crack a slight grin as he glared at the Skimmer trainer who was struck in his majestic pose. Then Borlin gave his shoulder a rough slap, as they headed back to the main room.

## Chapter 5
# A Cat's Tale —
# Or One Life Down, Eight to Go

Fletcher had spent half the night searching for Carrie, but she simply was not anywhere. A rumor reached him at ten that she had gone Ring Skating with Kim, but when he went back to the Spiral Run chambers it was long since empty. Finally, and with great reluctance, he turned in for the night, determined to apologize to her first thing in the morning.

Only first thing in the morning became much later as the alarm warned him that he was in risk of being late for class. He fought the inertia of exhaustion as he rubbed his bleary eyes, the alarm droning its warning into his head.

Quickly grabbing his armor, Fletcher was up and off towards the Spiral Run chambers, hoping that the long night had softened what his words never had a chance to.

The center arcade area was alive with activity in the early morning, with people milling about, intent on their day's activities. Fletcher paid them no heed as he raced to the training room. His mad dash, while still putting on various parts of his armor, drew more than a few curious glances from passersby. When he finally arrived at the Spiral Run control center he only saw two other people there: Tsunami and Checkmate. For a brief second relief swept into him, as the possibility that everyone was more late than he tried to soothe his tension; however, the vulture-eyed glare that the instructor fixed on him as he came to a stop drove any such hope deep into an early grave.

"Promptness is a skill that is extremely valued here, Phantom," the Brit said in an even but unmistakably firm tone, never wavering his glare in the slightest, "see that you acquire it."

Fletcher nodded while taking in a few deep breaths from his frantic run. It was then that the realization struck him that Carrie was nowhere in sight. *If all the trainees had paired up and gone to the chambers, where was his partner?* Then he glanced over at Kim, and wondered why she wasn't with Condor, as she was yesterday.

"Let's get you two off and going," the trainer instructed, as he motioned for them to head down one of the twisted corridors, and placed his hand on the major's shoulder.

Fletcher pulled his shoulder back from the large hand like it was covered in acid, the sudden gesture surprising the trainer.

"Phantom—"

"Where's Starfox?" the major demanded as he glared at the trainer accusingly. Then he shot a glance at Tsunami and froze. Her eyes were lowered, but there was no mistaking the emotion that she tried to hide from him. "What's going on here, Kim?"

"Starfox requested a partner change," Borlin informed him in the same straight tone. "It seems you two had incompatible personalities."

"*She* requested?" Fletcher asked.

"That's what the memo said," he confirmed.

"The memo? She sent a memo?" He took off his helmet and leaned against the wall, the wind taken out of his spirit.

"Sometimes partners don't work out, Phantom," Checkmate reminded him, his stern visage softening ever so slightly. "It's almost like a marriage in a way. Consider this an early annulment. After what happened yesterday, I'm sure it shall be for the best."

"And she's with Condor now?" he asked. "How do you feel about that?" he said as he faced Kim again.

"Starfox asked me to switch," she responded softly. "She's a good friend. Condor was fun, but I'm sure we can be a good team also."

So sure was he that he could win her back, that this unexpected defeat left him totally flustered; which quickly cultivated into annoyance, then simmered into anger.

"Fine," he finally stated as he pulled his helmet back on, "if that's what she wants. Alright, let's get going." He turned sharply and strode off down the hall, leaving Tsunami, who glanced at Checkmate and shrugged, then ran after him.

She caught up to him in the chamber, finding him already strapped into the chair.

"Don't you even want the mission docket?" she asked with a concerned smile, her small Asian features curved in light amusement. "Or do you just want to disappear into the Spiral Run without knowing where you're going?"

Despite the black cloud that hovered over his head, he smiled meekly, then reached out his hand for the mission card. "You probably think I'm an idiot," he said, forcing a grin.

"No," she said while returning the grin, "I think that you're just someone who is totally infatuated with a woman and don't know how to deal with her in a work environment. Maybe this team change will be good for the two of you, to give you a chance to get to know each other better."

His grin faded as his internal defenses returned with a vengeance. "I have no interest in her in any way *but* professional," he said as he turned away from her, angered at her perception, "and *you* have no idea what you're talking about."

Her smile turned to a frown as well as she crossed her arms in front of her chest. "I take it back," she said with a sigh of annoyance, "you *are* an idiot."

For a moment she stood there, then sat into the open Spiral Run chair and turned to him, her eyes softening again as she suddenly felt pity for his frustration. "I apologize, Phantom," she said as her smile returned, "there's no need to let any conflict between you and Starfox to spread to us as well. Let's start this team off right." Her small hand reached out towards his, the offer obvious. "I'm Kim Lee, call sign Tsunami…I'm your new partner."

He slowly turned to face her and stared at the hand for a minute, suddenly realizing that the only reason that he was mad was that she had hit a tender spot in him with her words that were too close to the truth. He reached out and took her hand and shook it, his own smile returning as well.

"I'm Fletcher Taylor, call sign Idiot."

They both let out a chuckle as she handed him the extra mission card, which he took with a smile and inserted into his WCD.

> *Spiral Run Chamber 3:*
> *January 20, 1950 — Chicago. Ten-year-old Johnny Monroe is a patient in the Chicago Psychiatric Ward, and has been for the last four years since the death of his parents in an automobile accident. He is now a ward of the state, who deem his condition as 'hopeless'. He has been in a state of catatonia since the accident, ignoring the world around him; though medically, there is nothing wrong with him.*

> *You are going back to save Scrambles, a calico cat that lives in the alleyway behind the institution under Johnny's window. She has made it part of her routine to visit Johnny every day now, and the Omni computer believes that continued exposure to the feline is the key to snapping Johnny out of his catatonic state. However, Scrambles was killed by a car on January 20, 1950, at 6:22 a.m., right outside the alley that is her home.*

Fletcher read it again, then a third time, just to make sure he was not misunderstanding the true parameters of their mission.

"We're traveling back in time to save a cat?" he asked, wondering if Kim's docket read the same information.

She nodded as she began to strap herself in. "It sounds great, doesn't it?"

"Is this serious?" he asked in disbelief.

"It most certainly is," Checkmate affirmed as he walked into the chamber and stood in front of both chairs. "Every mission has been carefully weighed not only by the Omni computer, but Justin as well. Don't forget, you are experiencing a luxury now that you will not have when on a real Time Skim. That luxury is time…time to wonder about the case, time to debate its impact on society and the people involved. When you are called to a real Time Skim there is only fifteen minutes until the window closes and the opportunity is lost." He gave them a hard look which dissolved their smiles like butter on a hot plate. "You have to be totally committed to this cause to be a Time Skimmer. You have to know—and truly believe that when you are called for a Skim that you are doing the right thing. Without that conviction you will be useless to us." He focused his gaze on Fletcher, who instantly realized the meaning behind what he was driving at.

"You're saying that this is what happened to me and Starfox on the last Spiral Run," the major said with an air of consent.

"You tell me, Major," the trainer asked quietly, his left eyebrow rising ever so slightly.

Fletcher nodded, realizing that Checkmate was absolutely right. This was really no different than flying his F-15 for the Air Force. Indecision in that case could be fatal, and he realized that it was the same here. "Thank you, Checkmate," he finally said. "This is something I need to work on."

A slight grin curled the edges of the trainer's lips, almost unperceived, but was not missed by the major. "Very well," the Brit said as he straightened like a taut bow string, all traces of his smile gone, "let's see how you two perform this time."

With that said he turned on his heels and left the chamber. The two trainees watched his departure, then glanced at each other in silence. Then they started up the equipment, each lost in his or her own thoughts.

"You all set?" Fletcher asked her as he made the last connection.

"Definitely," she said with a wide grin. "Let's go save that kitty."

"Yeah," he agreed as he activated the equipment, "let's."

This Spiral Run started out as the first one did, in the Departure Nucleus. They both appeared simultaneously and took a moment to get their bearings.

"Hello, Sender," Kim said with a warm grin to the figure behind the skim controls. "How are you today?"

"Just fine, Tsunami," he responded with a straight face. "You'd better get on the pad, you only have a few minutes left to depart."

The two trainees stepped up onto the raised platform and watched for the signal, as Fletcher leaned over to whisper in Kim's ear.

"Are you always this friendly to virtual reality images?"

"Virtual reality images have feelings too," she chastised him in a humorous tone. "Besides, we have to treat this run like a real one."

"How does talking to him help that?"

"I have no intention of being disrespectful to the real Sender," she said as she activated her WCD, "why should I be any different with the Spiral Run version?"

"True," he answered with a shrug as he activated his own WCD.

"Ready, folks?" Sender asked. When they nodded he activated the control panel as they touched their own buttons, leaping into the next Spiral Run.

Fletcher didn't feel quite as disoriented this time as he had on the last, but it still took him a few moments to get his bearings and figure out where he was.

The alleyway that he was in was only semi-lit, making him feel that night was falling. However, he quickly dismissed that idea, as the peaceful serenity of the empty city street ahead floated by him on a gentle breeze, holding the unmistakable aroma of fresh bread. The warm and sweet scent made it crystal clear that it was just past dawn for this large metropolis that was still asleep.

He felt Kim move up next to him, as they both surveyed the tiny alleyway that they were in. The scene was painted in shades of grey, from the dirt grey of the unwashed alley, and the hazy grey of the skyline, to the harsh gunmetal grey of the bars that secured the windows of the dark grey building to their right.

Fletcher found that both of them were staring at the windows, which were eight feet up from the cracked pavement.

"What do you think?" he asked, not even aware of the quiet tone his voice had taken on, as if its very sound could disrupt this almost tranquil scene.

"This must be the institution," she commented almost absently, her own voice's tone mimicking his.

The major glanced around, trying to look for clues as to which window belonged to little Johnny. There was a large pale dumpster that had long since lost any trace of paint, but it was on the other side of the alley, closer to the building on their left. At the far side of the narrow way, towards the dead end that was secured by a ten foot chain link fence, there was an abandoned sedan which appeared as if it was a leftover from some old gangster movie of the twenties. He stared at the rusted out, wheel-less hulk as a smile came to his lips.

"Tsunami," he said while pointing towards the car, "what about that?"

She turned to study the rusted vehicle and looked at the window that it was directly under. "Could be...but where's the cat?"

"Not sure," he admitted. "Let's see what the mission indicator says." He studied the WCD readout, then showed it to her. "According to this, we are right where we need to be to save the cat."

"Scrambles," she said with a smile.

"Right," he continued with a grin, "the cat. However, the accident isn't supposed to happen for another hour and ten minutes."

"That long?" she asked. "My last Skim was only a few minutes before the incident."

He nodded. "Same here."

She strolled over to the grey wall of the institution and leaned against it. "So, what are we going to do for an hour?"

Fletcher shrugged, then pulled Kim back into the shadows as a large bus drove by on the main street, followed closely by another sedan. However, it was sharp clipping noise of a horse's hooves on the pavement out in the street had caused him to retreat to the relative safety of the dark.

"What's wrong?" she asked, her voice now barely a whisper as they both crouched low.

"Do you recognize that sound?" he asked as he backed them further down the street.

She nodded. "A horse."

"Where are you from?" he asked, keeping his voice low.

"Korea," she answered, "why?"

"In America," he explained, "in a big city, the only horses that would be here are either pulling a carriage, or are working for the police. I don't hear a carriage, so I'm going to bet that it's a cop."

"Cop?"

"Police officer," he explained. "And if he's on horseback, he might take the time to check out the alleyway…especially if he spots two black armored people in it. Get ready to go into hazing mode."

"If we use up the hazer for this," she asked, "what will we do if we need it to accomplish the mission?"

Fletcher ran his tongue over his bottom lip, absently noting that it seemed to have assumed the consistency of sandpaper, then glanced over at the dumpster. "Over there," he pointed while standing up. "The trash container."

She nodded, understanding that it was their best bet. As they both got up Fletcher's boot struck an empty Coke bottle, causing it hit a loose piece of concrete. It shattered with a crash that echoed in the empty alleyway, breaking the relative calm of the city dawn. The sound of the horse's hooves abruptly stopped and Fletcher broke into a run, pulling Kim behind. Instantly the silence dissolved as the horse broke into a run and rounded the corner into the alleyway, the blue uniformed officer sitting erect in the tall saddle.

As the officer burst into view, Fletcher dove behind the container and rolled into a low crouch, hoping that he had been unseen.

"Hold it right there," came the harsh command from the police officer.

The major sucked in a sharp breath between his teeth, incredulous that he'd been spotted. Then he glanced back the way he came and froze; Kim was standing just shy of the dumpster, her hands in the air, a look of confused fear in her eyes.

"Haze," he hissed at her, not seeing any other course of action.

She glanced over at him and he read the indecision in her eyes, abruptly striking home how young she was, how young they all were. He had realized that he was, by far, the oldest of the cadets, but he wasn't taking into account experience, or lack of it. Suddenly the events that had occurred on his first run came to him in a new light, and he cringed at the words that he still couldn't take back.

"What are you doing here in that outfit?" the police officer demanded, snapping him back to the situation at hand. "Let's see some identification." Kim's mouth opened to speak, but nothing came from her almost imperceptibly quivering lips.

Taking a deep breath, Fletcher lurched forward, grabbing Kim and pulling her arms down. "*Haze now*," he instructed her again as he saw the cop starting to move in. She hesitated for another second, then numbly pressed the button that activated the hazing mode. Making sure not to lose his grip on her, he pressed his own button, as the two of them faded from view.

The police officer's horse reared up with a whinny of confusion at the disappearance of the two Skimmers, as the cop followed suit, pulling his revolver and waving it in the general direction of where he had seen them last.

"Where'd you go? Show yourselves!" his voice echoed in the small enclosure, as he slowly brought the horse further into the darkened alleyway.

Fletcher knew that they only had a few seconds, and the hazing still caused a fringe effect that might be detected if the officer got closer. Tightening his grip on Kim's arm so he wouldn't lose her, he started backing into the shadows.

"We have to get away from the cop," he whispered into the space he judged her head to be.

There was no response for a moment, then he felt her hand grab his, stabilizing his grip on her. "Which way?" she questioned, her quiet voice heavy with apprehension.

He glanced around quickly, feeling the time slipping away from him like sands in a hourglass. There did not seem to be any place to go that seemed apparent. He knew that if they stayed in view they would be easily spotted after the hazing effect wore off. Then his eyes settled on the rusted hulk of the sedan at the end of the alleyway. Without saying a word, he began walking at a quick pace towards the car, pulling his partner in tow. At first she struggled, not being able to tell which way her invisible teammate was pulling her, then she saw what she was heading towards, and moved that way as well.

The police officer thought he heard foot falls, but still nothing was in sight. Slowly he pulled his horse up to the trash container and looked behind it, a puzzled expression forming on his face.

The two Skimmers reached the car and slammed into each other as they both tried to enter the vehicle at the same time. Both hesitated for a moment, then hit each other again.

"Go in," Fletcher whispered, as he pushed her into the rusted frame, as his WCD vibrated softly, warning him that the hazing mode was about to expire. He gave her two seconds to get in, then dove in afterwards, pulling both of them below the seat level, just as they came back into view.

For a moment the two of them lay on the old bench seat, the springs sticking into their sides despite their armored protection. Fletcher took even breaths as he forced himself to stay quiet, and thanked numerous unnamed sources that Kim was following suit, as he listened to the slow clopping of hooves getting closer. His head snapped back and forth, searching for something, though he wasn't sure what. Then he spotted the dislodged rearview mirror on the floor of the sedan and grabbed it, amazed at his stroke of luck.

Slowly he raised the splintered mirror until the refracted form of the police officer came into view, no more than ten feet away from the car.

"Crap," he whispered, as Kim squirmed next to him, trying to get the same view from the mirror that he had.

"We could knock him out," she suggested quietly. "Our armor could be bullet proof, I think."

"Think?" he asked with doubt, then shook his head. "No...what if knocking him out affects the time flow? The Omni computer didn't mention him at all, so we've got to keep from interfering with him."

"What if he interferes with us, Phantom?" she asked as she finally saw him in the reflection, still ten feet away and looking back at the dumpster.

No answer came to Fletcher's mind as his ice blue eyes fixed on the police officer in silent judgment. Every movement, every sway of the cop's body as he searched around in vain, sent a hundred silent signals to the Time Skimmer, helping him make up his mind.

"Just stay still," he finally whispered, "we'll be fine."

Almost on cue to the major's words, the cop let out a disturbed sigh of frustration, then pulled the horse around and slowly left the alleyway, careful to glance behind him a few last times to be absolutely sure.

Kim let out a sigh of her own as she started to get up from the position that had left a cramped feeling in her neck, only to be yanked right back down by the strong arm of her partner.

"What?" she asked in annoyed surprise.

His only answer was to put a finger to his lips, then to point at the mirror he still held. She stared at if for a moment, her breath fading as the police officer appeared again around the edge of the alleyway as if stealing one last glance of assurance, then disappeared down the street.

She let out a soft hiccup as she caught the breath she had been holding, then slowly sat up in the back seat of the car.

"How did you know?" she asked quietly, as if her words could pull the police officer back.

Fletcher shrugged again. "It's what I would have done in his place."

Slowly the two of them climbed out of the car to stretch, as the noise in the city began its daily awakenings. They hesitated by the car a few minutes more, then began to relax.

"We've both lost our hazing ability," she commented softly.

"We didn't have much choice."

She nodded as she looked at the indicator on her WCD. "It's still in waiting mode, so the Skim wasn't blown or anything. I just hope we don't need to haze to pull this thing off."

Fletcher leaned against the car as her words sank in. The last thing he could afford was another bungled case—not to mention the ramifications to the Skim itself.

"Where is that damned cat?" he half whispered to himself.

"Not a cat owner," she said with a smile, "are you?"

His brow creased as he focused his attention back at her for a moment. "Is that necessary criteria for us to be partners?"

"Nope," she laughed lightly, her soft Asian accent almost taking on a British tone, "but you'd better let me handle the cat when we see it."

"No arguments here."

They stopped talking for more than fifteen minutes, as Fletcher continually checked his own WCD. "We've got over a quarter of an hour to go," he commented, "and still no sign of the cat."

"Scrambles," she reminded him again.

"Dumb name for a cat," he grumbled to himself.

"Definitely not a cat owner," she chuckled.

"Maybe we should check on the kid?" he suggested. "Just to be sure."

"Great idea," she agreed as she quietly climbed up the car, careful not to make any noises. She reached up to the barred window and pulled herself up to eye level, ever cautious of being spotted from within.

"Well, how about that," she muttered softly, her voice taking on an almost maternal tone. Then she glanced back down at Fletcher who was waiting below. "Phantom, come and take a look."

The major climbed up the car, then pulled himself up on the bars as she made room for him at the window. He stole a glimpse around the small sterile room that was little better that a sanitary prison cell, finally focusing on the cot. There, little Johnny slept peacefully, hardly a care on his tiny face. However, it wasn't the child's smile that brought a grin to the Time Skimmer's face, but the small ball of fluff that was peacefully curled under the boy's chin, softly purring in rhythm to his breathing.

"Well...I'll be."

"I think we found Scrambles," Kim said with a happy smile.

Fletcher lowered himself back to the car top, then slid back to the ground. "Yes, now all we have to do is keep her alive another ten minutes or so."

His partner lowered herself down to the street next to him, concern lacing her features. "Scrambles was killed by a car, according the Omni computer." She glanced up the long alleyway to the open street, which now had more cars passing back and forth, well over thirty miles per hour. "We have to keep him in the alley."

"Sounds easy enough," he commented as he evaluated the distance from the window to the street. "We just catch the cat and hold him."

Kim cocked her head to one side, then shook it slightly back and forth. "It may not be as easy as you think," she said with a sigh. "Remember, you're not the cat owner."

Fletcher made a little face, then sat on the hood of the car. "Alright then, what do you suggest?"

"We have to catch the cat," she commented, almost as if running it over in her own mind. "However, how long to hold it is the question. We could save it from being hit by a car, only to let it go to get hit by another one. How will we know when to let Scrambles go?"

That thought had not occurred to the major, and the question flung both of them back into silence as they each ran various scenarios over and over in their heads. Dealing with the human element seemed vastly simple compared to this, since the one being saved was an animal, and an unpredictable one at that.

In time, a slow smile began to creep along the corners of Fletcher's mouth as the answer dawned on him with a simplicity that made him laugh that it had not come much sooner.

"What's so funny?"

"It just occurred to me," he answered with a grin, "that all we have to do is hold the cat until our WCD indicators turn green."

Her grin reflected his own as she sat down on the hood next to him. "Great." Then her smile faded as she got back up again a paced a few steps away from him. Fletcher's deep blue eyes studied her carefully as she moved away from him, her sudden shift in mood revealing her concern.

"What's wrong, Tsunami?"

"I don't know," she said, the lack of conviction making clear the opposite. "It's this whole Skim…I mean Spiral Run. I have to keep reminding myself that this is virtual reality. When that police officer pulled his gun on me…" her voice faded away.

"This feels very real," Fletcher admitted, understanding her feelings more than he wanted to admit. "It's easy to get wrapped up in all of this."

Her eyes dropped slightly as her gaze hit the street. "I was scared, and it wasn't real."

"You were scared?" he asked, masking his tone with curiosity. "I hadn't noticed."

She glanced back up at him, the edges of her smile returning. "Really?"

He shrugged. "I guess I was too busy watching the cop. But you're right. These Spiral Runs are quite intense…it *is* easy to get wrapped up in it. But that's probably the point of the whole exercise. I used to do things very similar to this back at the Air Force Academy. Flight and combat simulations, I mean." He let out a low laugh. "Nothing quite this intense, though."

She started to join in, then froze, her brown eyes rising from her partner to the barred windows behind and above him.

"The cat?" he asked, his voice dropping to barely a whisper.

The sharp curve of her jaw gave the slightest nod as her body tensed up, ready for action.

"What do we do?" he asked, afraid to move.

She started to shrug, when her face lit up in shock and she started to move forward.

Fletcher was about to dive out of her way when he felt a weight hit the back of his shoulders, as needle sharp claws sank into the only thing they could get traction on—the sliver of exposed skin of his neck. He let out a yelp of pain as he shot up and reached behind his head, his arms flailing around as he frantically grabbed at the air, trying to catch his attacker.

The feline let out a hiss of anger and fear as the major's large hands closed on its back, retaliating by driving another set of claws into his neck, as the rear claws found the softer material of the scarlet latex body suit between the armored plates at his shoulder, and dug in deeply.

"Get this thing off of me!" he hollered as he spun around in circles, trying to get a firmer grip on it.

"Don't let him get away," she yelled in return as she danced around him, trying to see if she could grab the cat. "Let go of his neck," she commanded, "you're hurting him."

"Thanks for noticing," Fletcher said, as he tried again to pull of the cat without losing all his skin.

"I was talking to *you*, Phantom," she said sharply. "You're hurting Scrambles…and scaring him."

"Me? Hurting *him*?" the major asked in pained wonder as the cat continued to hiss and cry.

"Stop squeezing him," she ordered as she hit one of his arms away from the feline.

"Whose side are you on?" he snapped at her as he let go of the cat.

Instantly Scrambles vaulted off his scarred neck, clearing Kim's outstretched arms and landing on the dirt covered pavement of the alley. There she glared back at the two Skimmers, the fur on her tail and back erect, her ears flat against her head, as venomous daggers seemed to fly from her deep mustard eyes to her two assailants.

The Skimmers glanced at each other for a moment, as if unsure of who was going to act, then Fletcher dove at the cat, his arms poised to clamp onto her body. He hit the ground with a thud as Scrambles leapt straight into the air, dexterously avoiding the massive arms that threatened her. The cat landed firmly on Fletcher's head and immediately jumped off, digging in her claws into his neck again for more power in the leap.

The major let out another cry of pain as the cat sped just out of his reach, then began fleeing down the alley towards the street.

"No—" Kim yelled as she vaulted over her prone partner and tore down the alley after the cat, calling out her name in as soothing a voice as she could muster while running.

Fletcher forced himself back up to follow, but realized that any hope for saving the cat lay fully in his partner now. He quickly glanced at the chronometer on his WCD, which indicated that they had eight seconds left to accomplish their mission. His head snapped back up to warn her, but no words left his lips as he saw the cat run into the main street, Kim in hot pursuit.

Tires squealed in frustration as a milk truck bore down on the feline, who suddenly froze in indecision as the mammoth vehicle closed on her like an anvil of doom. Kim's eyes narrowed into determined slits as she forced the truck out of her mind and dove at the frozen cat, aiming just past it. Her hands closed firmly on its fur as she tucked her head in and landed in a somersault that barely cleared the milk truck as she came up in a crouch—right in the path of a bus coming the other way. Her head snapped to the left to verify the way back was clear and fell backwards in a reverse roll to end up back at the edge of the alleyway, the shivering cat still tucked tightly in her arms.

Fletcher had gone to the edge of the alley and grabbed her as she came to a stop. He pulled her back into the narrow way, as car horns blasted and the bus driver stuck his head out the window to chase them with a few derogatory remarks about her family's heritage. The two of them ran back to the rusted sedan and took a few deep breaths to calm down.

"Are you alright?" he asked, concern in his voice.

Kim nodded as she took in a few more lung fulls of air.

A small grin came to his lips as he reached out and petted the cat's head. "Actually, I was talking to Scrambles."

Before she could respond he looked at his WCD indicator, his grin turning into a wide smile as the emerald green light heralded their success and the return light illuminated. "We did it," he said with relief. "Let's get out of here."

"One moment," she said as she cradled the terrified cat. She climbed up the car with one hand, and then pushed Scrambles up to the bars of Johnny's window. The cat immediately jumped back into the room and onto the boy's bed, to curl up where she was before. Then Kim lowered herself back down to the street and sat on the hood with a grin. "Still green?"

He checked his WCD again to be sure. "Still green." Then a thought occurred to him that made no sense. "If Scrambles was running from us, didn't we create the situation that almost got her killed?"

Kim shook her head. "You didn't notice but a door slammed behind the cat…probably from Johnny's room. That's why she jumped on you. If we weren't here, she probably would have run into the street anyway."

He nodded, as he reached to the ripped skin on his neck to rub out the pain, his hand coming back covered in blood, causing him to frown. "Pretty real for virtual reality, huh?"

"Yea," she agreed. "Does it hurt?"

"Some," he admitted, "but probably not as much as it should. What about your crazy stunt? Think you would have done that if this was real?"

"I don't know," she answered quietly. "I wasn't really thinking about it, I just wanted to save the cat."

"I'm sure Scrambles appreciates that," he laughed as he picked up his helmet that had fallen off in the fray.

"You called him Scrambles," she said, her head cocked to one side in amusement.

"That's her name, Tsunami, isn't it?"

Her only answer was a slight frown.

"Let's get back," he said as he lifted up his arm and readied the return button. When he saw that she was ready as well, he pressed the button as she did, sending them back the colored spiral to the *Twilight* center.

When they came out of the Spiral Run they found Checkmate standing over them, a light smile on his stoic face. "Not bad," he admitted after a few moments of silence. "Not bad at all."

## Chapter 6
# Down Time

Fletcher had hoped to catch Carrie as he left the Spiral Run center, but she was nowhere to be found. He wasn't surprised, as he learned that each team of trainees finished their runs at different times. The part that had truly dazzled him was after he had disconnected from the system, he found that his neck suddenly did not hurt anymore.

"Of course there's no wound," Checkmate had stated bluntly. "You were in VR, not a real Time Skim. You think we want our cadets dying on us while in training?"

He had hoped that Carrie and Condor would have finished their Spiral Run after him, so that he could wait for her, but they had finished theirs successfully over an hour before he and Tsunami got out. Something inside told him to continue looking for her, but instead he ended up at the observation lounge, which was a dimly-lit bar of sorts with a panoramic window that displayed the multicolors of flowing time that constantly surrounded and encircled the *Twilight* complex. There he sat for hours, drinking and staring at the complex images that swirled outside the protective shielding, deep in his own swirl of thoughts more turbulent than the shifting currents outside.

"What are you drinking?" came a soft voice as he felt someone settle into the only other chair at the small table he was sitting at next to the window.

His gaze didn't alter, as he brought the glass to his lips, letting some of the bitter sweet amber liquid slide down his throat like liquid fire. "Tequila," he finally answered. "Want some?"

"Not my cup of tea," she responded, that almost undetectable British accent toning her voice once more. "Speaking of which…One cup of hot green tea, please," she said into the ordering receptacle on the table.

He finally glanced over at her and let out a soft sigh of annoyance. "Why don't you join me, Kim?"

"Why, thank you," she said with a smile. "You don't want to be alone anyway."

"Is that so?" he asked as he took another drink from his glass. "I thought I did."

She shook her head as her smile remained unwavering. "If you wanted to be alone you wouldn't be in the observation lounge, surrounded by people. You'd be in your quarters."

"My quarters don't have this view," he stated as a meek smile crawled onto his face. "I love this view."

"It *is* magnificent," she agreed as she gazed into the multicolored splendor. "But I don't think I'm the one you want to be sharing it with…am I?"

His left eyebrow rose slightly as he studied the young woman confronting him. "Dodging the point has never been a problem for you I'll bet."

"My father always told me to speak my mind if I wanted to be heard," she said happily.

"Your parents were Korean also, I'm going to assume."

She nodded.

"So what's with the British accent I catch you with once in a while?"

"Do I really do that?" she asked, seemingly surprised.

"Ever listen to yourself?"

She shook her head. "I guess I shouldn't be surprised. I tend to pick up accents easily and I was going to Oxford University when the accident happened that brought me here."

"Accident?" he asked. "Oh, you mean the incident that brought you to *Twilight*. What happened?"

"I was run over by a car in London while jogging one morning," she said, her voice growing quiet. "Or at least that's what was supposed to happen to me when I was saved at the last moment by a Skimmer."

"Which one?" he asked.

"Would you believe Checkmate?" she said with a grin.

"You're kidding me. I didn't know he still did active Skims."

She nodded. "Sure he does. It was a very upsetting experience."

"I'm sure it was," he agreed, remembering his own 'incident', when a thought occurred to him. "Then it was especially brave what you did today in the Spiral Run."

"Not brave," she half said to herself, "just instinct. The more I think about it the more terrified I become thinking about what could have happened if it had been a real Skim, instead of VR."

He reached out and put his hand on her arm and gave it a small squeeze. "You did real good today, you should be proud."

"Thanks," she said while lifting her head back up to meet his gaze. "Did you know I'm from your time? I left London just a few months after you were shot down in the Middle East."

Fletcher almost choked on the tequila he was drinking. "You've been checking on me?"

"I looked you up when I found out about the team switch," she admitted. "I hope you don't mind."

"Not really," he said with a shrug. "But that does put me at a disadvantage with you."

"I like it that way," she said as she let out a short laugh. "OK, here's the story…"

The undefined depression that had engulfed Fletcher slowly dissipated over the hour as Kim related to him the tale of growing up in Korea, of her family who were rice farmers, of her engineering scholarship to Oxford, and the eventual moment of the accident that brought her here.

"So you left our time months after me, but arrived in *Twilight* only two hours after I did," he said, happy to talk with someone who lived in the same decade as he.

"I guess that's *Twilight* for you," she agreed, then narrowed her eyes as a sly grin came to her soft Asian features. "And *you* totally managed to derail me from talking to you about what I wanted to."

"Me?" he asked with a smile. "Why would I do that?"

"Why indeed," she said while leaning forward on her elbows. "Perhaps you're just as evasive as I'm direct."

"Perhaps…" his voice trailed off as his good spirits lost their tenuous hold on his mood, and he turned back to the panoramic view that lay outside.

"So," she persisted anyway, despite the implied resistance to the subject, "what's the deal with the two of you?"

"I don't know," he said while bringing the glass to his lips again, only to find it empty. "Maybe it's some sort of chemistry. Something when I saw her for the first time…looked into her eyes…it sounds ridiculous."

Kim's eyes took on a misty sheen as she leaned forward onto her hands. "Not really," she almost sighed as romantic visions flashed in her head. Then her brow suddenly creased and she hit his arm. "So then why did you act like a jerk on your Time Skim together?"

"Who knows," he said absently while continuing to stare outside.

"You, if anyone," she commented.

Fletcher let out a deep breath and ordered another glass of tequila from the table and took a long drink when it arrived. "Relationships have never been my strong suit," he said quietly while holding the half-empty glass against his forehead, his face turned down to the table. "I've had plenty of dates, even had a somewhat serious relationship once when I was first out of the Academy…but it turned out bad."

"Everyone has a bad relationship," she said, trying to understand the emotions driving the major.

"Maybe so, but we were happy, and young…I thought we were in love."

"Weren't you?"

"I guess not," he said with a touch of sadness in his voice. "When it came down to the wire, I couldn't commit. I kept backing off until she wasn't there anymore. It's as if some insidious demon inside takes over and I say or do something that hurts the women I care about just to scare them off. And you know what, Kim…it works. It works too damn well." He drained the remainder of the glass and ordered another.

"How many is that?" she asked as he dove into the freshly-filled glass.

He shrugged. "More than I can count on one hand."

She studied him silently for a moment, judging his clarity and quickly decided that she was grateful that he had nowhere to drive that night. "So, if you know that you do it, why don't you do something about it?"

"Maybe it protects me," he said, his voice beginning to slur from the alcohol.

"The only thing it protects you from is having a good relationship with a woman that really likes you."

"Carrie likes me?" he asked, a silly smile coming to his lips as an almost glassy look sank into his eyes.

"What do you think?" she half scolded. "I'm her friend, and she tells me she can't figure you out."

"What about you?" he laughed quietly. "Can you figure me out?"

She stared at him in silence for a few moments, then nodded. "Maybe a little. Enough to know that you should be telling this to her and not me."

"That's what I'll do," he declared too loudly as he stood up, drawing stares from half the people in the lounge.

Sudden panic hit Kim at the thought of what he'd say in this state and she reached across the table and pulled him back down to his seat.

"Good idea," she reaffirmed. "However, the timing isn't that great. I'd wait a day or so to let her cool down. After all, she did request the partner change just this morning."

He glared at her blankly for a moment, then nodded, suddenly feeling like a complete idiot for the second time that day. "I think I'm going to turn in for the night," he half sighed, "before I really mess up my life." Then got up with a stumble.

"Good idea, Phantom," she agreed as she got up. "Um…would you mind walking me back to the quarters area? I hate going down the corridors alone at this hour."

He gave her a short smile of gratitude, pleased that she'd protect his pride even in this state. "I'd be honored."

A breath of relief escaped through her lips as she took his arm, and walked him out of the lounge.

## Chapter 7
# Spiraling Down

Being at ground zero during a nuclear blast would have seemed a less painful experience to Major Taylor then the way his head felt when the alarm went off the next morning, reminding him in the worst way that he was going to be late to class once again.

Stumbling from the bed to the bathroom, he barely let himself get wet in the shower before he was back out and off towards the Spiral Run control center, not taking the time to put on the armor plates over the scarlet suit. He arrived at the training area just as the cadets were beginning to head off in teams towards the chambers. Everyone hesitated to watch as he ran into the room, the ebony armor plates cradled in his arms. However, the opinions of the cadets were far from his mind, it was only the blank stare from Carrie that his thoughts managed to focus on. Despite the boiling feeling in his head as his hangover ripped at his central nervous system, it paled in comparison to the moment of sadness that he could read in her eyes as she stared at him from across the room, then grabbed a confused Condor's arm and led him down the corridor to their chamber. Fletcher took an involuntary step after them, seriously considering pursuing her for a half second, then stopped as the stares from the rest of the trainees finally registered into his mind.

"I see you are working on your promptness, Phantom," Checkmate's voice firmly rang, as he glared in disdain at the trainee's unassembled armor. "It would seem however that what you gained in speed, you have lost in preparation."

Sensing a conflict, the remainder of the cadets swiftly dissipated down the corridors like rabbits fleeing a hunter, leaving only the three of them. The major glanced over at Kim, who gave him a sympathetic shrug of her shoulders which was closely followed by the meekest of smiles.

Fletcher reached up his hand and rubbed his face that felt as if it was swollen to twice normal size. Then he looked back at the trainer, who noticed the sharp crimson tone to his eyes for the first time that morning.

"I see," Checkmate stated quietly as he approached. "Can you manage to function this morning, or are you still blotto?"

"I'm fine," came the response that lacked any sort of conviction.

"I suppose we shall find out shortly, shan't we?" He glanced over to Kim, who was patiently waiting to one side. "If you want to call off this joint Spiral Run I can send you on a solo one instead. No reason for you to suffer for this."

She seemed to consider for a moment, as she stared at the major, who was slowly putting on his armor plates. "We'll be just fine, Checkmate," she assured while stepping forward to pat her partner on the shoulder. "Come on, Phantom," she urged, "let's get going."

Fletcher nodded as he quickly attached the armor plates to his body suit, then pulled on the gauntlets. Taking the mission card that she offered him, he slid it into his WCD, absorbing the mission details for the day.

He took a few moments, to make sure he understood the parameters of the mission, as Kim started to urge him towards the corridor.

"Checkmate," he asked, moving back towards the trainer. "I have a question or two."

"Yes?"

He glanced down at the readout on his WCD. "It states here that we're going to Paris, in the year twenty-one, sixty-five. To slow down an assassination attempt that failed."

"Yes?"

"I thought we didn't got involved in important historical events. And this certainly counts as one."

The trainer took a moment to read a copy of the mission that they were to follow that day, then nodded.

"The mission parameters are clear here. This was the first time that the CEC, or Consolidated Earth Council met with an alien race in a peace talk. The Rateen of the Royal Valkeeran Dominion is visiting Earth for the summit talks. On the day of her arrival, an assassination attempt was made by radical Earth right wing isolationists. The attempt was foiled by her own personal guards. This attack seriously hurt the summit talks and delayed peace for another five years. However, the Omni computer believes that if the assassins were delayed one minute longer, the Earth military would have stopped them on their own, which would have been a great show of strength to the

Valkeerans."

Fletcher stared at the trainer for a moment. "I read the report," he said with a touch of annoyance. "However, you didn't answer my question."

"The level of involvement in this instance is actually quite minor," Checkmate argued, "and this is a very rare case where our involvement shouldn't have any negative effects for either people. Besides, earlier peace would benefit both races, and it benefits *Twilight* as well."

"How so?"

"With Earth and the Royal Valkeeran Dominion at peace sooner, Justin will have more resources for the station."

"Isn't that somewhat self supporting?" Fletcher asked, curious of the motives that guided Justin. "I thought we were only here to help the people, not ourselves."

"By increasing our resources," Checkmate's low British tone drilled, "we shall be able to continue to do just that. Don't forget, this is simply a Spiral Run of a Time Skim that already happened."

The major let this sink in for a few seconds, but his headache made it hard to concentrate. It was at that moment that the true ramifications of his mission sank home. "Wait a moment, this is a future mission, not a past mission."

"It's only a future mission if you keep your mind stuck in the twentieth century," the instructor reminded him. "Remember, we cover missions up to Justin's present time, which is in Earth's twenty-fourth century."

Fletcher considered it for a moment, then shook his head. "Doesn't that put us out of our element, going to the future?"

"As you pointed out yourself, every mission is out of your element," Checkmate tried to explain. "This is because every mission is in a time that is not entirely your own. Think of me, I'm from your eighteen hundreds, but I was the one who brought Tsunami here from the late twentieth century. We are Time Skimmers, Phantom...our element is *all* times, *all* places; you have to stop thinking linearly."

The major let out a soft breath, then grinned as he glanced over at Kim, his headache suddenly forgotten. "Alright, let's do it."

Inside the Spiral Run, the two trainees materialized in a narrow pathway behind a large white building that had many overpasses high above them, interlocking it with all the surrounding structures. They took a moment to acclimate themselves, as they kept to the shadows that early night cast over the street.

"We're in an alleyway," Fletcher noted quietly.

"Un-huh," she responded absently as she studied her WCD indicator to see what their time frame was, as well as to determine the direction they should take.

"Doesn't it seem that we always appear in an alleyway?" he continued, slightly amused. Then he glanced around, amazed at how antiseptic the street seemed. "Though I'll admit that it's the cleanest alleyway I've ever seen."

"It would seem like a logical place to drop us off," Kim commented quietly while reading the emerald letters on her wrist screen. "Alleyways are almost always abandoned."

Seeing that she had no mind for idle chatter, he changed his tone to one of business. "So, what does it say?"

"We have less than ten minutes to accomplish the mission," she informed him while verifying the pointer. "And we need to gain access to this building some how. That's what the mission indicator tells us."

Fletcher studied the tall monolith, and tried to consider a way for them to enter easily. "Stay here," he told her, "I'm going to check out the street and the entrance to this building."

"I'll look in the back," she said, and headed off that way.

The major nodded in agreement then quietly slunk up towards the main street, though he quickly noted that stealth would be next to impossible here. The streets were coated with a white, plastic material that was clean and obviously well maintained. The same material covered the building that they needed access to, and he realized that in his black armor he stuck out like a beetle on a white wall. That is until he reached the street and checked out the situation. There were many more pedestrians than he would have thought in a future city, most in states of dress that would have put the Jetsons to shame. Red neon shirts were tucked into metallic blue pants, next to jet black dresses with electrical highlights of moving energy. Fletcher shook his head a few times to make sure what he was seeing made sense, then laughed and turned back to find his partner.

He caught up to her as she returned from the back, a look of concern on her face.

"It's no good back there," she said with a touch of disappointment, "it's all locked up. What about out front?"

Fletcher started to open his mouth to explain what he saw, then started to chuckle again. "I don't think we'll have a problem out front. Come on."

Kim gave him a strange look, then followed as he led her back to the main street. Her mouth opened in surprise as he walked straight out into the street. Making a quick grab at his arm, she wondered if he had lost his senses, but he managed to pull her out along with him. For a moment she cringed, expecting people to yell and point at them immediately, then she started to look at the people around, her face showing her amazement.

"Excuse me," a passerby in a fluorescent yellow tunic said to them as he skirted around the two trainees, obviously in a big rush.

They watched him continue along the ivory sidewalk in amused silence for a moment, then a slow thought caught up with Fletcher's mind, and he almost did a double take.

"That man spoke to us in French," he stated, still amazed. "I think our helmets translated it instantly for us."

She pursed her lips for a moment as she tried to recall the incident, then nodded. "You're right. I did hear another language for a brief instant, but it was so quiet it was almost like background noise."

"You would have thought that Checkmate would have mentioned it," he said almost absently, then shrugged, overcome by a sudden wave of good spirits. "Well, no one seems to be noticing us, so let's try to get in."

The two of them walked up towards the large building that stretched up into the sky like an immense obelisk, and paused at the doorway. The building had what seemed hundreds of flags on the front, some totally unrecognizable. Under it, in large black letters, read *Consolidated Earth Council.* It was then that they noticed the guards in white battle armor, guarding the inside of the doorway. They carefully policed the widened doorway, thoroughly checking each person that entered or left.

"Hmmm," was Fletcher's comment to this development.

"They don't seem to be watching people once through the entrance," Kim noted. "Why can't we just haze thorough the checkpoint and then go on our way?"

He considered it for a moment, and could find no real flaw with the idea. Suddenly, he realized that he was anxious to get inside, but wasn't sure why. "Sounds fine," he agreed while readying his WCD.

"Great. Let's do it."

They activated the hazing mode on their WCDs, quickly fading from sight. One passerby stopped and shook his head in wonder, but quickly lost interest and kept on walking along. Kim reached out and groped for Fletcher's hand and held onto it when she found it.

"Let's stay together," she whispered.

He nodded in agreement, then realized that she couldn't see that. "Gotcha."

The two of them started forward, pausing at the electronically activated door as someone left the building. Before the door could close back up, they slipped inside and walked right by the heavily-armed soldiers, who had *CEC Guard* written on their armor. Once inside they quickly ran into the main concourse, to put as much distance between themselves and the guards as possible.

Kim paused at a reception table and grabbed two visitors' passes that were on it, closely guarded over by another soldier. Once inside the concourse they stepped away from the moving sidewalk, and swiftly searched for a private place to reappear. They gave each other a squeeze of the hand as they both noticed the rest rooms at the same time.

"How much time to we have left?" he whispered.

"No more than ten seconds," she blurted quickly. "I'll meet you in a moment."

He felt her let go of his hand and heard her run towards the ladies' room. Taking a swift glance around at the numerous people milling about the concourse, he bolted to the men's room and dove inside, just as he reverse faded back into view. It was only then that he took another look around, grateful that the restroom had been empty. Swallowing a deep breath, he strode back out into the concourse, just as Kim reappeared as well.

"How much time do we have?" he asked as she walked up to him.

"About five minutes now."

He was about to comment on their best course of action, when he looked up in amazement as they emerged into the center of the concourse. When he had first seen the *Twilight* center, he had been awed at its high tech splendor. However, that seemed minor in comparison to the hundred story mammoth that rose above him. The spiraling center was empty so he could see all the way to the laser-enhanced, multicolored, holographic image of the Earth, rotating slowly on its access.

"My God, Con would have loved this," he said half to himself, momentarily saddened by the thought of the friend he had left behind.

"Who's Con?" Kim asked as they continued to head in the direction their WCDs indicated.

"He was my partner back in my own time," he explained softly, the jump drained out of his stride, "he was also the best friend I ever had."

"Maybe you'll see him again some day," she said with a concerned smile.

He shook his head slowly. "He died right next to me on the day I came here."

Kim's eyes widened in surprise as she absorbed this news. She pretended to brush it off and looked at her WCD again. "We only have a few minutes, but it should be right up there." She pointed to a landing above them, which served as an observation level to the concourse, which they noticed was now being cleared out by the ivory-armored soldiers of the CEC.

"All personnel must clear the concourse now," came an automated voice over a loud speaker. "The Valkeeran delegation is arriving now. All personnel must clear…" it droned on, as the people quickly scampered to higher levels.

The two trainees found it easy to move with the crowd, getting into an elevator that dropped them off on the second level, along with a few dozen others who were there to view the historic occasion.

Kim's eyes twinkled as she stared down from the balcony at the open main doorway, as more white-armored guards started coming through.

Fletcher glanced over at her and smiled, understanding the feeling full well. "Amazing, isn't it?"

"Amazing isn't the right word," she said, her eyes riveted to the doorway, as a procession started to move in. "In a moment or two, the first aliens seen by Earth are going to enter, and we're here to see it."

The smile on his face grew at her youthful exuberance, driving away the sad feelings that remembering Con had dredged up. Such was his happiness he decided not to remind her that this was only a virtual reality experience, and that they weren't really there at all. Instead he put his hand on her shoulder and gave it a small squeeze.

"Tsunami, don't forget to keep an eye out for the bad guys."

"Right," she agreed as she checked the readings on her WCD. "According to the mission details, the CEC forces would have stopped the attempt if they had had only one more minute to get here. This is all supposed to happen in the next three minutes, right were we are standing. So…"

"So," he continued for her, "in theory, the CEC forces should have already been alerted to the danger and are on their way."

They started to search around on both the balcony and below, hoping to spot something wrong, which wasn't hard to do. Below them, running along the bottom level, was a squad of CEC soldiers, heading towards the elevator that was right next to them. The two cadets looked at each other in suspicion, then glanced straight down the outside of the elevator shaft to the first level. There below were two men in gold and red jumpsuits with rifles in their arms pushing their way towards the elevator. In another moment they'd be inside and the CEC forces would have to wait for the elevator to return to their level to continue the pursuit.

Before he could act, Kim reached up and pushed the elevator call button, summoning the elevator back up to the second level. The would-be assassins had almost reached the doors as they closed on them, sending the elevator out of reach. Instantly the mission indicators on their WCDs turned green, and the return lights illuminated, signaling that they could return at any time.

"Not bad, Tsunami," Fletcher commented, forcing his best Checkmate impression. "Not bad at all."

"Hey," she said with a grin that spread from ear to ear, "it's a gift."

"Shall we," he motioned back to the balcony railing, continuing his best attempt to maintain a British accent.

"Most definitely," she answered, following suit.

Together they returned to the railing, which was emptying as attention was drawn to the altercation below, while the CEC soldiers apprehended the armed terrorists without incident.

It was then that they saw the Rateen of the Royal Valkeeran Dominion come in, adorned in her white and blue uniform with a long, draped cloak, her wavy blonde hair cascading about her shoulders as she strode in with the pride of kings in each step.

"She looks human," Kim said, a touch of disappointment in her voice. "I was hoping for some bug-eyed alien."

"What does Rateen mean, anyway?" he asked her.

"I think it means queen…or something like that."

"Wanna get out of here?" he asked, patting her on the shoulder.

She let out a snort of disappointment, which drew more than one stare. Then they moved to the far side of the balcony where no one was watching and hit their return buttons, leaving twenty-second century Earth, or at least the VR version of it, far behind.

A small party was organized for the cadets in the observation lounge, to celebrate the complete success of all Spiral Runs done that day; a first time event for the class. A buffet affair was organized with food provided by the senior staff of the *Twilight* complex, to congratulate the students on a job well in hand.

Fletcher found himself in great spirits that night, despite an unacknowledged blackness that continued to scratch at his good mood. Like water eroding a rock over time, this thought continued to lay in his subconscious, unrealized, but there as he sat at a table with Kim and passed jokes about the missions that they had been on. Despite all this, his eyes flicked to a table on the far side of the room, where Carrie sat with Condor and a bunch of their friends, eating and laughing together. For a moment her head turned as her jade pools clashed against his blue sea, their eyes locking together, both hoping for a brief glimpse into the other's soul. Then the moment was shattered as Justin stood up at the makeshift podium and tapped the small microphone, testing it. Fletcher's eyes briefly diverted from their purpose to the *Twilight* leader, but as they darted back it was too late. She had turned back to her friends, and an inexplicable emptiness filled his heart, as that suppressed thought struggled to surface.

Justin cleared his throat twice, a seemingly innocent gesture that provided him with everyone's attention. "Good evening," the thin *Twilight* leader said with a warm smile, "Checkmate tells me that you are doing a fair job in the training center."

A few chuckles muffled through the room.

"But seriously," he continued, his grin never wavering, "you are all doing fantastically. Better than we've had in a long time, and I'm sure that this small gathering will transform itself into a graduation celebration in just a few days." He glanced around the observation lounge and made a wide sweeping gesture with his hand. "If you like this, you'll love the real party—a celebration that I'm sure you will all be attending in good spirits, knowing that a hard job has been well done. As for tonight, enjoy the dinner and the chance to relax. You earned them."

Checkmate stepped up to the makeshift podium and took the mike that Justin offered him. "Yes, enjoy yourselves tonight," he affirmed the *Twilight* leader's commands, "but you are all still expected to be at the training center tomorrow morning, ready to enter your Spiral Runs sharply on time." His eagle eyes briefly scanned the room, momentarily locking on the table Fletcher sat at with Kim. "This has not been a problem for *most*, and tomorrow should be no different." He started to walk away, when Justin cleared his throat again, the happenstance working in his favor once again. The instructor looked back at the *Twilight* leader, who cocked his head to one side towards the microphone, which Checkmate reluctantly picked up again.

"You don't need me to coddle you and tell you what kind of job you are doing in there," his British accent sharply noting each emphasis in his sentence. "You are all quite aware of what you are capable of. Just remember, it gets no easier from here on in. You still have three more Spiral Runs to go through before graduation."

Condor raised a hand out of classroom instinct, then quickly pulled it back when all eyes turned his way. "Only three more?"

"That's right," Checkmate affirmed. "You have two more standard runs, then your graduation test, which is your most important Spiral Run. Your performance there will have a big impact on our decision to put you into the field on an actual Time Skim or not."

Kim's eyes turned to Fletcher to share her excitement with the news of how close they were to graduation, but noticed that he wasn't even facing the trainer; instead he was staring off at the table on the far right. She didn't even have to look over there to know who he was watching. Her lips tightened for a moment as she shook her head, a spark of determination coming to her soft brown eyes.

"Enough with the speeches," Justin cut back in, taking the mike from Borlin. "I'll let you guys get back to enjoying the evening. Keep up the good work."

The *Twilight* leader hesitated at the podium a moment longer, his gaze resting on Fletcher's table, then flicking ever so subtly to Carrie's. For a moment he seemed concerned, then took a deep breath which turned back into his smile, and left the observation lounge, followed closely by Checkmate.

"You know you want to talk with her," Kim said quietly as the party resumed its previous noise level, "so go and talk with her."

The major's head snapped back over to his partner as his chiseled features wrinkled into a frown. "Excuse me?"

"Remember our little chat last night?" she reminded him.

He nodded, then looked unsure. "Most of it."

"Well," she continued while motioning with her hands for him to get up, "now would be a good time to tell her what you wanted to tell her."

"Right," he seemed to agree, though made no effort to rise from his chair. "What did I want to tell her?"

Frustration creased her youthful features as she rubbed her face with her hands. "Men," she groaned softly, then got up from the table. "Well, if you're not going to talk to her, I will." With that she strode off towards Carrie's table, grabbed an empty chair and joined them.

Fletcher's lips pressed thin with determination as he moved to get up and follow her, when a burst of youthful laughter from that table suddenly drained him of the will to rise. A sudden feeling of age struck him as he glanced back at the table of cadets whose mean age, with the exception of Carrie, was no more than the early twenties. For a moment he questioned if that was really the reason that he wasn't getting up, wasn't going to talk with them. Somehow he doubted this, but failed to convince his mind one way or the other. The only thought that consolidated was the one that had been trying to come out all night, and when it did he knew there was no longer an option to ignore it. Every twist of her head that caused her russet hair to shimmer, every light bend of her hand that sent her silken sleeve gliding effortlessly down the ivory skin of her arm, placed iron bolts on the foundation of these thoughts, and he doubted that he'd get any sleep this night.

"So who dubbed you the Lone Ranger?"

Fletcher turned at the new voice to see the med tech seating himself at his table, a drink in one hand and a slice of pizza in the other.

"Hi, Eric," he said, happy to see a friendly face.

"Hey, Kimosave," the tech said with a grin, "why not kick the 'solo hero' bit and join the others?"

"Actually, I'm enjoying a few moments by myself," he lied, immediately wondering why he did.

"Oh," Eric said as his face stretched in an exaggerated state of apology, "I'll split."

"No," Fletcher quickly said to stop the youth from leaving. "It's okay."

"Nah," the med tech said as he got up, "don't worry about it. I was going over there anyway…why don't you come too? You're one of us, you know."

The major's lips tightened for a moment as he took in a deep breath. "I know," he agreed, "but I'm still happy here."

Eric shrugged and sauntered off towards the table, anxious to join his friends, leaving Fletcher in silence.

For almost an hour the major sat there nursing one drink, not in any hurry to repeat his hangover from last night. Then an internal signal went off and he decided that it was enough for the night. He didn't feel comfortable going over to join the cadets, even though he knew he was more than welcome, and staying at the table alone seemed far worse. He was about to get up and leave, when Kim broke away from her friends and quickly scampered back to his table and sat back in her earlier seat.

"Looked like you were going to leave," she commented with a raised eyebrow. "Or were you finally going to come over and talk to her?"

"There's that problem you have again of avoiding the point," he said with a forced smile that hid his annoyance. "I'd prefer to talk with her alone."

"So ask her to take a walk or something," she suggested. "I'm sure she'd go with you."

For a moment he considered it, as he glanced back over at the table. However, the thought died a swift death as he watched the cadets joking with each other. "I have no desire to advertise the situation between Starfox and myself."

Her eyes widened in exasperation. "Hey, newsflash…you already have by sitting here alone all night and making moony eyes at her."

He glared at her for a moment, judging the validity of her words, and cringed internally as he considered the possibility that she was correct. Letting out a short breath, he half shrugged. "So what am I going to do? The last time I talked to her I wasn't at my best."

"So," she said as she placed her hand on his, "you make up for it. Nothing that was done is irreversible."

"She sure dumped me as a partner fast enough," he commented under his breath, immediately realizing how lame the statement sounded.

"I wouldn't be so sure," she contradicted him.

"What do you mean?" he asked, his curiosity peaked.

"I was just talking with her and she said that she was upset because you requested the partner change so quickly."

"But I didn't request it," he shot back. "You know that. You were there when Checkmate told me it was she that requested it."

"I do remember the moment," she said with a smile. "I'm not sure how this mix-up happened, but it did."

"Did you tell her that I thought it was her that made the request?"

"No," she admitted, "you're both my friends and I think that getting involved is the surest way to jeopardize that."

"You don't think you're involved already?"

"Not that deeply," she defended. "Not to the point where I'll speak for either of you." Then a quick smile flashed across her small mouth. "Besides, aren't you a bit old for that tactic? I'd figure you'd want to talk to her yourself."

He stared at her in silence for a moment, his eyes turning from a calm day to a hurricane in an instant, then he forced a smile. "You really think you know how to get under my skin, don't you, Kim?"

She shrugged. "I'm not doing anything but reminding you of what you already know. Unless I'm wrong…how do you feel about her?"

His eyes softened back to a calm sea as he finished his drink slowly, giving him the time he needed. "I think she's fantastic," he finally admitted. "I thought you knew that."

"I did," she agreed. "But she doesn't. So why don't you tell her?"

"It's not that simple," he argued, wondering if it was. "I *do* want another chance with her, but I've got to figure out what's going on first." With that he stood up. "Goodnight, Kim." With that he walked out of the lounge, as two sets of eyes silently watched him leave.

His intentions upon leaving the party had been simple in his mind; find Justin and get out of him what was behind the mysterious memo that it seemed that neither he nor Carrie had written. However, as he strode down the hall his conviction began to wane, as he considered the possibility that she had sent the memo, but perhaps regretted it. Either way, no matter how he presented the situation to the *Twilight* leader, he could not imagine himself sounding any less than ridiculous. In the end, he wound up back in his room; as he proved his prediction correct by staring at the ceiling all night from his bed, sleep the farthest thing from his mind.

## Chapter 8
# Spiraling Up

Fletcher was actually quite proud of himself the next morning for the speed at which he rose and prepared for class, that is until he actually got there to find Kim waiting alone in the Spiral Run control center.

"I'll bet you're not a morning person," she asked as he approached her, "are you?"

"I suppose not," he admitted, confused at the fact that he was still late when the chronometer on his WCD stated that he was just in time. "Was everyone early?"

"I suppose so," she said while they walked towards the Spiral Run chamber. "They've all gotten into the habit of getting off early."

"No one told me."

"That's 'cause you're never here when they are," she said with a grin. "Here," she handed him the mission card for the day. "We've got a cool one today."

He slid the card into his WCD, reading it as they walked down the corridor.

*Spiral Run Chamber 3:*
*August 10, 1266 — Cozumel. Yarel is a young woman belonging to the Mayan people that inhabit the Yucatan peninsula. Today is the day of her right of ascension, when she will take her boat to their holy island of Cozumel, considered to provide the fertility that changes girls into young women. She will arrive to this island fine; however, she has ulterior motives. She is really going there to meet with a young man from an enemy tribe, whom she has fallen in love with. The problem is that she is spotted with him by her sister, and reported back to her people. Consequently, her life was desolate and empty. The Omni computer believes that if she was*

*not discovered, she would have run away with this young man and lived an infinitely better and more fulfilling life.*

"Humph. You're right," Fletcher said, "this *is* pretty cool."

They settled into their chairs and hooked up to the virtual reality controls, finishing just as Checkmate came in to see them off.

"I see you're doing better with the time, Phantom," he said as he came in and checked the controls.

"I'm working on my lifestyle," Fletcher answered with a laugh.

"Very good," the trainer said as he flipped a switch. "Remember, no Skim is easy, and each has its own tricks and catches. Stay on your toes." With that said he flipped the activation switch, plunging them back into VR.

They materialized into the Departure Nucleus and gave each other a cockeyed glance.

"What do you think he meant by that?" Kim asked while stepping up onto the platform.

"I'm not sure," he admitted. "But I suspect we'll find out." He stepped up and joined her, as they both activated their WCDs and dove into the next Spiral Run.

Some say that the desert is unforgiving, and the polar regions are punishing by nature, but then there are the rain forests, full of light and life, in perfect harmony with nature. It is within this seeming paradise, underneath the emerald canopy, that the darkness can hide anything, holding the truth that struggles to escape.

It is into this concealing paradise that the two trainees materialized, deep within the jungle wilderness, unsoiled by the harsh hand of "civilization."

"Hey," Fletcher commented as he glanced about the lush rain forest that encircled them like a barrier, "we're not in an alleyway."

Kim let out a laugh as she checked her WCD indicator, then followed it with a soft grunt. "We have a few hours until we're needed, but I think we have a little distance to travel."

The major nodded as he confirmed the information on his own WCD, then glanced around as he breathed in the air that warmed his insides like hot creamed soup. It was then that he realized that despite the extremely humid climate, he wasn't uncomfortable in the least.

"The VR program must be off some," he commented as they started towards their destination. "I don't feel hot at all. But it must be over ninety out with high humidity."

"Actually, the program is running just fine," she observed while motioning towards his armor. "Take a look at your armor, it's covered in precipitation. It's the internal cooling unit in your suit that is protecting you. Why don't you try taking off your helmet?"

He tried just that, instantly regretting it, realizing that even though his face was exposed below the visor, the helmet still kept the environment stable around his head. Once outside the helmet's protection, he immediately began to perspire, his hair growing damp as the heated air blasted him full in the face. He put the helmet back on without hesitation, letting out a sigh of relief as the coolants kicked back in.

They walked in silence the majority of the way, for the most part enjoying the trek through the wilderness. Although not far from their intended location, it still took quite some time to get there through the dense forest. When they finally arrived they both sat down on thick roots which rose up from the ground like vines.

Fletcher almost considered taking his helmet off again, since it was somewhat limiting his field of vision, but opted to continue the environmental comfort instead. It was then that he noticed the snake.

"I don't want to panic you or anything," he said lightly, "but you are being attacked." He pointed at her foot.

She quickly looked down and almost jumped into the air. It seemed that she had stepped on an orange snake who was most unappreciative of the gesture and was repeatedly striking her boot, which she wasn't feeling through the armor plating.

"What should I do?" she asked, her voice suddenly strained.

"How about getting off the snake?" he suggested, his grin spreading at her apparent terror, despite the fact that she was in no danger.

She glared at him and tightened her lips. "Very funny, Phantom!" She lifted her ebony boot up and the snake immediately took off, disappearing into the dense brush.

"I didn't know you were afraid of snakes," he said almost absently. "They never bothered me."

"Well bully for you," she replied, her usually absent British accent ringing in as her arms crossed defiantly across her chest. "At least my fears are tangible."

"Tangible?" he asked. "We're in virtual reality."

"A difference which makes no difference is no difference."

"Excuse me?"

"Forget it," she said with a huff as she sat back down and buried her attention on her WCD. "We have a while to waste," she commented, apparently dismissing the earlier conversation as if it never happened. "What do you want to do?"

"Well, probably the best way to handle this is to intercept the sister some way, to keep her from finding out the truth. But that means that we'll have to keep an eye on everyone."

She nodded. "Alright, so we wait."

Without warning, rain suddenly began to fall in thick sheets of water, soaking everything in sight. Kim tilted her head back with her eyes closed and slid up the visor, letting the water strike her face through the now open helmet. Then she looked back at her partner and shrugged with a grin.

"Alright, so we wait in the rain."

Fletcher leaned back under the tree that was providing a minimal amount of protection and smiled. "I must admit that this one is definitely different than the other ones."

Kim took off her helmet, letting the water drench her hair as she shook her head, spreading the water around in spiraling sheets.

The water fell for over an hour as they sat there, trying to amuse themselves in silence, when it stopped as suddenly as it had begun. The major wiped off his WCD and pointed to it, drawing her attention.

"Almost time," he commented. "We should get ready in a few minutes."

She nodded, then caught his glance with a stare, trying for a moment of seriousness before the work began. "Did you mean what you said last night?"

"I usually mean what I say," he said with a guarded tone, wondering where this was leading to. "So what did I say?"

"You said that you wanted another chance with Starfox."

Still unsure of where this was leading, he slowly got up. "I not sure what your point is," he confessed, his tone sharpening. "Of course I would like another chance...I told you how I felt about her."

"Hey," she snapped back, "I'm just trying to help."

"I didn't ask for help."

"Maybe you need help more than you realize," her brown eyes darkened into swirling thunder clouds. "Remember...call sign, *Idiot?*"

His mouth opened to retaliate, but something inside held him back. Slowly he let out the breath he was holding and started gazing about the forest. "Call sign, Idiot…thanks for the reminder."

"That's quite alright," she said as her smile started to return, surprised by his calm.

"We only have a few minutes now," Fletcher reminded her, anxious to end the current subject. "We'd better get ready." He started to walk out of the clearing in the direction of the ocean smell that had been wafting his way.

"So you were serious about the other chance?" she insisted as she followed him along the makeshift path that was worn into the forest.

He glanced back at her then kept on walking. "What are you, Santa Claus? You going to make my wishes come true?"

Kim hesitated, letting him get a slight lead as she studied him with a mixture of annoyance and determination. "Maybe I am," she said under her breath, unheard by her partner. "We'll just have to wait and see."

She caught up to him again as they broke through the clearing onto the wide sandy beach. The hot sun burning off the white sand dazzled with a brilliance that made it hard to look at.

"This place is beautiful," she whispered. "It's almost sad to think that something this wonderful will be destroyed one day by civilization."

For an instant Fletcher considered telling her that the island was a great vacation spot, but instead pulled her back behind a tree as he pointed out into the peaceful Caribbean Sea. "Look, a canoe is approaching."

Kim stared out into the water which was so clear she could see straight to the sandy floor beneath. A long, thin boat was approaching with two women in it. They moved slowly across the water, determination on their faces.

"Those are really Mayans," Kim whispered all but silently in sheer delight, as she gazed at the two approaching natives.

Their features were delicate and slight, long ebony hair drifted down their bare red shoulders and along the simple garments they wore. Around their necks were jewels of gold and turquoise that caught the rays of the sun above. They continued on, methodically paddling as they approached the island that was sacred to them. When they finally reached the shore they both jumped out of the long canoe, their tiny bare feet splashing in the shallow water. Together they pulled the craft on shore, and turned to each other, the older of the two talking to the younger in a language long since forgotten.

Fletcher stared at them for a moment, amazed at how much like red porcelain dolls they seemed, neither could have been much over four and a half feet in height. It took a moment before he realized that the suit was translating what they were saying to each other.

"Listen to your sister, Yarel," the older of the two lectured the younger. "This is your ascension; this is when you become a woman. When we return you will wed with Malahais. The two of you will be happy."

"I will never be happy with him," Yarel insisted, her young voice singing like a dove. "Why must you and father force me into this?"

"Because that is our way," the sister insisted, "your way also. The same happened to me last season."

The younger one turned away from the other, defiantly showing her displeasure. It was then that Fletcher realized how young she must be.

"I don't want it to be my way," Yarel stated.

The major glanced over at his partner and saw anger in her face. Somehow, that feeling in her made him look back at the sisters in a new light as he put his hand on her shoulder to let her know that he understood. So engrossed were they, in the tale unfolding before them, that they almost didn't see the third native coming up from the forest behind them. Quickly they ducked down, as the male stealthily sifted through the forest like a panther on the hunt. He had a long spear in his hand, which he used to move the branches out of his way as he snuck up to the edge of the trees and hid, no more than three dozen feet from the concealed cadets.

"I will not marry him," Yarel stated again as a spark of defiance twinkled in her eyes.

"Go," her sister pointed into the woods along a rough path. "Go to the shrine and make your sacrifice to the spirits so that you can ascend. The sooner that is accomplished the quicker you can start to behave like a woman who obeys her duty…and less like a spoiled little girl."

It was then that the unseen warrior let out a soft whistle, like the call of a thrush, and Yarel turned towards the line of woods, a glint of hope on her oval face.

"What was that?" her sister asked as she cocked her head suspiciously.

"A bird, silly," the young Mayan said as she turned back to her sister, her whole demeanor instantly changed to one of happiness. "You are most wise, my sister," she said, putting her hands on her sister's. "I must act like a woman now and not a foolish child."

"Good," her sister responded, her tone a bit guarded. "Then go."

With the consent given, Yarel turned and ran into the woods, heading down along the path towards the sacred alter.

Immediately the warrior turned and pursued her, always staying close to the ground to remain unseen.

Fletcher glanced at his WCD, the chronometer stating that they had less than a minute left. "I'll slow down the sister here, you make sure Romeo and Juliet get away."

She nodded her agreement and slunk off after them, just as the older Mayan shook her head with resolution and began to pursue her sister into the woods.

Lightly hitting the hazing button on his WCD, the major started on an intercept course, mentally counting down the thirty seconds he had to accomplish his goal. Quickly running in front of the determined sister, he planted himself in her path and let her run right into him, knocking both of them to the ground.

In a flash Fletcher was back on his feet, as the Mayan woman slowly got up, obvious confusion on her face.

A sudden thought jumped into his mind, as he wondered if the translator worked both ways. "Leave her be," he said in his most commanding voice he could muster.

Fear enveloped her tiny features as she remained on the ground, but crawled back to gain a small distance from the unseen voice.

"Who are you who calls me?" she asked, her lips trembling.

"I am the guardian of this island," he continued, trying to deepen his voice even further. "Yarel is welcome here this day, but you are not. Wait at the boat and enter not these woods."

"Are you man or spirit?" she asked, as she slunk even further away.

He stepped up to her and lifted her to her feet, knowing full well that at that close proximity she would be able to easily see the distorting fringe that surrounded his body in hazing mode. "What do you think?"

She let out a small shriek, and fled back to the boat, where she prostrated herself for a few seconds and then jumped into it, once again taking on a penitent posture.

Satisfied that she was going nowhere, he turned and went after Kim, just as the hazing effect wore off. He found her not more than a few hundred yards down the rough path. She was crouched behind a bush as she watched the two young lovers hold each other in a tight embrace. A smile crept to his lips at the simple innocence of what he beheld, then he glanced down at his mission indicator, which shone a bright emerald green.

"All set?" she asked, keeping her voice low.

"All set."

The two of them slunk back from the couple, so as to not bother them when they Skimmed, and then pressed their return buttons, bringing them home again.

"Interesting approach," Checkmate commented stoically as the two of them came out of VR and realized that he was standing over them in the Spiral Run chamber.

"It worked," Fletcher said with a smile. "Isn't that what counts?"

"Not necessarily," the instructor said as he shook his head. "Your primary task was to accomplish the mission parameters. However, you are also not to interfere with the lives of others who are around when you Skim."

A sheen of concentration settled on the major's face, as he got up from the chair. "Since our mission was to save Yarel and her warrior by keeping her sister from finding out, the very parameters of the mission dictated that we would have to interfere with her life in some way."

"What did you do?" Kim asked as she finished disconnecting herself and stood up as well.

"He played god of the island," Borlin said, a lecturing tone to his voice.

"You didn't?" she asked her partner.

"Look," Fletcher defended himself, "I saw the risk as slight, but the potential for gain high. I had to stop her from going after her sister, and she already had accepted that Cozumel was their island of spirits, so my presence would be deemed odd by her, but not out of the realm of possibilities. This way I was able to allow my partner to stay with Yarel, and guarantee that she was undisturbed. That was our mission goal, wasn't it?"

The trainer studied him in silence, then glanced over at Kim.

"Makes sense to me," she said with a big grin.

"I suppose it does," Checkmate reluctantly agreed. "Very well, this shall be counted as a success."

Fletcher's grin grew as large as his partner's, as he patted her on the back and followed her out of the chamber.

There were a few activities that several of the cadets were involved in that night, after all the review classes were over, but Fletcher had a greater plan in mind: sleep. This was the first time in a while that he felt really good about himself and with being here, and instead of the urge to celebrate, the equally tantalizing feeling of drowsiness came over him, reminding him that he hadn't really gotten any sleep for three days. The idea was great, the execution flawless; however, the results fell shy of the intention, as he tossed and turned most of the night away. The only advantage to this was that he ended up waking a good hour before he had to, and decided to be early to class that day.

The morning shower struggled to waken him, but his limbs still felt like leaden weights were firmly affixed to them as he pulled on the armor plating that seemed mysteriously to have tripled in weight overnight. Finally finishing with his preparations, he trotted off to the training center, forcing his body to motivate.

The first sign that made him feel better was the two cadets he passed on the way to the class. Despite his exhaustion, a small smile crept onto his tired face at the thought that for once, he was not going to be late.

He entered the training facility with purpose in his stride, a feeling of accomplishment flooding through his veins as he reached the room full of cadets, and a very surprised instructor.

"Congratulations, Phantom," Checkmate said with a smile. "I see some of Tsunami is finally rubbing off on you."

Despite the dig, Fletcher found it easy to laugh along with the cadets, even at his own expense. He glanced around, expecting Kim to be waiting for him, but when he didn't find her, he expected that she was late.

"Your partner is waiting for you in chamber three," Borlin informed him when he saw him glancing around. "She has the mission docket. Go ahead and I'll be right there to send you off."

Fletcher smiled as he headed down the winding corridor, wondering what this mission would be since it would be the last before the test. Although he enjoyed the Spiral Runs, and it was easy to get caught up in the realism of *Twilight's* brand of virtual reality; he was looking forward to his first actual Skim, and equally nervous about it as well. Even in the Spiral Runs, he was starting to understand the grand scope of his actions, and the possible effects they could have on many people.

He entered the chamber and saw her sitting in the far chair, hooking up to the system. "Morning, Kim," his cheerful voice greeted, "I'm actually on time today."

"That's good," she said, turning to face him, "because I don't like waiting."

Fletcher's jaw dropped as his stomach tightened into thousands of microscopic knots. It was Carrie in the chair next to him, an expectant look in her bright jade eyes. A thousand words came to his mind, and a few hundred even made it to the back of his tongue, but none passed through as anything other than a few "ums."

"Kim wasn't feeling well this morning," Carrie explained as her eyes seem to judge his every expression, "so she asked me to take her place. Condor didn't mind waiting, so they'll take their mission together later. That is if it's alright with you."

More words struggled to form themselves on his tongue in such a flurry that they bottle necked in his throat, allowing none to get through. In the end he settled on nodding, as a slight smile came to his lips. Suddenly, he didn't feel so tired after all.

"Alright, trainees," Checkmate said as he came in and glared at each of them with as judgmental an eye as he could muster, "you've both proven that you can do the job, and work with a partner...now let's see if you can work together. Is this going to be a problem for either of you?"

They both quickly shook their heads.

"Good," the instructor responded with a nod. "Then take a look at the mission docket so we can get started."

Fletcher took the clear plastic card from Carrie and slid it into his WCD, a sense of deja-vu coming over him as he read the details of the mission. "This is the Brenda Sykes mission again," he said, his smile growing, then he made a sly face at the trainer. "I thought you never got a second chance here in *Twilight?*"

"This time is an exception," he said, allowing a brief smile as he activated the controls for the Spiral Run. "Ready?"

The two cadets glanced at each other, their eyes locking as they struggled to sift past the glistening barricade that barred the way into the other's soul. Then they looked up at the instructor, each signaling their readiness.

He pushed the button, launching them back into virtual reality.

The slight disorientation that occurred while adjusting to being in a Spiral Run seemed extra long to Fletcher as he waited to appear in the VR version of the Departure Nucleus. When it finally came into view, he glanced over at his teammate to make sure he hadn't imagined the change.

"Ready, folks?" the virtual Sender asked them from behind the controls.

They both nodded as they activated their WCDs, spilling azure light across the departure platform.

The hauntingly familiar New York alleyway came into focus at the end of their time Skim. Nothing seemed different to Fletcher, as he knew that it shouldn't, except, perhaps, for the confidence that hadn't been there before.

"Another alleyway," he half whispered to himself.

"What was that?" Carrie asked.

"Oh," he said, surprised that he had said that out loud. "Just a little joke with Tsunami about how we're always popping into alleys."

She glanced around and let out a soft laugh. "You know, I guess you're right." Then she checked her WCD to re-familiarize herself with the situation. "We have just under fourteen minutes to help Sharon kidnap her daughter Brenda, or else the kid grows up with her jerk father."

"Right," he agreed. "Let's do it."

She nodded and started to move out of the alley when a sudden impulse overwhelmed Fletcher and he grabbed her arm, turning her back to face him.

"I know we're pressed for time," he started to explain, trying to get out as much as possible in his rush. "It's funny, Kim and I had over an hour to waste in our last Spiral Run and had little to say. But despite the lack of time, there's something that I have to tell you before we go on."

Her eyes opened wide in un-expectant apprehension.

"You remember last time we were here and you said that I just didn't get it…didn't understand what you wanted?"

She nodded silently.

"It was respect. That's what I wasn't giving you, and you had every right to be angry. I was way out of line that day," he continued, "and I'm sorry." His throat felt like autumn leaves that just fell from the tree. He tried to swallow to overcome the feeling, but it had little effect. "That's it, I guess. I just wanted you to know that."

Her lips followed his throat's example, and she pulled the bottom one in with her tongue and lightly bit it. "I don't know what to say," she admitted, holding onto the warm feeling that suddenly was within her.

"You don't have to say anything," he told her, then glanced down at his WCD and realized that they were talking their precious time away.

"I know," she agreed as if reading his thoughts, "we have to act now. If we blow this one we're both out of the program…but thanks." She touched his arm lightly as her lips formed a shy smile. "So how do you want to handle it?"

He thought for a moment, then nodded. "We'll stick with your original plan. We'll go to that alley that I found you in last time. It was a good hiding place, and very close to where Brenda and her father were."

She pursed her lips in surprise, and then smiled. "Alright, then let's do it."

Following her lead, the two of them quickly scurried along the deserted street as the booming sounds of the bicentennial parade rumbled just two blocks over, echoing like a thunderstorm. She led him to an intersecting alley that was extremely narrow, too tight for a car, and swiftly darted up it. A transient was passed out halfway down, but he didn't awaken as they jumped right over him, continuing on their way. As she reached the main street where the parade was, she stopped just behind the six row deep throng of spectators and paused, as Fletcher came up behind her.

"Any ideas now?" she asked, trying to keep quiet but unable to do anything but yell to be heard over the pandemonium in front of her as the bicentennial parade continued down the street.

"What was your plan last time?" he asked while verifying on his WCD that they had only a few minutes left.

"No one seemed to notice me last time," she observed. "I moved past a few of them, but so many are in bicentennial costumes that our armor will most likely be unnoticed."

"I see," he said as he watched the crowd. "We get up to the Dad and the girl, then wait for Mom to make the attempt...then pow!"

She grinned. "Exactly. If we haze at the right moment, he won't stand a chance. You watch Dad—"

"And you'll help Mom," he finished for her, as they both nodded in agreement.

They started to move into the crowd, Carrie leading the way with the directional signal on her WCD. As they drove deeper into the masses he began to get this sensation that started down low, and began to fill his body. He couldn't identify it at first, but as it grew he realized that it was a simple feeling of "rightness." Working with Kim had been fun, but this seemed like he and Carrie were suddenly in sync with each other. It was as if she could complete his thoughts, and he hers. He chuckled silently. *As long as I don't act like an idiot*, his thoughts reminded him. He tried to fathom what had gone wrong the first time they worked together, and came up with the only possible answer: him.

They continued to move further away from the relative safety of the alley, as more and more people began to stare at them. Carrie's hope that the pandemonium of the bicentennial parade would grant them anonymity in the crowd had worked so far, but he was beginning to think that their luck could be fading out.

"What the hell kinda outfit is that?" came one call from a bystander.

"This is Independence day, you morons," answered another, "not Halloween!"

Fortunately, none of them paid further attention to them once they had passed, but Fletcher began to doubt that would continue long, especially if one of the many scattered law enforcement officers were to spot them.

"We can't last long in this," he called to her, trying to get his head near hers so that she would hear him over the rising din of the parade and the masses.

"I know," she agreed as they closed on their targets. She glanced down at her WCD which indicated that they had under two minutes left. "Get ready," she called to him.

He checked his own WCD as he scanned for where the arrow was leading him. The luminescent pointer jumped wildly back and forth, trying to get a bead on a target that was being moved about in a packed crowd. Finally he spotted where he wanted to be as a man near the front row caught his attention. Although well groomed and dressed, his dark demeanor was translated easily on his face and body stance, as he held the young girl firmly in his hand, his fingers like iron claws gripped tightly around her frail wrist. Fletcher turned to draw Carrie's attention to him, when he saw Sharon directly ahead, no look on any other bystander's face could rob him of that instant conviction. There are times in a person's life when everything that has meaning is stripped away, when the only chance they have is one desperate stab at regaining what was taken, even if only in part. It's that moment, when their one and only chance is at hand, that the true nature of fear and determination can be defined. It was that look, on Sharon Sykes' face, that clearly defined her to him more certainly than any WCD indicator ever could. Fortunately, Carrie saw her as well. They gave each other one last nod of readiness and both hit the hazing buttons on their WCDs, vanishing from sight.

Their instant disappearance had a disorienting effect on the immediate crowd as people that were next to them did double takes and head snaps to make sure that they had seen correctly. Fortunately for the cadets, the city breeds a certain numbness to its dwellers, since the startling can be common place in a city of this size, and most of the people in the crowd that noticed the disappearance soon forgot as they became engrossed in something else.

This recognition, or lack thereof, was far from Fletcher's mind as he slipped through the crowd, trying not to hurt anyone since they couldn't see him coming to get out of his way. Simultaneously, Carrie cleared a way for Sharon to reach her ex-husband, gently moving the pedestrians to one side or the other.

Sharon's face tightened in a pure sheen of furious wanting as she finally saw the two of them, her fierce hazel eyes fixed on her only child. With a sudden lunge she reached forward and grabbed Brenda's other arm, pulling her towards her.

The young girl's face beamed with renewed hope as she saw that the person that had grabbed her was her mother. She tried to pull free of her father, drawing his attention to the play at hand. It was then that he tightened his grip further on the soft flesh of his daughter's wrist and pulled her back to him, a glare of pure contempt displayed in the harsh sneer on his cruel lips; that is until Fletcher's fist contacted squarely on his jaw.

The major had been unsure up to that moment as to exactly how he would get Sykes to release his daughter, so that Sharon could claim her. However, all doubt drained out of his mind like water in a sieve when that hurtful sheen covered the father's face, and in an instant he read every hateful thing that Brenda would have to endure in her young life written clearly in those soulless eyes. That's when his fingers curled into an unseen fist and flew forward, the hard gauntlet striking like a hammer against the unsuspecting chin.

Sykes flew backwards out of the crowd and into the cleared area of the parade, where a police officer on horseback instantly rode forward to grab him, thinking him a possible threat to the actors and models on the floats.

Instantly their mission indicators went green, as Sharon pulled her daughter into an embrace, tears streaming down her face.

"Mommy," young Brenda cried as she gripped tightly onto her mother.

"I've got you, Pumpkin," she said with relief, as she picked her up in her arms and watched out for her ex-husband.

Carl Sykes instantly dove back into the throng of people, violently pushing and striking people as he tried to get back to his daughter.

"Sharon," he screamed at her while pushing an elderly lady to the ground, "you whore! The kid is mine!" He almost reached her again, except for the fact that there was one area that he simply couldn't pass through, despite how many people he hit.

Fletcher worried that the hazing would wear off before help arrived, but just like the cavalry, the mounted police officer reached into the crowd and grabbed the maddened Carl and yanked him back.

"You're under arrest," the law officer commanded, as the two cadets quickly faded back deeply into the mass of people. When they both reappeared they were halfway back to the narrow alleyway, laughing and cheering along with the other New Yorkers who were thrilled to see the madman taken into custody.

"Damn straight," Carrie said with a tight shake of her balled fist.

He pulled her into the alley, gripping her shoulders tightly. A thousand witty things came to his mind to cap the event, but his lips stayed silent, as he grinned widely at her, the twinkle in his eyes mirroring the elation in hers.

"Let's go home," he finally said, and she nodded in agreement. They both pushed the return button on their WCDs, then clasped each other's hands as the blue light took them. They arrived back in the simulated Departure Nucleus and she threw her arms around his neck and gave him a tight hug.

"Was that as good for you as it was for me?" he asked, his wits returning.

"It was amazing," she said, squeezing him close.

"I guess it was," he agreed with a laugh as he returned the surprise embrace.

Then the moment passed and she quickly disengaged herself from him, a light pink flush covered her face as she realized what her impulse had driven her to.

"I really envied you that punch," she said, trying to brush off what she had done. "I couldn't see what you did, but the way he jerked back you must have really laid it into him."

"I guess I did at that," he agreed. He was about to elaborate on his emotions at the moment of the punch when everything faded out, as the Spiral Run drew to a swift close.

They opened their eyes to find Checkmate turning off the last of the switches in the small chamber. When he saw them stir he looked at them, a stern glare fixed on his face. However, before Fletcher could even voice a defense the trainer let out a warm laugh that startled both cadets, as he offered his hand to the major, pulling him out of the VR control chair.

"I did the exact same thing to that bloody bastard during the real Skim," Borlin admitted with a chuckle. "Felt great, didn't it?"

Fletcher returned his smile, his good spirits heightened by this revelation. "It damn well did."

Then Checkmate turned to Carrie and offered his hand to her as well. "Excellently done, Starfox, you handled yourself as fine as my own partner did in the real Time Skim."

"And Brenda?" the major found himself asking, unsure as to why.

"She lived a fine life," Borlin said as he started to walk the cadets out of the chamber. "Her father lost custody and spent a number of years doing community work...not that it softened his soul any."

With that the three of them laughed again, as they left the Spiral Run chamber behind.

They emerged back into the control center, stopping short as they spied Tsunami and Condor, laughing and joking about the Spiral Run that they had obviously just completed.

"Kim?" Fletcher asked, suddenly confused. "What's going on? I thought you asked Carrie to fill in for you."

"Yeah," Carrie voiced her agreement.

The young Asian gave a quick shrug and a disarming grin. "Maybe I was playing Santa Claus after all."

They both gave her a questioning stare, as the instructor stayed to one side, silently observing.

"Look," Kim tried to explain, "you both wanted another chance to work together, and Juan and I wanted to give it another kick as well," she defended, patting Condor on his shoulder. "I figured that this way everyone would be happy...and judging from the way you guys left your chamber, I'm going to assume I was right, wasn't I?"

Everything in Fletcher's gut told him that he should have been furious at her for totally manipulating him, but all that came to him was that he realized what a great friend he had that day. "You're a sneaky bastard, Kim," he said with a laugh. "I think you owe us a drink in the observation lounge."

Carrie's face was blank with shock, but as the moments passed with the major's good humor, she found it hard to hold onto any of the anger as well. "A drink, hell," she added with a grin. "I think a dinner is in order as well."

"I take it then that this temporary round in musical partners is going to take on a permanent status?" Checkmate asked, interjecting into their camaraderie.

"I guess it is," Fletcher agreed, as he glanced over at Carrie. "What do you say? Think you could stand to work with me?"

"I think so," she laughed as her eyes shined warmly up at him, "as long as we continue to work together as a team, like we did this time."

"Sounds like a done deal," Kim added as she and Condor came in closer to the pair and she patted each on the arm. "Now let's go talk about that dinner on the way to debriefing," she said while leading them out of the center. "The way I see it, shouldn't you guys be treating me?"

## Chapter 9
# Trial by Fire

The alarm that sliced into Fletcher's sleep hit like a bottle in a bar fight, jarring him awake with a dream shattering start. He numbly reached for the alarm clock that for a moment he was sure that was there on his night stand in his Air Base barracks, and tumbled out of bed and onto the cold floor in a flurry of sheets and blankets. He lay there for a moment, as the alarm focused, reminding him of where he was.

"Phantom," the alarm changed to computerized voice, "report to Departure Nucleus immediately in full gear. *Repeat*. Report to Departure Nucleus immediately in full gear."

Fletcher shook his head for a moment, as he absorbed the alarm and subsequent order, then he let out a soft curse and pulled himself to his feet. Quickly pulling on his scarlet suit, he began attaching the protective armor that made up his uniform. Then he ran out of his quarters and down the short corridor that was becoming more and more familiar to him every day. He wondered what the emergency was, to call him to the chamber in such a manner, but resigned himself to the fact that he would find out shortly.

His eyes struggled to stay open as the night of revelry flowed back to his mind. The four of them had ended up arguing about the dinner check for hours, a moot point since no money was used in *Twilight* at all, but the debate had kept them all in good sprits through the evening, as they bantered their points back and forth. Once again, Carrie and he had formed an excellent team, as Juan came to Kim's defense, evenly pairing them off. He couldn't remember a better time since his arrival in the *Twilight* facility. They had all stayed up far too late, comfortable in the statement that Checkmate had made to them during their debriefing, that their last Spiral Run would be in the afternoon so they could all sleep in.

With this thought in mind, he dashed through the abandoned cafeteria, struck by the fact that no one else was in the corridors with him. He checked the time chronometer on his WCD and realized that it was only four in the morning. Letting out another curse, this one a bit louder than the last, he sped through the empty rooms and down the hall that led to the Departure Nucleus, his mind focusing since he reasoned that the reality of the emergency had to be genuine. He entered the room, and paused to finally catch his breath. Two figures stood waiting for him, one on the platform, and one behind the launching controls.

"You've got to be faster when the alarm sounds, Phantom," Sender scolded from behind his controls. "You've been trained to know that the launch window is only open for fifteen minutes."

Fletcher stared, dumbfounded at Sender, then glanced at Checkmate, who he realized was the other person in the room.

"Come, on," Borlin urged from the platform, his lilting British accent taking on a demanding tone, "we've less than three minutes to launch."

"Checkmate," Fletcher asked, confusion flooding his system like a burst dam, "is this an actual *Time Skim*?

"Yes," Sender answered quickly. "Now let's get going."

"But I'm not certified yet," Fletcher protested, certain that this was some huge mistake. "I haven't taken the final test yet."

"There's no time for that," the nucleus controller informed him in a harsh tone. "All certified Skimmers are out already. I've got a situation here and of all the cadets you have the most real life experience, so you're it. This is a two person Skim and I can't send Checkmate alone." Then he smiled reassuringly at the major. "Don't worry, Phantom, just do what your partner tells you to do and you'll be just fine. Consider this a baptism under fire."

One thing Fletcher always prided himself on was his ability to make a quick decision, for better or worse. With a curt nod of his head, he pulled his helmet on and stepped up onto the platform next to Borlin. "Does Justin know about this?" he asked as he nervously activated the WCD's power crystal, the reality that this wasn't a Spiral Run starting to really sink in, causing his hand to shake ever so slightly.

Sender nodded as he powered up the chamber, illuminating the two Skimmers with the iridescent glow. "He wishes you could have completed your test first, but he trusts you to do what's right."

Borlin handed Fletcher the plastic mission card, which he promptly slid into the WCD, sparking up the tiny emerald letters that sprang across his wrist, instructing him on his mission. His eyes flashed across the tiny wrist screen as he tried to catch all that it was telling him, then shook his head in frustration.

"What's this about some woman falling?" he asked as he glanced back up.

"I'll explain upon entry," Checkmate assured him as his face grew serious. "Let's do it."

Before Fletcher could muster an objection, Sender pushed the power levels up all the way, blinding them with the luminous floor lights. Their WCDs screamed for attention as the activation buttons furiously flashed, signaling their readiness. With a gulp of resignation, and a thumbs up from Checkmate, he pressed the button, as his world turned inside out.

The reentry was harder than it had been in the Spiral Runs, and Fletcher felt his legs go out from under him as the multicolors of Twilight Space solidified into hard earth. Feeling like he had just stepped out of a washing machine on full rinse cycle, Fletcher felt himself sway as the room they were in came into focus. He instinctively reached out a steadying hand, only to have it grabbed by his temporary partner.

"You alright?" Checkmate asked while regarding the first timer.

Fletcher managed to nod as he closed his eyes to settle his equilibrium, and forced himself to swallow back down the bile that had slipped up his esophagus.

"You going to be sick?"

With a shake of his head, the major strained his eyes open and finally took in his surroundings, as the last waves of nausea slowly passed. "That was a lot rougher than the Spiral Runs."

Checkmate smiled, remembering the sensation of first Time Skim all too well. "It gets better each time," he laughed quietly. "Kind of like sex."

Fletcher turned away from his partner as the steady drone in his ears lowered but never actually faded away, which made him realize that it was the continuous sound of a crowd of people talking, muffled by many walls and a ceiling. He studied the simple room he was in, which apparently was a large coat closet of sorts. The plain wooden racks in the small area were filled with long coats of a style left behind long before the nineteenth century gave way to the twentieth. Ebony top hats lined the shelves above, as well as some ivory canes. However, it was to the lavish officer's jacket that Fletcher's attention was drawn. The sparkling gold buttons and decorations on the field of blue made him reach out to the jacket and pull it off the rack. The bright brass buckle caught his attention as it swayed free, proudly displaying the bold letters U. S. that were engraved in it.

"This is a federal Army officer's uniform of the mid-eighteen hundreds," Fletcher said with wonder.

"Cavalry, actually," Borlin corrected him as he studied the uniform himself. His eyes moved down to the indicator on his WCD then glanced at the door. "We're not far from where that woman falls down," he informed him. "Let's grab some of these coats."

Fletcher started to take the officer's coat off the hanger when Checkmate put a hand on the coat and shook his head. "Too conspicuous," he whispered while grabbing two long plain coats from the closet. He handed one to the major, and signaled him to put it on.

For a moment, Fletcher gazed at the federal officer's coat with sorrow. This period had always been a favorite of his, and he felt as if an opportunity had slipped by. Then with a shrug of feigned indifference, he placed the blue coat back, and slipped on the plain tan one, and followed Checkmate to the door.

"Are you going to explain the situation now?" he asked, remembering to keep his voice low. "The mission description seemed vague."

For a moment, the Brit seemed to ignore the request, as he quietly opened the slim wooden door and glanced quickly up the narrow service staircase that led to the main floor. Seemingly satisfied that they were in no danger of being overheard, he turned back to the major and nodded. "We're here to save a woman from falling down a flight of stairs."

"I got that much from the mission docket," Fletcher said with annoyance.

"Then what's your question?" Borlin asked, then smiled at the frown he was getting from his temporary partner. "She's a young woman who is attending the show at this theater." He then glanced down at his WCD. "In exactly one minute and fifty-seven seconds there will be a major incident in the theater which will cause most of the people to run out the exits. She'll trip at the top of the mezzanine stairs and fall all the way to the bottom, breaking her back and causing brain damage."

Fletcher took in a short breath as he considered the situation. "So we have to keep her from falling?"

"Exactly," Checkmate confirmed. "We'll position ourselves at the top of the mezzanine stairs or so, and enter hazing mode the moment the shot fires. Then as she comes out, we'll grab her so she doesn't fall. With luck, the whole episode will take less than our thirty second window and we'll return here to Skim back out." He looked at his WCD again and opened the door. "We now have one minute and ten seconds until the incident. Let's go."

With Borlin in the lead, following the homing arrows on his WCD, the two of them slipped onto the hard wooden stairway and slowly crept up the steps. They reached the top of the stairs and paused at the door for a moment, as the sounds of conversation were diminishing, making it seem apparent that the production had started. Being ever so careful, Checkmate pulled the heavy wooden door open a bit, revealing the Union soldiers that stood guard in the main foyer.

"Lots of guards for a small theater," Fletcher said in a sotto voice, but fell silent when Borlin gave him a signal to remain quiet.

"The guards are facing the ticket counter," the experienced Time Skimmer pointed out. "Let's slip to the mezzanine stairs now."

The two of them slid through the doorway, keeping their long coats pulled around themselves to cover their armor. The main lobby was brightly lit, but there was a good distance between the two Time Skimmers and the guards at the front entrance. Without hesitation, they crept around the sharp turn to the curtains that lined the bottom of the mezzanine stairs. A long curved staircase rose above them, with a landing halfway up. Checkmate nodded to the major, then they quickly climbed the crimson-colored velvet steps.

They reached the top and hesitated, seeing that there was little to conceal them up here, as the mezzanine opened right out to the patrons' seats. Borlin moved them back down a few steps, keeping them from view. Upon reaching the landing, they paused for a quick breath, as Checkmate examined his WCD.

"How much time do we have?"

"Forty seconds. We'll wait here until it happens, no one should see us here in the dark."

Fletcher nodded, determined that nothing would go wrong on his first official Time Skim. He then smiled, wondering what the young woman that they were here to save would think if she knew of the events that were about to unfold. Then his mind went taught like a rubber band springing back into place. He grabbed Checkmate's arm with one hand and lifted his own visor with his other so that he could clearly see the Brit. "What is this *incident* that causes the panic?"

The tall Skimmer glanced back at the first timer with apprehension as his eyes narrowed. "I told you, a shot is fired."

Suddenly the significance of the guards in the lobby struck home, along with the date that was stated on his mission docket, as the instincts of an Air

Force major took over. "This is Ford's theater, April fourteenth, eighteen sixty-five," Fletcher stated half to himself. "We're standing here while a United States President is about to be assassinated."

"We're here to save Linda Davenport from falling in a panicked run and ruining her life."

"We're talking about Lincoln here," the major said as he started to move back up the stairs that led towards the presidential box.

"Phantom, wait," Borlin said quietly as he grabbed his arm. "Think about what you're doing."

Fletcher turned back to his partner and shrugged off his grasp. "I'm going to save the President of the United States."

"You can't just bloody well go about changing the past the way you want to," he tried to remind the major. "Think of the unknown ramifications. Remember what Justin taught us about destroying our own futures, remember the Spiral Runs. The Omni computer has only calculated out Linda's future, not the entire future of a nation. The assassination of the President is a major event in time, but the crippling of Linda Davenport is important also. Our computer indicates that she could have written great children's novels if she hadn't been hurt."

"She's not the President," Fletcher insisted, trying to keep his tones low.

"And what makes her life any less important than his?"

Fletcher stood dumbfounded for a moment as he stared across the mezzanine, from the safety of the stairs, at the Presidential box where he knew that Lincoln was enjoying the production. Visions of the oath he swore when he joined the Air Force dominated his soul, screaming at him to protect the office of the President: *any* President, followed by the pledge that all the Time Skimmers had given to Justin, not to interfere. He agonized silently from the weight of the decision, then he lowered his eyes and stepped back down to the landing where he was waiting before. He gritted his teeth causing a muscle to jump in his cheek, as the shot rang out that ended an era.

Suddenly, the dimly-lit theater was alive with panic, as the two time travelers slipped behind the curtain that rested like a tapestry along the curved wall of the landing. First one, then dozens of fleeing patrons ran past them in a blind daze, as Union soldiers struggled to make their way up the stairs against the wave of people, desperately trying to get to their commander-in-chief. All this seemed like a dream to Fletcher, who watched with passive detachment. He hadn't even noticed when Checkmate had reached over and pushed the button on his WCD that activated the hazing mode. They stood like two specters, as the throng of people passed back and forth in confusion, oblivious to their presence. But Fletcher saw none of it, his thoughts and dreams ringing with the flintlock shot that he knew he could have stopped. Then he saw her, silhouetted against the mass of fleeing people. He didn't know how he knew it was her, but even before Checkmate had verified her identity on his WCD, the major had started back up the steps, carefully avoiding the people as they ran by. He vaguely heard his partner yell something at him, but all was lost in the deafening roar of the crowd and the distant shots that were being fired at the fleeing assassin. His attention focused on her, as she lost her grip on her handbag, and paused at the top of the stairs to grab it—and was struck by two men trying desperately to get down the stairs quickly. She lost her footing as her handbag flew in the air, and she tumbled into the mass going down.

Fletcher felt as if he were in slow motion as his hand reached out to her, then he was hit by a running soldier and he felt his own footing give way. The world spiraled out from under him as he went down, but he never took his focus off of Linda's arm. Forcing his body to shift as he fell, he lunged out and felt his armored hand contact her wrist. Yanking her to his hazed torso, he hugged the terrified woman in closely, as he let his armored body take the brutal force of the tumble all the way down the long stairs, as panicked people kicked and stepped all over him. Then he was on the ground floor, as another foot smashed blindly into his face. Shaking off the dizziness that threatened to overcome him, he pulled himself to his feet, never releasing his hold on Linda, who had fainted halfway down. Then he felt strong, armored hands on his shoulders, and he was pulled out of the throng to the safety of the service stairs that led back down to the cloak room.

"Phantom?" his partner asked with concern as the hazing effect wore off. Then Borlin grimaced as he saw the darkened bruise on Fletcher's face, and the blood that came from his split lower lip.

Fletcher shook his head one more time, forcing back the pain as he nodded in acknowledgment to Checkmate, then looked at the limp form that was still clutched in his arms. They both stared in amazement when they realized that she didn't have a scratch on her.

"Is, she...?"

Checkmate answered his partner's question by checking his WCD and noting that the mission parameter indicator was a luminous green. With a smile of genuine relief, he looked back up and nodded. "She's fine," he laughed. "I guess your thick head took it all."

Fletcher's laugh turned into a wince of pain as his lip started to really hurt. Then he glanced down at Linda, who was just starting to blink her eyes as consciousness returned to her. "What do we do now?"

"First you put the nice lady down," the Brit said with a grin, "then we get the hell out of here."

Gently sitting her down on the hardwood stairs, he held her arm for a moment longer, making sure that she was steady enough that she wouldn't fall over. For a moment her eyes fluttered open and tried to focus on the armored men, then she closed them and raised a hand to her face. She shook her head twice to clear the dizziness, and when she opened her eyes again, the strange men were gone.

Back in the coat room, the two time travelers quickly shed their coats and replaced them on the hooks where they had come from.

"We really did it," Fletcher said with a huge grin, regardless of his split lip. He couldn't get over the elation he felt, despite what had happened. "We actually changed her life."

"What I can't get over is that save you made on those stairs," Borlin said with a warm laugh. "Not one in a hundred Skimmers could have pulled that off." He adjusted the WCD on his wrist, and activated the return circuits.

The major opened his eyes in wonder, and then thought about what he had done back on those stairs. "I was lucky," he admitted as he activated his own return circuits. "Very, very lucky."

Borlin put his hand on Fletcher's shoulder in a manner which reminded him of a brother. "Welcome to the ranks of Time Skimmers, Phantom. You've earned it." Then he glanced at both of their WCDs, which had begun to flash their cobalt readiness. "Let's go."

They looked at each other to set their timing, then both pressed the buttons, flooding the coat room with a blinding light.

Linda stared at the closed coat room in wonder, the azure light coming out from under the doorway was impossibly bright. Mustering up her courage, she opened the door, half expecting to see the strange men in the black and red armor again, but the room was empty. Taking one last look around, she shrugged her shoulders, deciding that she had imagined the whole thing…but at least she felt it would make a good night time story for her sister's children.

## Chapter 10
# Return

The Departure Nucleus came back into view as the two time travelers returned from their journey. Waiting patiently aside Sender, Justin watched with eager anticipation.

When the light finally died down, Justin raised an eyebrow at Fletcher's disheveled appearance.

"I hope everything went well," he asked, watching Checkmate more than his companion.

Borlin nodded. "Phantom handled it fine," he informed his leader, his British accent calm despite their ordeal. "Target goal was achieved, no other subjects interfered with."

Justin's pleasure was obvious, as he turned back to Fletcher. "Well done, Phantom. I'm sure that was very hard."

The major was about to agree readily, when something in Justin's eye struck an inner nerve like fire on ice. Sheer coincidence suddenly became planned convenience in his mind, and the answer seemed ridiculously plain. "This was my test," he finally said, though it was hardly a question.

Justin's smile broadened into what Fletcher could only deem as pride. "You are quite right, Phantom."

"I thought it was supposed to be another Spiral Run. Why didn't you warn us?"

"Then it wouldn't have been a very good test."

A thought surfaced in Fletcher mind. "Was Linda really in trouble? Or was this whole thing rigged for me?"

A questioning look covered Justin's face, as he glanced side longingly at Checkmate.

"Linda Davenport," Checkmate answered his unasked question. "She's the young woman at Ford's Theater."

Justin nodded, then looked back at Fletcher. "No, Phantom, this wasn't rigged. Time Skimming is far too dangerous to *create* a situation just for you." He took a deep breath, as the two time travelers stepped off the platform. "However, there will be many times that you will be in a situation similar to what you went through, where you might want to take it upon yourself to change history for what you think will be the better. I had to be sure that you would follow the mission plan and not interfere."

Fletcher nodded, realizing the gravity of what had just happened to him. He glanced over at Checkmate, a questioning look in his eyes. But before he could speak, his mission partner and former trainer nodded.

"Yes, Phantom," he said seriously, "I would have stopped you at all costs...if you had made the wrong decision."

"But then Linda might not have been saved," he answered.

"There's no need to dwell on this," Justin said as his smile returned. "You made the right decision and Linda Davenport was saved. She went on to be a great writer, and lived a long and happy life."

Fletcher shook his head in wonder. "Talking about her in the past seems so strange, when I just saw her."

"Get used to it," Checkmate laughed as he slapped him on the shoulder. "Why don't you visit the med center and get cleaned up and then get some more rest. Tonight's going to be a great celebration."

"I'll see you both then," Justin said as he glanced at his watch. "I have to stay here to greet the next trainee who will be returning from her test in a short while."

Fletcher's eyes widened as his thoughts raced to Carrie; it could be her test. His lips parted slightly as his heart tightened into a knot. *What if she didn't do the right thing?* But even as he wondered, he knew she would be fine. Something about Justin's cavalier attitude told him all he needed to know.

Justin let out a sigh, then patted Fletcher on the arm. "Go and get some rest, you deserve it. Let me worry about Starfox for now."

Fletcher let out a long breath, then glanced over at Checkmate. "How about a drink?"

"How about you see a med tech first," his mission partner suggested. "I'll take you up on that drink tonight."

The two Skimmers left the chamber, as Justin silently watched. Then Sender gave him a nudge. "I just got the return signal from them. All lights coming up green."

"Bring them home," Justin said with a smile.

*Chapter 11*
# Twilight Skimmers

Fletcher waltzed into the observation lounge with a sense of elation that was difficult to contain. Although he was just arriving at the celebration party, the news had spread like wildfire that all the cadets had passed with flying colors. The assignment rosters had been displayed in the classroom, and with the exception of four of the younger cadets, everyone's partner remained the same as it had on the last Spiral Run. Somehow, seeing his call sign next to hers had been like the cherry on a sundae, making the day complete, and he found he couldn't wait to be with her that night.

Justin intercepted him as he entered the party, his hand held out towards the major.

Fletcher grinned and accepted the hand, shaking it firmly.

"Well done, Phantom," the *Twilight* leader said with a warm smile that filled the new Skimmer with a sense of belonging. "You've come a long way since that morning you arrived in my office."

"I guess I have," Fletcher admitted, then his grin turned into a forced humorous stance of seriousness. "I still haven't figured you out though, or why getting me here was so important to you."

"I trust that won't stop you from trying."

"Not in the least."

"Good," Justin laughed, and patted him on the shoulder. "Have a great evening, Phantom."

"I'll do my best," Fletcher promised as he headed for a table where he saw that Carrie, Kim, and Juan were already seated.

The *Twilight* leader watched him walk towards the other new Skimmers, his head tilted slightly as if contemplating an event of great occurrence, then let out a soft breath, and walked towards the bar area and signaled for the music to be cut off.

As Fletcher approached the table, Carrie stood up to greet him and offered her hand as well, which he took with an exuberance not quite felt with the *Twilight* leader.

"Congratulations, partner," she said with a wide smile.

"And you as well, partner," he returned happily.

Further congratulations were shared throughout the four of them on their success, as they sat back down. Just then the music died away, bringing the room to a sudden silence.

"I'm not going to bother you long," Justin said to the crowd of happy faces. "I just wanted to tell you all how proud I am of you. You all know what it means to be a Twilight Skimmer now, and the great responsibility you share, and you have all proven yourselves worthy of that responsibility. All of your WCDs have been activated in the central Omni computer, this way we can page you at a moment's notice. I'll be honest with you, there will be times that you may go some time without going on a Skim. Then there will be times that you get no rest at all. The Omni computer validates the proposed Skim and immediately pages me, so that I can give the project my OK. Once that happens, a team of Skimmers will be alerted. There will be rare occasions that we will send a Skimmer out alone, but only in extremely special cases."

Fletcher found himself staring at Carrie's silhouette as she watched the *Twilight* leader with captive attentiveness, remembering how she had appeared in his cockpit, all alone.

"There may also be a time when we will send two teams at once to handle a huge situation," Justin continued. "But I ramble…"

A low beeping cut into his words and he glanced at his watch, which served as a mini computer link. He studied it for less than ten seconds before pushing a button on the watch, then glancing back up at his audience.

"It would seem that circumstance wishes to impose on my speech." He pushed another button on his watch, setting off two more beepers on the WCDs of two experienced "on duty" Skimmers who were at a far table, waiting in full gear. Immediately they got up and darted out of the observation lounge, all the new Skimmers' eyes on them as they left. "As you can see," the *Twilight* leader resumed, "there will be different shifts when you are 'on duty', at which time it is best to be in full gear…just in case. There will be rare times when a second mission will arrive when the first team is out. At that time another team will be randomly chosen, from a list of backups. So," he laughed, easing the tension in the room that had developed from the sudden call, "just like the Boy Scouts, I'd advise you to always 'be prepared'. Thank you."

He stepped down and signaled the music to resume.

"Who are the Boy Scouts?" Carrie asked.

"An American youth group from my time and earlier," Fletcher told her as he continued to stare at his partner in wonder. His body was here, but his mind was still in the cockpit of his F-15E at that last moment.

Feeling his electric blue eyes on her, she turned to face him, her crystal clear pools of jade returning the stare. "What?"

"What do you mean?" he asked, the smile never leaving his lips.

"You're staring at me again," she said as she gently reached out and touched the firm lines of his jaw, and softly pushed his chin to one side, hoping to break the connection. However, this attempt failed as his eyes never left hers. "What is it that you're thinking when you do that?"

For a moment he considered telling her the truth, about how he was instantly drawn to her as his angel of mercy, but swiftly reconsidered, discarding the idea as the wrong time in the wrong place.

"I'll tell you later," he said as his smile softened, suddenly conscious of the two pairs of eyes on them, from the other team. He made a somewhat discrete gesture towards their friends, hoping she would get the idea.

"Very well," she agreed, understanding his apprehension. "But mark this, Fletcher, I will know the secret behind all this."

The major let out a small "humph" as he thought of all the unanswered questions he had as well, concerning the *Twilight* Leader. "I know what you mean."

"Do you really?" she challenged, a sly smile planted firmly on her lips.

Fletcher considered a few responses, but found that he was far more distracted by the new music that came on, representing his era on Earth. "Care to dance?" he asked her as he offered his arm towards her.

She took in a short breath, unsure as to whether or not to let him escape this easily, then nodded as she accepted his arm and they got up, moving to the area that had been cleared as a dance floor. There were a few other couples there, mostly veteran Time Skimmers and a few *Twilight* civilians that had been their guests. As they moved onto the dance floor he pulled her body closer to his, as he took her right hand into his left and moved her into the hypnotic rhythm of the song.

"You're not a bad dancer," she observed quietly as she moved to the tingling pressure of his other hand against the small of her back. "If I'd known it was going to be a formal affair, I'd have worn a dress."

"It's a good thing you didn't," he whispered softly in her ear as he moved his cheek next to hers.

"And why is that?"

"Hey," he admitted as he pulled his head back slightly so that he could gaze into her eyes, "I've just gotten used to how to treat you as a professional."

"So?"

"So," he continued, a devilish smile edging his lips, "if you'd worn a dress, I'm not sure that I could have kept up that perception of you…or to say the least, my thoughts would have been most un-professional."

"A dress makes all the difference to you?" she asked, returning his wicked grin. "Not too demanding, are we?"

"It's not the dress I was worried about," he admitted. "It was the woman that would be inside that dress that was on my mind."

She cocked her head to one side as her cheeks flushed pink. Then she let her eyes wander along his full torso, obviously appraising him.

"What's that look for?" he questioned, suddenly very aware of where her eyes were staring.

"Just imagining you in a tux," she said.

"You like tuxes?" he asked, pulling her close again.

"Actually," she admitted, "I was more intrigued by the man that would be inside that tux."

Now it was his turn to blush, the tips of his ears turning a bright pink.

They continued dancing through the song, and into the next. As the evening progressed, it slowly occurred to Fletcher that what he had felt before was merely the hot fudge on his sundae: it was *this* that was truly his cherry.

Despite staying up until late into the night, talking and laughing with his new friends, Fletcher felt fully alive and ready to go the next day, as he donned his suit and armor, ready to go on duty. He had arranged with Carrie to meet her in the Departure Nucleus to start their shift there. He realized that it seemed extremely over-zealous, but when he was around her he didn't feel like holding back. The flare that he felt burning inside gave him a new energy within that seemed to glow brighter each day. It was how he had felt when he first graduated from the Air Force Academy, only this time it seemed ten times more intense, and the reason always came back to her. Everything felt so right that it was almost frightening, and it was that underlying feeling that was starting to edge at the back of his thoughts. He easily dispelled the unsettling shadow that threatened his great spirits, but lurking in the distance was the question of whether or not it would so easily disperse the next time.

He met her on schedule in the Nucleus, a flash of her smile dissipating all his nagging feelings as she walked through the door.

"All set?" he asked her.

She nodded vigorously then waved to Sender, who was performing some diagnostics on the control panels.

"Ah, new graduates," the nucleus controller said with a chuckle. "Always so eager. You know that you may not even be needed today?"

Fletcher shrugged, the same thought had occurred to him, but she had been so exited at the prospect of meeting here.

"But we might, Sender," Carrie defended. "You never know."

"That's true, Starfox," he agreed, "But—"

His words were cut off as both her's and the major's WCDs beeped for immediate attention.

A quick smile formed on her small face, as both men glanced at each other and let out a light laugh. Then they looked over at her and she shrugged while getting up on the platform. "Women's intuition," she suggested with a sly grin, "I guess."

Instantly two clear plastic cards emerged from the Nucleus control panel. Sender ran them through a swift verification process, then handed both of them to Fletcher, who was still near the console. The new Skimmer took them over to her, and handed her one, as he slid the clear card into the slot on his WCD.

> *Time Skim 10194:*
>
> *October 13, 2006 — London. Kyle Brighton is a member of a street gang that is known as the Vipers, a group of juvenile delinquents that prey on the darkened streets of the city. On the night of October 13, 2006, they mugged and beat an old man that was on his way home. It wasn't until afterwards that Kyle realized that the old man was his grandfather. This will distress him so much that he will eventually commit suicide.*
>
> *The Omni computer believes that if Kyle never mugged his grandfather, he would have pulled himself from the gang eventually and led a productive life. Preventing this mugging will also have the benefit of making the grandfather's last few years a good deal more peaceful.*

"That poor old man," Carrie said as she took in a short breath through her teeth. "How could that kid do that?"

"It says that he didn't know it was his grandfather," Fletcher said as he stepped up on the platform with her."

She glanced up at him sharply. "I meant, how could he do that to *anyone*? Not just his grandfather."

He shrugged then activated the WCD circuits. "I don't know, but either way we have to stop him."

She activated her own WCD as Sender tuned on the main switch, bathing the platform in an iridescent glow.

"You folks ready?" the nucleus controller asked as a fatherly smile crossed his lips.

"As ready as ever," Carrie said with a grin of determination.

Fletcher nodded his readiness as well.

"Have a safe trip then," Sender said as he threw the main switch. "Remember, just get the green light and get out. Don't hang around any more than necessary. And if you get a red light, get out right away."

"No problem," the major said as he brought his WCD chronometer up to hers to make sure they were synchronized. "Ready?"

She nodded this time, as she held her finger over the button. "Let's rock and roll."

They pushed the buttons as the Departure Nucleus flooded with azure light, and they both vanished into seeming oblivion.

The first thought that Fletcher had as he materialized back into view was that Checkmate had been right, it did get better each time. He fought down the waves of nausea that were diminishing very quickly, as he glanced over at his partner, who was holding a hand to her head to steady herself.

"You OK?"

"I've been better," she admitted. "But I think it's getting easier each time."

He let out a quiet chuckle as he glanced around, taking in the surroundings. As he would have expected, they were in an alleyway that was small and deteriorated by the passage of time. It was late at night, and the streets in the area were poorly lit. What little light they had came from the soft glow of their WCDs. They started to move forward, the rubber soles of their armored boots lightly scraping against the cobblestones that stood steadfast, despite the age and neglect that had been heaped upon them.

"We have just under a half an hour," she indicated as she studied her

WCD, "but it's a distance away."

Fletcher verified this on his own WCD, then moved up to the edge of the alleyway and looked out. There was barely the sliver of a moon overhead, leaving the streets in virtual darkness. A low fog covered the narrow and winding streets like an aura of gloom, concealing the scant few passersby in tenuous anonymity.

"This place gives me the creeps," she whispered as she glanced around.

"I thought you said that you were born in London," he said with a slight grin.

"Not this side of London," she replied with almost an air of disgust. "This is not a good area to be in, and it doesn't look like it's gotten any better since I was last here."

"Well," Fletcher said with resignation as he watched the last passerby dissipate into the grey mist, "at least we can move about pretty much unseen by anyone. This stuff's as thick as water."

"I'll bet it's nice and damp out," she said with an air of nostalgia as she absently rubbed her arms. "Twilight is always so dry."

"The words 'nice' and 'damp' are rarely used together in my vocabulary," he said with a forced frown, then grinned has he touched her shoulder, a tingle shooting up his arm despite the two layers of armor that separated their flesh. "Let's get going."

The two Twilight Skimmers headed out into the dank night, the soft luminous numbers on their WCDs their only guidance and comfort as they stole through the streets of the dark side of London. There was a narrow park that housed a few drooping trees, and a wide stone bridge that went over a dry sewage tunnel. They paused near a large entangle of dense foliage to check their WCDs, when a scrape of metal against stone caused Carrie to put her hand on Fletcher's arm.

"Did you hear that?" she whispered while gesturing into the fog. "Someone's coming this way."

He pulled her behind the clump of trees, as they slunk down to a kneeling position and watched and waited.

"We only have a few minutes left," he told her in a voice that was barely audible. "And it should happen right ahead."

Together they continued to peer into the murk, struggling to make out anything in the thick, soggy night air.

Fletcher felt his heart thumping within his chest as the adrenaline poured through his veins. He had considered the Spiral Runs exciting, but there was always the underlying safety factor there. *It is like being on a roller coaster*, he silently considered, *thrilling, but controlled. Even when on my first run with Checkmate, it had that same sense, since he was our trainer...but now—*

"I've never felt anything like this," Carrie's whisper sliced into his thoughts, echoing their very sentiment. "I feel like I'm on a high wire walking without a net."

Despite the attention the situation demanded, the major let out a soft chuckle. "I know exactly what you mean."

Suddenly she tapped his arm and pointed ahead. There in the darkness was a group of teenagers, the youngest no more than thirteen, the eldest, maybe seventeen. Their attire was like a clash between cults and bondage, all chains and black leather, with dyed hair of numerous colors that nature never intended for a human to have on their head. In the darkness they seemed like demonic imps, laughing in shrill high voices as they pushed and prodded each other, slowly moving the group along.

"I count eight of them," he whispered, as he recounted again to make sure. They had stopped at a trash can, which they seemed to be trying to catch on fire as one of them absently threw lit matches into the paper, while the one that seemed the leader pushed a few of the smaller ones around. The paper in the can finally lit, adding to the hellish vision as the orange lights from the flame danced along their darkly-clad bodies.

No answer came from Carrie for a few seconds and he glanced over at her to see if she was alright. When she realized that she had his attention, she pointed up the walkway, where they could just make out an elderly gentleman, who was slowly making his way with his cane, on a path that would take him right to the gang.

"What do you want to do?"

Fletcher glanced at his WCD and saw that they had less than two minutes until the occurrence. Then he studied the teenagers, judging that they probably wouldn't notice them at all if they moved from their hiding place.

"I think we take the direct approach," he suggested.

"Should we haze?"

He shook his head as he put his hand gently on her arm and pulled her up with him. "Just follow my lead."

Checking to make sure that the youths hadn't noticed them, he began walking up the path towards the man they could only assume was the grandfather. Carrie kept in close behind him, continually checking behind her to see if any of the kids had noticed their movement.

The elderly man stopped as the two Skimmers approached, a look of confusion covering his care worn face.

"Who are you," he asked, his cockney accent dominating his aged tones, "some kind of soldier?"

A big smile came to Fletcher's lips at the intonation as he moved up to the old man to stop him from proceeding.

"You are correct, sir," he said, trying his best to fake an English accent, but falling short of the mark.

Carrie winced at his words, as if he had pulled nails across a blackboard, then she stepped forward and took off her helmet, letting her long russet hair cascade like flowing silk across her face and shoulders. She softly touched his hand while flashing him her quirky grin. "You must not go that way, sir," she said, allowing her long suppressed accent to come through. "There are some nasty men down there that we have under surveillance. Is there another route you can take, perhaps?"

The smile that came to his elderly lips defied his age, as he took in the youthful beauty before him. Eagerly he accepted her hand in his as he let out a soft chuckle. "Certainly," he told them as he glanced around. "I can cut through that tunnel and still get home in plenty of time."

Fletcher studied the stone bridge with the tunnel under it, judging it for safety. He looked over at his partner and nodded.

"That would be fine, sir," she said as she returned the grandfather's open smile.

The two of them started to walk that way, while the major lagged behind, keeping an eye on the path towards the kids.

"Interesting uniforms," the grandfather said, as they walked with him.

"They're new," she explained as they neared the tunnel. Then she stopped, and pulled her hand back slowly. "Will you be alright now?"

"Certainly, dear," he said, his smile never wavering. "You two have a good night." Then he leaned in close to her and lowered his voice to a whisper. "You tell your Yank friend to work on that accent of his," he laughed softly, "I haven't heard anything that bad since the last big Robin Hood movie."

She continued to grin, as she watched the elderly man walk into the darkened tunnel, then she turned back to find Fletcher catching up to her.

"I think we're OK now," he suggested, then noticed her expression. "What's so funny?"

"Nothing," she said as she checked her WCD, her amused smile fading quickly into a frown. "We're past the deadline, but the mission indicator hasn't turned green."

"It's not red either," he commented, "which means that his fate is still up in the air."

"But the gang is back that way," she said, her tone growing softer with concern, "and he went through the tunnel…unless."

"Unless the gang has moved and they are heading that way as well," he finished for her.

Instantly they ran after the grandfather, desperate to avert what seemed an impossible turn of events. As they hit the edge of the tunnel they glanced down its length, amazed at how long it seemed in the dark. They could clearly see their charge, about halfway down and moving at his usual pace; however, they both saw the slight movements at the far end, as chains caught on the smallest flickers of light from a distant lamppost.

"My God," she whispered, "they'll ambush him."

"Go into hazing mode," he commanded, as the only possible solution came to him. "We'll run in and grab him and bring him back to here."

"Gotcha," she agreed as they both hit their hazing buttons and vanished.

Fletcher reached out blindly and managed to grab her hand so that they could keep their pace together, instantly feeling her fingers entwine with his as she seemed to share his sentiment. Together they ran down the darkened tunnel, two specters who could only be detected by the splash of water as their unseen boots hit the occasional puddle.

They reached the grandfather just a few paces from where they saw him and didn't wait to introduce themselves. Each of them took an arm and turned him around, as Fletcher placed his finger against the elder's lips.

"Keep silent," he warned him, forgetting the accent this time, "and come back with us to the other side of the tunnel."

"I can't see you," their charge almost whined in fear. "Why can't I see you?"

"Don't worry," Carrie cut in, keeping her voice low for fear of it echoing in the tunnel. "Our black uniforms are meant to blend in to the darkness, when we reach the end of the tunnel you will see us." Her voice edged slightly with concern. "Please trust us, sir, you are in grave danger."

He seemed to relax at the sound of her voice, and he let them lead him back down the tunnel as they each held an arm, half carrying him to quicken his pace. They started to rematerialize as they emerged into the soulful mist.

"There you are," the grandfather said with relief, as the three of them left the tunnel behind. "I thought it was safe that way."

"So did we," Fletcher said as he watched the tunnel to see if any of the kids had followed. He strained for a moment against the silence, almost imagining the sounds of running feet, then he decided that it wasn't his imagination at all; the gang was heading down the tunnel at a quick pace.

"We could run," Carrie suggested, fear starting to edge in her eyes as she stared at the approaching menace.

"With *him*?" the major asked, doubt in his voice as he searched around. "No offense, sir, but they'd out distance us quickly."

"No arguments here, son," the grandfather hastily agreed.

"Then what?"

Fletcher pointed to a group of barrels near the tunnel entrance that were piled quite high, over his sight level. "Let's hide there."

"Hide?" she asked while glancing first at the elderly man, then at the dark shadows closing in swiftly in the darkness. "Hide," she agreed.

They quickly escorted him behind the large plastic containers and waited, knowing that the next few seconds would determine their fate. Fletcher had no doubt that, if confronted, he and Carrie might be forced to protect not only the grandfather, but themselves as well. The results of which could not be anything but disastrous.

He could feel his heart pounding in beat with the drumming of the gang members steel-tipped boots. Despite the temperature controls in his armor, a droplet of perspiration formed on his forehead, as he tried to weigh all the options. The obvious kept hitting him in the face, as he stared at his WCD indicator, which still was left unanswered despite the fact that they were already eight minutes past the original occurrence time, and that obvious answer was to abort the mission. If they Skimmed out now, only the grandfather would be affected, and the mission would be a failure. However, if they were all discovered, who knows what damage the time stream could take.

His hand inched out almost unconsciously, as he sought reassurance in his actions, and contacted hers as their two hands instantly clasped together. He glanced over at her, reading the same concerns and questions in her shimmering jade eyes. There was no doubt in his mind that she was asking herself the same questions, and coming up with the same lack of answers.

It was then that the kids emerged from the tunnel and stopped running, as they hunted all around like wolves on the scent, searching for their prey.

"So where's the old geezer?" one youth asked, obviously annoyed at this game of cat and mouse.

"He was supposed to come out of the tunnel," another said in what must have passed as an authoritative voice, though Fletcher clearly detected the almost hidden whine of a confused kid who was playing tough.

Carrie glanced sharply at her partner, her thoughts once again mirroring his own.

"Well, he's not there now," the first one complained.

"What about the running?" a young girl's voice asked. "He must have come this way, and no old man is going to outrun us."

"Unless he never was there," the leader tried to reason. "Let's forget it, mates, there's plenty of pickings in this park."

There was a general grumble of consent, as they started to reenter the tunnel, disappearing back into the consuming darkness from whence they came.

"That's the last time I listen to a bloke in some stupid high tech costume…" the leader's voice grumbled as they vanished from sight, "not even all hollows eve yet."

Fletcher's eyes quickly darted down to his WCD, relief flooding his body as the mission indicator turned a bright kelly green. He glanced up at Carrie, whose smile clearly showed her mirrored state of mind.

They escorted the grandfather back around the barrels, each still glancing around to validate what their WCD assured them was fixed.

"You'll be safe now," Carrie told him. "I'm sorry for the trouble."

"That's quite alright," the elderly man said with his own smile of relief. "You two kids work well together, you make a sweet couple."

The Skimmers glanced at each other, then Fletcher smiled and patted the grandfather on his shoulder. "You take care, sir."

With that their charge headed back off into the mist, swiftly vanishing in the thick night air.

"What the hell happened here?" Carrie asked after she was sure he was far away.

"Beats me," Fletcher confessed. "It was as if they were tipped off somehow."

A distant flash of azure light at the far end of the tunnel caught Carrie's attention in the edge of her peripheral vision.

"Did you see that?" she asked, pointing to where the light had been.

"See what?"

"I'm not sure," she admitted as she strained to recall exactly what she had seen. "If I had to make a guess, I'd say that there was another Skimmer here who just left."

He turned to stare down the way she had pointed, but there was nothing in sight. Checking his WCD one last time to comfort himself with the green light, he let out a long breath and patted her on the shoulder.

"Let's get out of here."

"No arguments here," she agreed. "We've got to tell Justin about this."

They readied their WCDs and activated their return controls. With a push of the button and a flash of light, they gratefully left the dank scene far behind.

Back at the *Twilight* center, the news of how the Skim had fared cut sharply into Justin's elation at the team's first success together.

"Starfox, are you sure it was another Skimmer?" the *Twilight* leader asked, grave concern in his usually jubilant voice.

Carrie considered it again, trying to relive the moment in her mind, but she shook her head. "Pretty sure, I saw the flash of light just like ours…but I can't say for certain."

"Someone was playing with us down there," Fletcher commented as he took a seat in the *Twilight* leader's office. "We successfully contacted our goal and diverted him, then the damn kids circled back around to get him again. The WCD indicated that we were still there after the fact, but it hadn't turned red or green. Unless the Omni computer was wrong about the time table."

Justin shook his head. "I sincerely doubt that. The computer's never wrong, yet I know for a fact that no other Skimmer was sent to that time with you, unless he came from *Twilight's* future." He paced around behind his large desk, then sat back down, obvious worry creasing his thin features. "If you ever find yourself in a similar situation, I want you to abort the mission. It's simply not worth the risk."

They sat in silence for a moment, each in their own thoughts.

"Could it have been this rogue Skimmer that Checkmate told us about?" Fletcher finally asked, breaking the quiet.

"I've considered the possibility," Justin admitted, "but his existence is still only a theory. We have no proof."

"What about today?" Carrie suggested. "Isn't that proof?"

"Only of the fact that something went wrong with the Skim," the *Twilight* leader stated, "not of the existence of this rogue."

"If the rogue Skimmer exists," Carrie asked absently, almost as if voicing her thoughts aloud, "what would his motives be…why try to hurt the grandfather?"

"I don't think that those were necessarily his motives," Justin commented thoughtfully.

"Then what?" the major questioned, as he tried to formulate his own answers.

"If such a person exists," the *Twilight* leader continued, "I would think that he is playing around…testing us…maybe testing me and *Twilight* as a whole."

"To what end?" Carrie asked.

"Why does anyone try such tests?" Justin queried rhetorically.

"To see what he can get away with," Fletcher interjected, "while he plans for something big."

"Makes sense to me," Justin said as he let out a low sigh. "I want you to be extra careful on your Skims until we learn more. I'll pass the word on to the rest of the teams. I don't want any of you taking any unnecessary chances out there."

Justin had little to be concerned about, as the Omni computer found few things to occupy the Skimmers with over the next three weeks. Fletcher discovered that the *Twilight* leader's feast or famine theory panned out with regards to Skims. It was either quiet or crazy, and for the most part, it was remaining dead quiet.

Despite his anxiousness to get back into the field, the major found that he was enjoying the downtime. He spent a good deal of it with Carrie, Kim and Juan, hanging in the observation lounge or other sections of *Twilight*. He even tried Ring Skating, enjoying the virtual reality exhilaration of skimming along at phenomenal speeds on the rock-filled, icy-slick rings of Saturn, jet skates flaming at his feet. But most of all, he enjoyed being with her. Every day he looked forward to seeing her in the mornings. Even when they weren't on duty, which was every other week, they still met for breakfast, and ended up spending most of the day together. Sometimes he would catch Justin watching in the distance, and he even asked him to join them for breakfast once. However, their stalwart leader had too many things to accomplish that morning to afford the luxury, as he called it, of a leisurely meal.

Twice, Carrie and he had ventured out into the actual *Twilight* facility, leaving the Skimmer sections behind. Outside their little sanctuary was a much larger complex, filled with many living facilities and a shopping mall.

Although there was no actual money used here, work done by the citizens of *Twilight* gave them credit that they could use at these shops. Fletcher had seen no real difference, though Carrie had defended the system emphatically, which didn't really surprise him since she practically grew up here. All this time he was aware of what was growing between the two of them, but he resisted trying to define it, instead simply enjoying it. However, still lurking far in the backwaters of his mind was the demon that would cause him to question whether or not partners that had to rely on each other for their job and for their survival should ever consider being more than that, and what consequences there could be. But he accepted a simple cure for this, which was to tell Kim about his misgivings and let her scold him for a short while, and he would usually feel much better. Sometimes he would wonder why thoughts like that would creep up, but chalked it off to his own fear of commitment, which he never really tried to hide from himself, though he often wished he could.

Despite how much he enjoyed these days, he still spent more than a few sleepless nights, deeply locked in consideration of how he felt about her, and wondering if she ever experienced the same.

It was far into one of these sleepless nights that their first call in almost four weeks came in, just as he was beginning to nod off.

When the alarm went off, he almost ignored it, then slowly came out of his daze as it sounded off a second time.

Before he could even force himself out of bed, there was a quick knock at his door.

"Come in," he called while pushing back his blonde hair, noticing for the first time how much it had grown out from his normal crew cut.

The door swept open with a light whoosh, as the outside corridor light framed her curved silhouette in a darkened outline.

"Carrie?" he asked as his eyes tried to adjust.

"Let's go, partner," she said gleefully as she walked into the room, "we only have ten more minutes to get to the Departure Nucleus and Skim."

"Yeah," he half grumbled as he stood up to look at her, noticing that she was in full armor already. "What'd you do…sleep in that thing."

For the first time since entering his room, Carrie noticed that Fletcher was only wearing undershorts. Her eyes briefly caressed his tight, muscular body, pausing on his broad chest, then quickly darted down to the ground.

"Um…" she half stammered. "I couldn't sleep so I was doing some exercises in my armor when the alarm went off."

He half nodded, not noticing the shade of pink that his partner had become.

"You should get chest—I mean dressed," she quickly shot out as she turned back to the door. "I'll wait outside." With that she stole one last glance his way, then retreated to the corridor, leaving him alone with a puzzled look covering his face.

Swiftly donning his scarlet body suit and ebony armor, he grabbed his helmet off the night stand and left his quarters, finding her waiting outside, the slightest traces of pink still in the tips of her ears.

"We'd better run," she suggested while checking her WCD. "We have less than six minutes."

Together they ran down the corridor and through the open cafeteria, finally entering the Departure Nucleus with barely two minutes to spare.

"That's calling it close, folks," Sender scolded as he quickly handed them the plastic mission cards.

Fletcher quickly slid his in and took a brief glance.

> *Time Skim 10198:*
> *June 14, 1990 — Amherst. Chester Bloom is a twelve-year-old boy who is on his way home from school. He will arrive just in time to witness the murder of his mother at the hands of his father. After this he ran away and it was three days until the police found his mother's body, because she hadn't shown up for work. Chester buried his anger over the incident, never really accepting what had happened. This incident so traumatized the young boy that he grew up to be a wife beater himself, spending much of his adult life in and out of prisons. The Omni computer feels that if he hadn't had this first hand experience of his mother's death by a beating of his father, that he would have been better able to deal with the trauma and would not have become the person he was.*

"My God," Carrie whispered as she read the mission docket as well.

"You've go to go now," Sender ordered them. "You only have a minute left to get on this time stream."

Not wasting any time to discuss the case, they both activated their WCDs and Skimmed out, dissipating into the azure flash.

They both materialized in someone's back yard, which was dense with trees. Taking a quick glance around they realized that they were in a suburban development, with houses occupying every quarter acre of land or so in an even disbursement.

Fletcher took another look to make sure they hadn't been seen, then checked his WCD. "It's about twenty after three in the afternoon," he commented thoughtfully. "Odds are that most these people are still at work."

"Except for the Blooms," Carrie said solemnly as she checked out the picturesque scenery that surrounded them. In the distance, they could hear a dog barking sporadically. "I don't know, Fletcher," she said as they started to walk from the back yard around the two story colonial house, "this time I'm seeing things the way you did back in that first Spiral Run. Couldn't we just save Ms. Bloom from her husband instead? Wouldn't that solve Chester's problem just as well? If not better?"

"I don't know," he said as he reached out and softly touched her arm, causing her to gaze into his eyes. "Who's to say he wouldn't just kill her next week then, or she could have killed him."

"Sounds like he'd deserve it."

Fletcher nodded, then checked his WCD again. "We have a very narrow window this time, the incident is going to happen in just a few minutes."

"But where?"

"I would guess a few houses over," he suggested, "by the mission indicator. Let's go."

Together they came around to the front of the house and crossed the deserted street, quickly moving to the back yard of the next house along the way.

"We really stick out here," Carrie commented as they jogged along, trying to make up for lost time. "Where are we, anyway?"

"Massachusetts, I think," he said while keeping one eye on the WCD and one eye on where he was running, trying to avoid such pitfalls as gopher holes or divots. He stopped them as they passed the sixth house, as he tried to get a definite reading on the direction. "It could be that house right there." He pointed at a small, two story Cape Cod, just a few dozen feet away.

"You're not sure?" she asked, checking her own WCD.

"What do you think?"

She checked it again and shrugged. "The arrow points that way all right, but I don't see Chester."

"Let's check out the windows," he suggested. "If Chester saw it through the window, all we have to do is wait for him, haze, and then keep him from seeing the event."

"Sounds simple enough," she agreed, time ticking nervously past them as they started searching the windows of the small house.

"Something's wrong," he finally offered. "We only have half a minute left and there's no sign of—"

The high-pitched woman's scream across the street punched into his words like a hammer through glass.

"Jesus," he whispered as his face lost color, "we're at the wrong house."

Caring little if he was seen or not, he took off at a full run, crossing the street in an attempt to avert the disaster that was unfolding before him.

"Phantom," she called after him, then quickly followed in close pursuit.

He could hear the blood rushing in his ears as he tore across the carefully manicured lawn, as the last scream from inside the colonial house died out. Rounding the corner to the back yard he stopped dead in his tracks, as his eyes fell painfully on the young boy who stood like a ghost as he peered through the window, the unspeakable horror of what he'd witnessed written on his face in pained lines that went far past his age. A stab of failure registered in his heart as his peripheral vision caught the bright glow of cherry red on his WCD, as the micro computer declared the mission a failure.

Carrie caught up to him, having already registered the red light on her own WCD. For a moment she glanced at the child in silence who still stared at the ghastly vision with an intensity that almost pleaded for time to reverse itself, to undo what had been done.

"We'd better get out of here," she whispered to her partner, who was as still as marble. "There's nothing more that can be done here."

"I don't accept that," his voice hissed quietly in a low guttural tone, as he glanced at the bright red light again, his own WCD signaling the return light as well. "I don't accept *that* either." Before she could stop him, he crept up to the boy and placed a hand on his shoulder. The youth turned to face the stranger, his eyes vacant and non-responsive to the outlandish dress of the man kneeling next to him.

"My mother," he said, his voice hollow and empty.

"We have to get out of here," Fletcher told the boy, as he grabbed his hand and then picked him up and brought him back to Carrie.

"What are you doing?" she asked, her eyes wide in shock. "We have a red light, we have to get out of here."

"No," the major stated flatly, as he began walking through the back yard, to the next house that seemed deserted. Then he placed the boy back on the ground, who just stared at the two of them in blank non-recognition.

"What are you doing?" she asked again as she shook his arm, trying to draw his attention.

"I have an idea," he tried to explain, but felt he didn't have the time to go into details. "Break into that house, find their phone and dial nine-one-one. Tell the police that this is an anonymous tip about the murder and give them the address."

"Are you crazy?" she questioned, staring at him in disbelief. "Do you have any idea of what Justin would say?"

"A this moment, I don't give a rat's ass what Justin will say," Fletcher almost shouted, but managed to keep his voice low. "Right now all I care about is this boy." His bright blue eyes stared deeply into hers, pleading for understanding. "Please, Carrie…you've got to trust me on this."

Taking in a deep breath, she snuck up to the back window and put her helmet though it, shattering the glass easily. Within a moment she was inside and out of his view.

All this time the boy remained silent and vacant, as if lost deeply in his own world.

"You have to listen to me, Chester," Fletcher said as he knelt back down to the boy's height and lifted his small chin to face him. "What happened to your mother was not your fault. And what your father did was wrong…very, very wrong."

Chester stared at the Time Skimmer, seemingly oblivious to his words. Then he turned his small head away and tried to leave. Fletcher held on his arm tightly, and pulled him back to face him again.

"You can't run away from this. You try to run from this and you'll be running your whole life, until one day you become the man your father was…Is that what you want, to do to other women what your father did to your mother today?"

The slightest spark of anger struck young Chester's eyes, as he turned back to face his captor.

"Maybe that *is* what you want," Fletcher taunted, seemingly carefree of the hurtful words he was dealing to the child. "Maybe you like pushing around helpless people, maybe you like your father for what he's done."

"No!" Chester screamed at him and struck out with his free hand, as tears began streaming down his reddened face in sheets of previously contained grief. "No!"

Fletcher let the young boy strike him a few times, as he took off his helmet so that the boy could see his face better.

"I'm not my father and I never will be," Chester cried, as he pounded on the Time Skimmer again, this time with less energy.

Taking this as a sign, the major pulled the boy in and closed his arms around him. "You don't have to be like him, Chester. You can do whatever you want with your life."

"I hate him," Chester continued to cry, his tears running down the chest of Fletcher's armor as he laid his small head on the major's shoulder.

"It's alright to hate him," Fletcher comforted, as he rocked the boy in a gentle motion. He continued holding onto Chester, swaying slowly back and forth for a few minutes, until he realized that his partner was standing to his left, her own eyes clouded with water.

He wanted to explain to her, to make her understand why he did what he thought he had to do, but was cut off by the distant sound of sirens swiftly closing in on their location. Carrie sniffed back once then snuck around the side of the house, to witness the three police cars pulling up to the front of Chester's house. Then she came back to tell her partner what was happening.

Fletcher nodded at the information as he continued holding the boy. They listened to the struggle next door, as the police took the father into custody. Once the major felt that the danger was over, he slowly pushed Chester to arms' length, and gently wiped away a tear from his youthful face. "It's up to you now, Chester.... Still want to run away? Or do you want to take charge of your own life?"

Chester nodded silently as he sniffed back his own tears. Then his tiny voice spoke, the slightest hint of determination within it rang of a newfound maturity. "I'm *not* like my father."

Carrie let out a short gasp of hope at the boy's words, as she moved in slowly and knelt next to him as well.

"You can do it," she assured him, adding to Fletcher's comfort.

"Now I want you to go over to the police officers at your house and tell them what you saw your father do, and they'll take care of you. Can you do that?"

Chester nodded as he glanced back at his house, no longer the safe place he'd always known it to be. "Are you a cop?" he asked, unsure of his savior.

"Sort of," Fletcher confirmed with a warm smile. "You can just tell the police that we were concerned people that happened to pass by." Then he turned Chester towards his house and gave him a gentle push. "You go ahead now."

The boy took one last look at the two Time Skimmers, and then ran towards the police cars that were still in his driveway.

Both time travelers were so wrapped up in watching the boy leave, that neither of them noticed the harsh red indicator on their WCDs turn to a gentle kelly green.

"My God, Fletcher," Carrie whispered as she finally noticed the indicator. "You did it." She knelt down next to him, as she drew his attention to his wrist.

They both stared at the green indicator for a moment, then back up at each other, smiles growing on both their faces.

"No," he said, his voice a bit haggard from the stress, "*we* did it."

Carrie put her arms around his neck and held him against her chest, as he took a few deep breaths to bring himself down from the emotional rush that was still coursing though his veins like fire. He returned the embrace and held her tightly as well for a few moments, then she noticed some of the police starting to check out the back yards.

"We'd better get out of her," she suggested as she reluctantly pulled away from his hold.

"I guess so," he agreed, as they both stood up and activated the return circuits.

Fletcher leaned over and picked up his helmet and put it back on, then signaled his readiness. A moment later they were deep in the time streams, safely on their way home.

*Chapter 12*
# In the Heat of the Night

The Twilight Skimmers rematerialized back in the Departure Nucleus, to find their leader standing with arms crossed, a stern look covering his usually warm facade.

Both of them felt drained from the experience and the last thing that Fletcher felt he wanted, or needed, was a lecture on what could have gone wrong, and he doubted that his partner felt any different.

"Look," the major instantly spoke up as he read the emotions clearly on the *Twilight* leader's face, "I'm sure what we did was wrong, but it was all my idea, Starfox didn't know what I was doing."

Carrie shot a look of surprise over at her partner, as a warm smile came to her lips. "That's not true," she denied, "we were working together—"

"Starfox," Justin cut in as he held up his hand for her to stop, "Phantom, it's alright." He lowered his arm as the two Skimmers glanced at each other in surprise. "What you did today I'm sure was very, very risky…and I don't ever want you to try it again. I'm not even going to touch on what could have gone wrong." He held up his hand again, stopping Fletcher's words before they escaped his open lips. Then a smile came over the *Twilight* leader's lips as a low chuckle sounded from within. "However, I'd love to hear what really went on down there, 'cause I'll be damned but no Skimmer team has *ever*, in the history of *Twilight*, reversed a red mission light."

Both team members smiled at the approval, as Fletcher flashed a wink over at Carrie.

"I'll bet you guys are beat, though," Justin suggested. "Why don't you try to catch some sleep?"

Fletcher glanced at his WCD and let out a soft breath of surprise. "It's only three in the morning."

Carrie suddenly found herself in a prolonged yawn, which infectiously spread throughout her companions with relentless abandon.

"You can easily forget the real time," she said with wonder. "I just got used to it being the afternoon."

"Hazards of the trade," Justin said with a laugh. "Now go and get some rest you two. Remember, when it rains it pours here, so I'll bet you'll be quite busy the next few days."

The two Skimmers gave no argument as they bid the *Twilight* leader good night and headed back to their quarters. They reached hers first, as he gave her a short smile and continued on. However, her hand reached out and grabbed his, causing him to look back.

"You didn't have to take the blame for what happened," she told him, her voice soft with the warm feelings that were still in her from the Skim.

"Yes, I did," he said with a smile. "It was a big risk, and I did it without consulting with you first. I shouldn't have done that."

"Everything turned out fine," she reassured him. "I'd like to think that I'd do the same sometime."

"Justin was right," he confessed, "a lot could have gone wrong..." He shrugged and let out a short laugh, then took a small step back. "I'm going to get some sleep." He started to turn, when he felt that she had touched his hand again.

"You were great tonight," she said as she gave his hand a squeeze, "partner."

He lost himself in her green sea for a moment, as his smile grew. Then he squeezed her hand gently in return, then let it go and continued on to his room.

Sleep came easily to him that night, and when he awoke he felt invigorated and rejuvenated, which was good, since Justin's prediction of the downpour hit them full on. Before either he or Carrie had half a chance to eat, or take a breath for that matter, they had gone on four Time Skims. None were all that difficult in any way, but the pull on their systems with each Skim taxed the body worse than any G-force stress that Fletcher could ever remember back in his flying days. There was a house fire in the early eighteen hundreds that was easily quelled with a small amount of water while the family slept, and a baby who was almost kidnapped that was protected simply by calling the mother's attention to her at the right moment. The car accident that they got next seemed like it was going to be difficult but when they both Skimmed into a sedan where the driver was sound asleep, it was an easy thing to take control of the car and park it in the parking lot of a fast food restaurant. Fletcher's personal favorite for the day, so far, was the dog that they saved from drowning in a swimming pool, who was an intricate part of a young couple's life together.

By the time late afternoon rolled around, they were both pretty exhausted, and the thought of another Skim that day made them a little punchy. However, when they realized where they were going, all traces of exhaustion vanished.

"Rome?" Carrie asked, as she checked her own WCD to read the details of their sixth skim of the day.

"Imperial Rome," Fletcher confirmed with a grin, his excitement rising at the thought of visiting this great era. "The mission seems like another simple one, keeping this young boy from being trampled by a runaway horse."

"How do you two feel?" Sender asked from behind the control panel. "You've been quite active this day. If you want, I can call in your backup. But it has to be quick."

The major looked over at Carrie, who shrugged her head with a grin.

"Let's do it," she suggested. "It'll round out the day."

He nodded and then stepped up on the pad with her.

"I guess that means that you folks are going ahead," Sender said with a laugh. "All ready?"

They both gave the thumbs up signal.

Sender activated the Time Skim platform, illuminating the room, as the time travelers gave each other a last glance, then Skimmed out.

There was always a moment or two of disorientation as the Skimming effect wore off, though Fletcher felt that it most closely resembled vertigo. Then there was that next moment of confusion, as the brain took in the new surroundings and adjusted to a whole new world. He had come to call it the "fly in the car" syndrome, where a fly enters a parked car, then travels with the owner a few miles, and then leaves the car when the owner does. What that fly would suddenly be faced with was what gave him the analogy. Carrie's opinion of this theory was somewhat less than flattering.

There was also the tenseness, not knowing if you are appearing in a situation that could be somewhat hazardous, but that was far from the situation here, as the two Skimmers materialized, finding themselves on an abandoned rolling meadow.

The night was just starting to overcome the waning sun, and the sky was filled with its multicolored splendor, streaking in indigos, scarlets, and golds as the day fell away. The air was clean in such a way that each breath felt like sweet violets, and the gentle sound of a flowing brook nearby put them instantly at ease.

"It's magnificent," Carrie whispered as she took in the placid scene, almost as if a loud noise would break the spell and spoil the vision somehow.

"Yeah," Fletcher agreed as he checked his WCD to see what their status was, "it's amazing what going back in time a millennium or two can do for your environment." He examined the mission parameters again, satisfied that they had plenty of time. "Well," he said as he studied the arrow indicator. "It's seventy BCE, and we're a couple dozen or so miles north of Rome. The accident happens a little ways off that way," he pointed towards a distant hill, "but not for another ten minutes."

"If he's run over by a stray horse," Carrie spoke her thoughts aloud, "couldn't we just divert the horse? Or delay it?"

"I don't see why not," Fletcher commented as they started walking towards the hill, surprising her since she hadn't realized that she was talking. "If we do this right, we may never even see our target at all." He studied the WCD as they continued along, then pointed at a cleft in the hill. "That's where the incident happened, so all we have to do is find the horse."

Almost as in summons to his words, they heard the distant whinny of a horse in distress, and the clattering of hooves on cobblestone. Instantly they broke into a run as Fletcher led them to a point far to the left of where the target incident was to happen, hoping to intercept the horse on its way to the boy. They reached a cobblestone road which served as an artery connecting Rome to its provinces, as they looked around for any sign of the horse or boy.

"The kid should be way down that way," Fletcher said as he pointed south.

"Right," Carrie agreed as she grabbed a loose branch that was still covered with leaves and held it ready. As if on cue, a black stallion appeared over the crest of the hill, seemingly on a wild run. The saddle was empty, and it wasn't hard to guess that the rider was most likely far back on the road, trying to catch up. "Make some noise," she instructed, as she started yelling at the horse and waving the branch wildly. She then started jumping up and down in front of it as it bore in on them. Almost at the last moment, the stallion reared up in front of them, confused by the two armored people that had appeared in his way. It retreated a few steps, then turned and trotted into the field, running a few paces then stopping in the tall grass, suddenly more interested in grazing than whatever had panicked him not long ago.

Fletcher stared at her in wonder for a moment, then glanced at his WCD as the mission indicator turned green. "Interesting approach," he said with a chuckle, as he checked to make sure that no one was coming in either direction.

"Hey, it worked," she defended as she noticed that the return light was lit on her WCD. She looked at it sadly for a moment, then gazed about her at the quickly darkening field that was slowly being illuminated by the rising full moon. "I guess we should get back."

Her tone caused him to look back at her, as he read the longing in her jade pools as she took the surrounding in, not wanting to let it go.

"We could stay a little while," he suggested as he walked off the road towards the horse.

"Are you kidding?" she asked as she ran to catch up to him. "Justin would kill us."

"Normally I'd agree," he said as he approached the ebony mount, who was still concentrating on its dinner, its head low in the grass. "However, the area is abandoned, and the night is beautiful." He glanced at her as he examined the horse. "Why couldn't we? Just for a short time."

"It is kinda romantic here," she half commented to herself, as she took off her right gauntlet and knelt down to pet the horse's nose. "I guess it wouldn't hurt for a few minutes."

Fletcher gazed down at her as she took off her helmet, her russet hair shimmering in the glowing moonlight. Then he removed his own helmet and let it fall to the soft grass, as he knelt down next to her, catching her gaze as his own eyes reflected the last colors of the day in sparkling intensity.

Her eyes became lost in his as she looked up at him, her free hand caressing the horse's soft nose as she smiled warmly at him. Suddenly a low grumble sounded from within her body, causing both of them to laugh.

"I guess I'm hungry," she said as her face flushed pink.

"It has been hours since we ate anything," he admitted, remembering the breakfast that had been interrupted by a Skim. He glanced up at the round bundle, tied to the horse's saddle and raised an eyebrow in curiosity. "Perhaps…" He stood up and opened the cloth bag, instantly grinning as he examined the contents.

"Is it food?" she asked, suddenly very hopeful.

He pulled out a bottle of wine, and a long loaf of bread, then set the bag down next to her. "It's full of grapes."

Her lips curled in a wide grin as she reached into the bag and came out with a handful of the sweet white grapes, and slowly ate them. "Is the bread fresh?"

Fletcher gave it a short squeeze, pleased at its pliability. Then he broke it in half, instantly hungering at the sweet odor that rose from inside. He handed a half to her, as he sat down next to her again, and took a bite of the loaf. "This is fantastic," he said as he swallowed their newfound bounty. "Try the bread."

She studied it for a moment, then glanced back down at the grapes and bottle, suddenly feeling guilty. "Isn't this kinda like stealing? What if someone is waiting for this food?"

"I doubt it," Fletcher responded, as he considered the implications. "This horse was supposed to run that boy down and would most likely have kept on running. This means that the owner still would have lost the food. Besides," he said as he noticed the inlaid gems on the saddle, then pointed them out to her, "I somehow doubt that the owner will be hurting for a meal."

Her eyes reflected the inlaid emeralds, as she took in a deep breath and held it, then gazed shyly at her partner. Their eyes locked momentarily, then she glanced down, taking a piece of bread and eating it.

They ate in silence for a few minutes, each deep in their own thoughts, while enjoying the peaceful quiet of the lush scenery. The last of the sun vanished, leaving the meadow gently illuminated by the soft light of the full moon, which reflected off the tall grass, turning it into long strands of jeweled sapphire.

Fletcher finally uncorked the wine, which was simple since it was a multi use decanter. He paused, smelling the sweet fragrance, then took a short sip, letting the nectar slide down his throat with a satisfying warmth. He then offered the bottle to her, which she took gratefully, following his example.

"This wine is amazing," she confessed. "I can't remember any better. But then again, all the wine I've drank was at *Twilight*...and everything is reprocessed there."

"I was wondering why this tasted so good," he admitted.

Silence descended back upon them for a few more minutes, and then he checked his WCD, noting that they had been here for some time now, and started to wonder when they should return.

"You know," Carrie said as she flashed him her quirky grin, "this would be a great time to resume our previous conversation."

"And which one was that?" he asked, suddenly wary.

"The one where you explain why you were staring at me with those puppy eyes at our graduation party."

"Puppy eyes?" he exclaimed. "I wouldn't call those puppy eyes."

"I would," she said as she let out a warm laugh. "But either way, you said that you would explain it later…so, now it's later."

Fletcher scrambled for a way out of this, hardly wanting to dwell on something he had thought she would forget about. He glanced at his time chronometer again, trying to make it obvious that they should perhaps get back.

"Won't work," she said, her grin never wavering. "Staying here a little while more won't hurt anything. Besides, we haven't seen anyone and we've been here a half an hour already. So tell me…"

He took in a slow breath and held it, as his face creased in concentration, and then it finally hissed out. "I was just thinking…"

"That I looked so familiar?" she asked, as if anticipating his response.

A grin came to Fletcher's lips, despite the uncomfortable feeling that had come over him. It still amazed him how in sync they seemed to be. "Alright," he finally continued after a short delay as he assembled his thoughts, "I guess I'd have to tell you this some day anyway. You remember the first day we met?"

"In the classroom," she said with a nod. "You gave me that same look then."

"That's because the classroom was not the first time I saw you," he confessed, suddenly feeling as if a weight was lifting off his chest as the truth edged to come out. "I had met you before then…you're the one who brought me to *Twilight*."

Her lips parted slowly, as she absently bit the lower one in shock. "That's right…I'd forgotten that you were saying something like that when we met."

He nodded, reaching out to her hand and taking it into his. "You're the one who pulled me out of my burning F-15, and I haven't been able to get you out of my mind since."

Carrie absorbed this slowly, as she felt the warmth of his hand on hers and put her other hand on top of his, holding him tighter. "Do you know when I did this?"

He shook his head. "No, and I'm glad I don't. I don't think it's something that you should worry about. You seemed older in the jet. What about me? You said that I seemed familiar to you also?"

"It was just a feeling," she admitted. "I can't pin it down to more than that." Suddenly she realized what he had told her, and the feelings that were concealed behind his words, feelings that mirrored her own. "So," she said as her smile returned, "*that's* where the puppy eyes came from."

He made a slight face, and rolled his eyes a bit, but ended up laughing anyway. "Well, maybe I was staring at you," he consented, "but let's drop this puppy eyes thing."

"So I guess that makes me your hero?" she said as she pulled herself closer to him. "Like you owe me your life and such?"

"I suppose I do," he said, as he took his free hand and let his finger trace a delicate line across the gentle slope of her jaw. He felt his own lips dry, and wetted them as he felt his heart pound deeper, its throb echoing in his ears so loud that he wondered if she could hear it. Their eyes locked firmly this time, neither wanting to look away as they moved in closer, barely a breath away from the other. Then both closed them as their lips lightly brushed each others, not as if either had maneuvered it, but as if it had come as a force of nature, something that just seemed right. For a brief moment they separated as their eyes opened and met again, the moonlight joining her sea of jade with his thunder sky blue. Then they shut again as they embraced, this time their lips closing in ardent fire as they pulled the other tightly into their arms. Carrie lay back as Fletcher came down on top of her, their lips never separating as they rolled in the grass, each hoping to pull the other closer. Without really being conscious of what they were doing, they continued to roll on top of the other, with her on top, then under, as piece by piece their armor plates came off.

She felt his smoldering kisses move from her lips to her neck, causing a soft cry of pleasure to escape from her, as she pulled herself onto him again. Her hands found the front of his now bare scarlet body suit and pulled the zipper, exposing the tightened muscles of his chest. She ran her fingers through the silken hair there as she brought her wanting lips to his pale skin.

For the briefest moment, Fletcher's mind wandered to the *Twilight* leader, and what he would think of this complete abandonment of sense and safety, and he even wondered what the hell they were doing, but as her soft mouth left a warm trail of kisses down his torso he quickly decided that he suddenly didn't care.

His hand ran along her sides to her front, as he pulled her own scarlet body suit open and down, and rolled back on top of her. Their mouths joined again as their bodies squirmed in methodical rhythm, slowly slipping out of the remainder of their second skins, as she rolled back on top and pulled herself up to gaze on him. Their eyes locked once more, all the emotion flowing through them as she lowered herself onto him. His mind spun in ecstasy as he looked up at her, a flawless vision framed by the naked full moon. His deep breaths were echoed by her soft cries as they brought their passions together in perfect harmony, finally crescendoing in a downpour of musical jubilation.

## Chapter 13
# In the Thick of It

Some time passed before either of them said anything, as they lay there on the moonlit grass, holding each other, both swimming in their own thoughts. The only sound was the slow crunching as the horse munched grass a few feet off, ignoring his new companions' nocturnal activities.

A thousand thoughts flooded Fletcher's mind as he felt her head resting on his chest, his arm cradling her small body as his finger lightly traced along the gentle swell of her breast: this was a perfect night—I can't believe she's in my arms—the moon overhead is fantastic—I wonder what would happen if a cohort of Roman soldiers came by—and on and on. However, mostly his thoughts revolved around her, and what had changed between the two of them this night.

Carrie squirmed slightly, then slowly raised her head up and glanced at all their equipment that was scattered in the high grass. "Um…I can't believe we did this here," she said with a shy smile as she gazed back into his eyes. Then she lowered her lips to his and softly kissed him, as if in a closing gesture. Then she grabbed her scarlet suit and pulled it up over her front as she stared into the darkness around her, hoping that the lack of noise confirmed her wishes that there were no nighttime spectators. Once satisfied, she quickly began getting dressed, swiftly donning her armor plates with driven purpose.

Taking her lead, Fletcher let out a soft sigh, still not finding the right words for the moment, and got up. He quickly pulled his things back on, making sure the left gauntlet went on first. For a moment his heart stopped as he saw that the WCD looked dead, but as he touched the screen it immediately sprung back to life with the current mission status clearly displayed. "Whew," he whispered with relief.

"It must be like some computer screen saver," Carrie commented after experiencing the same moment of terror. "All mission parameters are still on green."

"Did you expect otherwise?" he asked with a wry grin as he snapped his last piece of armor on.

"Who knows what time-altering effects this night could have," she said with a girlish giggle as she crossed back over to him with a skip and jumped into his arms.

He caught her lithe body in his hands and brought her down to him, his mouth finding hers as her arms wrapped around his neck and held him tight. Then he lowered her to the ground and gently pulled back from her.

"We're sure to catch hell for this already," he said with a forced air of seriousness. "We'd better get back."

Her lower lip protruded in a pout as she glanced around at the magnificent scene. "We may never get to come back here again."

"Carrie," he whispered as he lifted her chin up to face him, "the place isn't what made it special." Then he gave her nose a light kiss, and disengaged from her.

Her eyes followed his movements for a moment, shimmering with the radiant moonlight, then she activated her WCD and gave him a nod. "Let's go."

Making sure they were both in sync, Fletcher gave her the ready signal and they both hit the buttons, vanishing in a flash of azure brilliance.

The perplexed expression on Sender's face was almost comical, as they reemerged in the Departure Nucleus. He studied his readouts a few moments, then glanced back up at the now solidified Time Skimmers.

"Did you two have a problem down there?" he asked, as he tried to make sense out of the readings.

The two of them looked at each other for a moment and shrugged.

"No," Carrie said, her eyes wide with seeming innocence. "Why do you ask?"

"It would seem that you two spent a long time down there after getting the green light...almost an hour and a half."

They glanced at each other again, their grins obvious.

"Hey," Fletcher said with a cavalier air about him, "it's Rome. We had to take in some sights. You know, the coliseum, gladiators, Caesar, the whole bit."

Sender's eyes went wide with shock, then narrowed as he realized the joke that he was at the receiving end of. "You two know the rules. Get in, do your job, and get out; fast as possible."

"Thank heavens it wasn't like that," Carrie whispered side longingly to her partner, causing him to laugh.

The departure coordinator gave them a suspicious glare, and then let out a short breath. "You two have had a rough day, why don't you get a shower and hose off."

"Great idea," Fletcher admitted, as they stepped off the platform and walked out of the room. As they passed through the door they brushed each other and paused, smiling as their eyes met. However, a short "Humph" from Sender sent them going on their way.

They walked down the main corridor in silence, each deep in their own thoughts. When they finally reached Carrie's room, they paused, as she opened her door.

"Want to come in for a while," she suggested with an inviting smile, "we could talk about...well you know."

A lump settled in Fletcher's throat, and before he knew it he shook his head. "I really need a shower, and I'm kinda beat," he said, wondering if his answer sounded as lame to her as it did to him.

Her face showed some disappointment, but she recovered quickly. "Then I'll see you later...or tomorrow."

"Tomorrow, then," he quickly agreed with a nod. He leaned over and gave her a short kiss, then turned and was on his way to his quarters. She watched him for a moment, her eyes studying him as if in silent judgment, then she went in and closed the door.

Fletcher hit his bed with a thump as he threw his body onto it in frustration. His hair was still wet from the shower, but he didn't care as he stared up at the ceiling which he had become all too familiar with. He couldn't believe that he had not gone in with her, but knew that he had to sort this all out in his head. What had happened on that Skim still buzzed in his brain at an almost dizzying speed. He couldn't believe this turn of events, which had culminated his dreams. Yet he also feared what this would do to their relationship. *What if this affects how we work together?* his mind questioned as he lay there. On one hand he feared that this could have been a mistake, but on the other hand, the thought of terminating these feelings seemed impossible.

Acting on impulse, he stood up and slid on his shorts. Before he allowed himself to reconsider his actions, he left his room and was at her door, quietly knocking on it.

The door opened with a silent whoosh, as Carrie tightened the towel that was wrapped around her body. For a moment she stared at him, surprised at his appearance, then a warm smile curved the corners of her full lips.

"Lose your towel?" she asked as she watched the water drip from his still soaked hair.

Seeing her again removed all doubts from his mind, and he marveled at how her presence could do that to him so easily. He reached out and touched her arm, lightly resting his fingers on her, as his eyes caressed her ivory skin that was barely concealed by the terry cloth.

"Could I borrow yours?" he asked, his face curving in a devilish grin.

She pulled him into her room, as the door closed silently behind them.

Life stayed busy for the Time Skimmers over the next few weeks, as an almost rash of calls broke out, keeping all the teams going at full steam with little time for rest. Fletcher managed to spend as much time as possible with Carrie, but it was mostly in snatches that slipped between the calls and sleep, which seemed to be the only downtime they were getting these days. His fears of what had happened on the Skim in Rome affecting how they worked together seemed to have been in vain, since they continued to work as the well-oiled machine that they were becoming. In fact, he felt more in tune with her than ever before, almost sensing her around him which made working with her all that much easier.

They had hoped to keep their private life a secret, but the walls of *Twilight* seemed to have ears, and soon their friends were making small innuendoes that solved nothing but to embarrass the two of them; though Fletcher often wondered if that was their purpose to begin with. Worst of these was Kim, who had a smug "I told you so" grin on her face whenever she saw the two of them together, which was more and more often as the work load finally began to ebb down. For the first time in what seemed far too long, Fletcher felt that everything was going right, which scared him more than anything he could remember, as that "relationship demon" of his started once again to edge at his soul. At first it was easy to ignore, as their relationship budded and grew, but as she moved closer to him, it became apparent to Fletcher that a commitment was inevitable. When this happened his actions started to change, almost too subtle to notice. And it wasn't he who finally realized what he was doing, Kim had to point it out to him.

"So what's your problem, Phantom," the small Asian woman asked with a knowing grin, as they walked towards the observation lounge where they would catch up with their partners for dinner.

"I don't know what you're talking about, Kim," he declared, though he doubted the validity of his own words.

"Carrie tells me that you stood her up for dinner three times over the last week."

"Did I?" Fletcher asked, not remembering it being that many times.

"You know what it sounds like to me," she said as they approached the lounge. "You're getting close and that pattern of yours is kicking in."

He stopped at the doorway and looked at his friend, and feared that she was telling the truth. Sometimes he could understand what happened with him and women in the past, but this time it was different, he had never felt for any of them the way he did for Carrie. "Did you tell her about what I told you?"

Kim shook her head. "That's not my place, Phantom...that's yours." Then she reached out and laid her hand on his arm. "It's not a place you'll have long it you keep acting this way."

There had been no words necessary after that, and the two of them had gone into the lounge, finding Carrie and Juan having drinks at a table. When he saw her his eyes fell down, suddenly ashamed of the way he had been acting. The two of them sat in practical silence through the whole evening, as Kim and Juan made up for their lack of input by telling stories of the various and bizarre Skims that they had been on, reluctantly pulling Fletcher and Carrie into the conversation with direct questions. Cautious glances passed between the two of them, but no words were really spoken, except for when they had to help each other with a point on the telling of one of their Skims. Finally the evening waned on, as Kim gave up with an unconcealed sigh, and threw up her hands in resignation.

"Come on, Condor," she said as she got up. "Let's leave these two sparkling conversationalists to themselves for a while." With that the two of them walked off, but not before Kim made sure to give Fletcher one last warning glare.

A few minutes passed by, then Fletcher took in a deep breath and touched Carrie's hand, instantly causing her to smile at him.

"Want to get some air?" he asked, motioning towards the door.

"Sure," she agreed, as they got up and left the lounge.

They walked along together towards the public sections, pausing at one of the panoramic windows that opened out to the multicolored void. Slowly she took his hand and gave it a squeeze, pulling his attention to her.

"It's been almost three weeks since our night in Rome," Carrie half whispered as she stared out into the endless swirls of light. "Are you regretting what happened that night?" Then she turned to him, her deep jade eyes shimmering as they searched into his, seeking the truth. "Please be honest. If we don't have that, we have nothing."

"Of course I don't," he defended, upset that she would think that, but even more upset that he was the one that had created that doubt.

"Then what?" she asked, her eyes almost pleading as they misted over. "I see a gentleness in you that calls to me. It's as if I can almost see your thoughts through those soulful eyes of yours, but something is in the way…and I'm like an open book to you…and I think I'm falling in love with you."

He felt his body stiffen at her words, as the demon fueled his fears. Before he realized what he was doing, he dropped her hand.

"That scares you, somehow," she stated more as a fact than a question, "doesn't it? Or maybe I'm the one being the idiot here, and I've totally misjudged how you felt about me."

"That's not true," he defended as he tried to force down the turbulent thoughts in his mind. "I really care about you."

"And that's all?"

"Isn't that enough?"

Her eyes fell from his towards the floor with a feeling that he felt in his bones, but she took his hands back into hers, and gave them a gentle squeeze.

"We're great partners," she said, slowly glancing back up at him, "and we work as a fantastic team."

He smiled, despite the confusion within. "I know."

"I also know that when I look into your eyes there's something there," she continued, as her eyes locked back on his. "Don't you feel it also?"

He nodded, mesmerized by the light within her pools of jade.

"Then tell me," she asked once again. *"How do you really feel about me?"*

His mouth ran dry as his lips parted to speak, but nothing came out.

Her lips pursed in anticipation for a moment, but when no response came, she let out a soft breath. "I see. Then I guess that's that." She gave his hands a last squeeze, then slowly let them go and started to walk back the way they had come.

She hadn't made it two feet before he reached out and grabbed her hand as his mind scrambled for the right words to say.

"Breakfast…"

"Excuse me?"

"Give me until breakfast tomorrow to sort this out in my head…can we talk more then?"

"I'm busy in the morning," she quickly responded, her thoughts elsewhere for a fraction of a moment.

"Then lunch."

She started to object but he squeezed her hand tighter.

"Please."

Carrie searched his storm blue eyes deeply for some hint as to his feelings, and then nodded, as she started to understand the battle that was waging within the man that she had fallen in love with. "Alright," she agreed, hoping it was the right thing to do. "I'll meet you in the cafeteria at noon."

"You won't regret it," he promised, though he wondered what he was going to tell her then, and wondered even more so why he couldn't do it now. "Let me walk you back to your room."

"Actually, I'd enjoy some time alone," she told him as she dropped his hand again. Then she smiled softly. "But I'm looking forward to tomorrow." Then she turned slowly, and left the promenade area.

Fletcher stood like a statue as he watched her dwindle down the corridor, an ache in his heart that half wanted him to run and grab her as he had that night in Italy. "I'm looking forward to tomorrow as well," he whispered to himself, as he turned and gazed out the window at the endless streams of time.

## Chapter 14
# The Fall

Carrie's thoughts drifted haphazardly, as her body mimicked the aimless directions she traveled. She had walked the neon halls of *Twilight* for hours, ever since talking with Paula earlier that morning. Somewhere in the back of her mind, she reminded herself that she had promised Fletcher that they would meet for lunch, but it was already past dinner time, and she knew he would be worried. *Not that he didn't deserve it, after the way he has been acting lately.* Kim had tried to tell her that he was just having commitment doubts, but if that was so, then this was the last thing he would want to deal with. But none of this changed the way she felt about him, and she had put this off too long. Finally she shook herself, trying to rid her body of the feelings that were in her. She knew what she had to do, but sometimes the simplest of tasks seemed monumental. Taking a deep breath, she headed towards the Skimmers' quarters, hoping to catch him looking for her there.

Fletcher's face creased in soft lines of concern as he headed towards Carrie's room. The fact that she had stood him up for lunch was certainly disturbing, but he had assumed that she had gotten a solo assignment. However, it was now past dinner, and no one seemed to know where she was. They were both on duty now, he reminded himself, so he doubted she was too far from the Skimmer sections of the station. There was a hollow pit in his stomach as the lift let him out on the circular living quarters floor. For a moment he considered going back down a level, to see if Dr. Kesseler had heard from her, but then shook his head, certain that she would have let him know.

Suddenly that thought echoed in his mind. *Why do you assume she would let you know if she was in trouble? After the way you've acted recently, it would serve you right if she stood you up.* But a gentle smile curved the edges of his lips as the answer seemed obvious in his mind. There was no mistaking the look in those crystal jade eyes when she gazed at him. A warm glow replaced the hollow pit as he quickened his pace, suddenly overwhelmed by the desire to hold her in his arms and feel her soft breath against his chest.

He could no longer question the feelings that had grown and developed within him for her, yet he slowed again as he wondered why such simple words sometimes felt as if they carried the weight of the world upon them. *"How do you really feel about me?"* had seemed like such uncomplicated words from her lips, but the tone was unmistakable: she wanted to know where they stood, and he couldn't blame her.

The gentle curve of the living quarters floor slowly gave way to the observation hall, a long room which overlooked the lower part of the complex, and the warm feeling in his stomach tightened back into a knot when he realized she was standing by the window.

"Carrie," he called out, still unsure of what to say to her. But all doubt vanished, as it always seemed to, when her eyes met his. For a moment he stood still, his lips parted slightly, and all he could hear was his own breath reverberating in his ears, and all he could see was the vision of her perfect smile in his mind as she was framed by the full moon on that Italian night not so long ago.

Then he quickly closed the gap between them, never losing her gaze. Taking her into his arms, their lips joined in impassioned heat, and it was in that moment that he realized that words were only as hard to say as you let them be. He pulled back from her slightly, still holding her in his arms, his eyes beaming wide with his inner joy.

"There's something I want to tell you," he said softly, his voice a warm whisper in her ear. But then she looked down, doubt crossing her ivory face.

"I have something to tell you also," she said, even quieter than he.

For a moment that pit threatened to open in his gut, as warning signals were frantically displayed. Could he have been wrong in his assumptions?

"You seem upset," he tried to soothe her, as his hand came up and gently lifted her chin so that her eyes came to his. "Tell me."

She took a short breath, as the strength of his manner hit her. Suddenly she sensed the change in him, and a warmth filled her as a newfound hope was born.

"I was at the doctor's this morning," she started, deciding on simply getting it out.

The sudden concern that struck Fletcher dissipated in the brilliant flash of azure light that unexpectedly filled the curved hallway. So close was the flash that it wasn't until moments later that they realized that someone was actually Skimming *into* their hallway next to them.

"What the hell?" Fletcher whispered, as he took a step back and shielded his eyes, feeling Carrie move out of his arms.

The glow faded around a tall Skimmer, at least that is what they had to assume he was. He stood all in black, without the scarlet body suit that all Skimmers wore. His helmet fully covered his face, leaving a sheen of mirrored ebony to conceal his visage. The telltale markings that identified all Skimmers were missing, but there was no mistaking his stance as he stood shoulders squared, with the lethal weapon held at arms' length, leveled directly at them.

Soldier's instincts kicked instantly in, flushing the Air Force major's body with adrenaline, but before he could even ask to derive the intruder's meaning, the weapon fired. The intense ruby beam struck Carrie square in the face, and Fletcher only caught a glimpse of her in his peripheral vision, as her smoking body was flung back by the explosive blow like a broken rag doll.

The intruder then leveled the weapon at Fletcher, but his intended target was already moving fast. The first chop struck the ebony Skimmer in the wrist, sending the weapon flying to the ground, then the major's foot swept up in a swift back kick, striking the assassin in the neck, bringing him down with a firm thud.

Fletcher paused for a moment, hovering over the intruder like a lion on freshly killed prey, and waited to see if he was getting up. Seconds ticked by without movement, then Fletcher's head snapped back down the hall, to the woman who lay crumpled against the far wall. He felt his heart pounding with a dread he never knew he could experience as he raced to her side, practically falling down beside her to lift her still smoldering head into his lap. Her soft jade eyes were frozen in fixed perfection, as she gazed lifelessly towards the ceiling.

For a moment he stared at her in disbelief, then he shut his eyes and pulled her tightly to his chest as if the force of his embrace could bring back what had just been viciously torn from him. He felt the slow sting of grief flow down his check, leaving a bitter taste of salt in his mouth, as he struggled to hold in the sobs that wanted so desperately to escape his body.

"Touching," came the cruel voice.

Fletcher opened his eyes and fixated on the intruder who now stood over him again, his weapon pointed at his head. He wanted to lash out, to destroy this man who had robbed him of his very life's blood, but no words came out. He stared at the attacker in silence, as if his very glare could rip out his enemy's heart.

"Vengeance is sweet, Phantom," the ebony-clad Skimmer whispered with contempt. "I hope you rot in your hell."

Fletcher's mouth opened in silence at the mention of his call sign. Within his mind, the world seemed to blur into slow motion as he watched the intruder fire the weapon again, sending the deadly plasma beam directly at his head. His arm came up by sheer instinct, taking the brunt of the blast as his armor sizzled and his WCD flared into explosive flames.

The blow knocked him down on his back, as the mortally wounded circuits in his WCD struggled to contain themselves. Distantly he heard his own mind yelling at himself to get up, to fight back, but all he could do was force himself back to a sitting position, as the assassin moved in closer, and raised the gun again. But his attention drew from the intruder who prepared to deal his last blow and fell on his shattered Wrist Control Device, which was crazily flashing lights around the charred remnants of his wrist armor. The gun leveled at his head and the finger whitened on the trigger, as the circuits of the WCD finally gave way to the loose charge within and flared a blinding cobalt blue. The last thing that burned into his mind was the frozen face of the one person he didn't know if he could live without, then his world turned inside out.

## Chapter 15
# Aftermath

Eric ran through the halls of *Twilight* in a near panic. Something dreadful had happened, he wasn't sure what, but the ramifications were unmistakable. The people were in a state of near hysteria, as lights fluttered on and off in sporadic waves. Distant explosions echoed where there was nothing to cause it, and worst of all, was the periodic pockets of *Twilight* space that appeared and disappeared throughout the center.

"Eric," Checkmate yelled as he ran to the young med tech. "What in bloody hell is going on?"

Eric strained to hear the Skimmer above the din, relieved to see a familiar face.

"The rogue Skimmer was here," Eric called back. "He killed Starfox and vaporized Phantom—"

"Where is he now?"

"I dunno," came the frantic response, "I think he's gone."

"I can't get a hold of Justin anywhere," Borlin said, a deep worry etched into his tone.

"Did you get his answering service?"

"No," Checkmate explained, his voice straining as more people ran by in a confused frenzy, more than one knocking into him. "There was no service at all; it even rejected his personal codes. I asked the computer where he was, and the computer kept repeating 'malfunction', then shut down."

"The Omni computer's down?" Eric asked with fear. "Do you think the renegade got to it?"

"There's no way to tell yet," Checkmate answered as he quickly pulled Eric out of the way of a hulking alien that was running past. "I can't even imagine why another Skimmer would want to damage the computer, it keeps this place running."

"Unless he wasn't a real Skimmer," the med tech said, his eyes going wide.

"Get all the Skimmers together," Borlin ordered, his face turning grave. "We'll meet in the training room in ten minutes to go over a plan of action."

"I don't know if we have ten minutes," Eric yelled over another explosion that caused him to turn back towards the main gallery, but all he could see was a mass of *Twilight* space infiltrating the large center. "We're breached in the gallery," he told Checkmate as he turned back, but the Skimmer was nowhere to be seen. "Checkmate?" he called again as he looked down the hall; he couldn't have moved that far that fast.

A sudden noise behind him caused him to pivot on his heels to avoid another lumbering alien that was running past, but when he looked up again, the alien had vanished as well.

"What the…" he whispered, confusion dominating all his thoughts now. Then he turned back towards the main control center and ran, hoping to find Justin, or any of the Skimmers. Suddenly, ahead of him the corridor dissipated into *Twilight* space, causing a loose beam to roll into his path. Eric caught his foot on the displaced steel as he tried to jump over it at the last moment, and came down hard, but no sound echoed since there was no one to actually fall.

A moment later, *Twilight* ceased to exist.

*Chapter 16*
# Full Circle

Fletcher thought his head would explode as the turbulent currents of *Twilight* space threatened to tear him apart with half his armor off. When he finally came to consciousness, he was sure he would vomit, but a few moments of deep breathing calmed him down; then he opened his eyes.

The world slowly came into focus as he became quite aware of the protective value of the Skimmer armor while in *Twilight* space. His body ached in a dozen different places, but the pain was dominated by the burning sensation in his left wrist, where the still sparking WCD uttered its death throes like a wounded animal. For a moment Fletcher stared at the destroyed circuits and wondered if it would even be possible to fix the time travel device. Taking another deep breath to shake the last of the nausea, he gazed around and came to the slow realization that he was on a military air field.

The sun had just cleared the distant horizon, and already Fletcher could feel the hot desert wind permeating the clothing he wore. An all too familiar scent of paprika waved over him and he got up with a start to look at the field again. His mouth fell open as the certainty of what he was looking at struck home: he was back at the Air Base in Saudi Arabia where he had been stationed—*but when*?

He started to walk across the air field, towards the large hangar building some few hundred feet away, the sensation of deja-vu no longer possible to suppress. The blinding glare of the Arabian morning sun crested over the roof of the tall building, keeping him from making out details in the structure. He could see workers moving about in the open doorways, and the large shadows of planes loomed in the background. The thought of how he was dressed struck him as he heard a low engine start up. A moment later a tow vehicle started to pull one of the planes out of the hanger. Instinctively, he reached for his WCD, to activate the hazing function, but he was only rewarded with a short crackle of static electricity as a few lights flickered on and off in the crippled system.

"Damn," he cursed quietly as he swiftly moved to the side of the building to avoid being seen. Here, on a military base, it would be quite difficult to explain away the strange clothes and armor he wore. Trying to stay under cover, he peered around the front of the hangar, just as the jet came into view. Brilliant gold washed across its surface as the sunlight struck it from over the rooftop, illuminating the sleek craft with the morning light. Fletcher stared in wonder as the unmistakable silhouette of the F-15E etched itself in his mind, and he found himself involuntarily stepping closer for a better look. Then his gaze fell on the cockpit to the words stamped in identification just below the canopy. He felt his lips go dry as he stared at the words again, just to make sure he wasn't hallucinating:

*Major Fletcher "Phantom" Taylor*
*Captain Conrad "Jackal" Striker*

He turned back from his jet as the realization of what had happened occurred to him. He was home.

When the WCD circuits in his armor had blindly sent him spiraling through time, he had realized that he could have appeared anywhere, at any time. Then he recalled Justin telling him once that all people were tied to their own time streams, it was time's way of trying to mend itself.

He took a deep breath as he tried to let all of what had happened sink in, when he felt a hand fall on his shoulder from behind.

"Excuse me," came the hauntingly familiar voice, "who are you?"

He turned around as warning sirens began screaming in his mind. Too late he realized what he had allowed to happen as he stood facing a shocked version of himself. For what seemed a short eternity, they stood, facing each other in silence. The Fletcher who was in the right time and place shifted uneasily in his flight suit, as he tried to understand the unsettling feelings that were washing over his body. The Fletcher who had invaded this scene watched in fascinated horror as the strict warnings that Justin had given him came to his mind.

It only took a few moments for the younger Fletcher to fade totally away. At first he just seemed blurry, and the time traveler had to blink to make sure he wasn't simply getting dizzy again, but then the younger Air Force major went totally out of focus and dissipated, almost as if fading into the wind. The initial nausea came back to him as the ramifications of what had just happened sank in, and he fell against the steel wall of the hanger and slid to a sitting position. It wasn't until a few moments had passed, that he realized that someone was approaching.

"You all right, Phantom?" came the cheerful voice that held the trace of concern lingering in its edges.

Fletcher gazed wearily up, as his line of sight fell on the friend he thought he would never again see.

"Con?" he whispered as a smile curved his lips and he felt a warm rush push out the strange feelings that had overcome him. "Is it really you?"

A look of amusement cocked the younger man's eyebrows as he offered a hand to his superior officer. "You on something?" he asked half seriously. "What's with the getup?"

The major looked down at his Skimmer armor as he prepared to come up with some excuse, but nothing came to mind, leaving him staring at himself with a blank look.

Jackal shook his head and let out a sigh as he checked his watch. Then he pulled his friend back to his feet and patted him on the back. "Don't worry about it, Phantom," he said with a devilish grin. "We all have days when we can't remember what we're wearing when we wake up." He took a serious look at his friend, not failing to notice the charred screen on the armor of his left wrist. "We're supposed to take off in a half hour, are you up to it?"

Fletcher found himself nodding instinctively, then caught hold of his senses; what if the time streams had not only brought him back to his own time, but to the very moment of his departure from his life here. "What mission is this?"

The look of amusement on Jackal's face began to turn to worry, as he started to walk his friend towards the bunkers. "Mission 57-X," he said as he led him into the officers' quarters area, and towards their shared room. Taking a moment to check that no one was watching them, he pushed Phantom into their quarters and grabbed his extra flight suit.

All the while they were moving, Fletcher sank further into his thoughts. *I've taken over my own life*, he realized, *even if I went back now, I would have never left in the first place*. Then the image that he had struggled to keep out of his mind sliced back into view like a rusted razor, painfully cutting as it settled back in. "Carrie," he whispered in a half groan, as he sank onto his bed.

"I see..." Con said as a grin came to his tanned face. "I knew this was because of a girl."

"You don't understand," Fletcher tried to explain, and then reconsidered even trying.

"You can tell me all about it in the air," Jackal laughed as he backed up to the door. "Now suit up and I'll see you on the field." Then he chuckled to himself once again and left their room, closing the door behind him.

For a moment Fletcher sat in the room in silence, uncertainty threatening to suffocate him as its waves flushed over him. Then he remembered Justin's training and it all seemed simple to him. All he had to do was go on the mission again, and the older Carrie would come to save him and take him to *Twilight* again. A forgotten smile came to his lips at the thought of seeing her alive again. Once back in *Twilight*, he knew that he could talk with Justin and get himself back to the right time in *Twilight*, at least he hoped it was that simple.

He quickly shed his Skimmer armor and put it in his aluminum brief case, pausing for a moment to study the charred WCD. Upon looking at it closely, he realized that it was actually mostly intact, but the power crystal was hopelessly destroyed. He laughed silently as he thought that all he needed was another power crystal and he'd be fine. *No problem, I'll just hang out until the twenty-fourth century.* With another chuckle he zipped up the flight suit and gazed out the window. He could see Jackal down on the field near the jets, laughing and talking with Warlock.

Despite all that had happened to him, he couldn't lose his smile. It felt as if he'd been gone a lifetime, not the few months it had actually been. Suddenly he felt himself slipping back into place, as if putting on a long lost favorite shirt that was always comfortable. All this had been torn from him when that missile had cut into his jet. He felt his lips tighten with anger as the thought of that day came back to him: Warlock's last shout of confusion before dying, then the blast that had destroyed his own jet, and killed Conrad as well. He closed his eyes and tried to shut out the memory, but all he could see was Con's lifeless body slumped in his flight harness. Their laughter, comforting before, now stung his ears like venomous wasps, as he realized that to get back to his life in *Twilight*, he had to let them die again.

Taking a determined breath, he picked up his flight helmet and slid the briefcase with his armor under his bunk. Then he opened the door and strode into the hallway. His gaze fell to the right, towards the open field and his waiting friends. But that's not the way he went, as his eyes narrowed in anger and his fingers whitened over the helmet. Without thinking of the ramifications, he turned to his left and broke into a run, jogging down to the war room.

"Major?" came the surprised voice of the airman guarding the doorway, as he was pushed back so that Fletcher could get past.

"Phantom," the colonel said with a slight annoyance as the major entered the room and broke up the staff meeting that was being held there.

For a moment the only sound was the ceiling fan as it rotated far too slowly to break the permeating humidity that allowed no one to escape. All heads turned towards the man who had interrupted the meeting, as they waited for the explanation that would sanction the intrusion.

"Aren't you supposed to be on the field?" the colonel said as he forced a smile to his dry lips. "That target won't wait."

Fletcher stared at the blank faces, faces that used to be his whole world, faces that didn't understand that their orders had cost three men their lives that day—this day.

"It's about this mission," he finally broke the silence as he raised a hand to wipe the perspiration from his head. The heat was dizzying, causing his thoughts to buzz with an almost deafening roar that dwarfed the constant drone of the desert flies.

"Yes?" came the impatient response.

Suddenly Fletcher snapped back to the reality of the situation, and realized just how his intrusion was being viewed by his superiors. He quickly straightened to attention, pushing his shoulders back as well as his fatigued body allowed.

"Colonel," he began again with a renewed formality to his tone. "I believe that there is something that we are overlooking in our enemy's defenses."

"And what is that?"

He paused for a moment, as he realized that he had no idea of what type of missile had destroyed his F-15E that day. However, he knew that if he didn't come up with something fast, history would prove itself to be unbreakable.

"A new SAM that is undetectable."

They all stared at him in silence for a moment, then a few of the junior officers shared secret smirks, with an occasional whisper that betrayed the feeling that the major had perhaps flown one too many missions. However, the colonel had known this pilot for many years, and although his mannerisms seemed unorthodox, the sincerity was genuine.

"A new surface to air missile, huh?" he repeated thoughtfully. "All right, Major, let's check the updated intelligence files."

Fifteen minutes went by slowly, as Fletcher constantly checked his watch.

Each mission was timed precisely, not only with the Air Force, but the other branches of the service that made each operation a success. In another five minutes, the mission would have to be scrubbed totally, and he was not quite ready for that possibility yet—he still had a monumental decision to make.

"Well, I'll be," the colonel said with wonder as the new data was given to him by his aide. "Army intelligence has some data about a new stealth missile that runs by image recognition."

"Image recognition?" one of the lieutenants asked.

"That means it is homing in on the silhouette of its target, and not the heat source."

"Of course," Fletcher said with sudden understanding, "that's why neither the chaffs nor flares did anything to shake that bastard."

The colonel stared at him blankly. "Major?"

"Oh, sir," he coughed with embarrassment, "I was referring to some data tapes I was going over."

"I see," the colonel said with mixed feeling of belief. "Good work though. If they had used those on our planes today, we would have been totally unprepared." He turned towards his aid as he put the report down on the table. "We'll suspend all missions until we find a counter to this weapon."

A feeling of panic gripped Fletcher as realized what he had done. Then he looked back down at the report, his eyes widening at the final paragraph.

"That won't be necessary, sir," he informed the colonel. "It says here that the missile's guidance system is totally unreliable under five thousand feet. We'll fly the mission low and end this threat now, before they can use it at all. Otherwise they may have time to develop it further, and we'll have lost our chance."

"That's very low to cruise at super sonic speeds, Major," the colonel said with obvious skepticism.

"We can handle it, sir," Fletcher assured, gaining back his confidence over the whole situation.

The colonel gauged the risks versus the importance of the mission, and decided to follow his faith in his flight leader. "Very well, Phantom, take the target down."

It was less than fifteen minutes later that the two F-15Es were safely in the air, cruising over the desert sands of Saudi Arabia at slightly over Mach one.

"What was the big hold up?" Con asked as he adjusted the communications equipment.

Fletcher glanced back over his seat at his co-pilot and shrugged. "We were going over some of the enemy's weaponry, nothing much." The lie burned in his throat, but he still wasn't sure of what to do. The obvious choice seemed clear. Ride out the mission the way it went the first time and let the jet be hit by the missile. Carrie will appear and then he's home free. Even racked with conflicting choices, the thought of her jade eyes formed a clarity in his mind that made all other options seem impossible. *Simple*, he agreed, *all I have to do is nothing...and let three close friends die*. His gaze drifted over to his left, to the jet that hovered less than a few dozen yards off his wing. Warlock had a wife and two children; his co-pilot, Ranger, had a young fiancée waiting for him back in Vermont. He had met the girl once, and a smile came to his lips at how happy they seemed together. Then there was Conrad, his best friend. He had a wife as well. They had no children, but not through lack of trying, it was just one of those things that they were hoping for, but never had got.

Fletcher lowered his head as the weight of it all came crushing down, and he realized with painful clarity what he had to do. Give up the one woman that he had ever even considered sharing a life with, so that three men could continue the lives they already had. *But to let her die...* his thoughts ached, then a new concept surfaced. *If I never was in a life threatening situation in the first place, then Justin would never have had cause to send a Skimmer back to get me...Then I would never have met Carrie in Skimmer training.* The words of the rogue Skimmer echoed in his mind. *'Vengeance is sweet, Phantom,' he had said. He had called me by name.* It suddenly seemed obvious that *he* had been the target, for whatever reason, and not Carrie at all. *If I never go to Twilight*, his thoughts instantly concluded, *then the assassin will have no reason to kill her*.

"Hey, Fletcher," came a concerned voice from behind, "you all right?"

"Sure," he responded quickly, realizing that his silence would seem strange to the captain. He tried to brush it off with a half laugh. "Why?"

"You're not usually this quiet on a mission," his friend laughed in return, trying to lighten the obviously dark mood that surrounded his co-pilot. "How about some tunes?"

Fletcher turned on his tape player with almost numb reflexes, then shut it off before one chorus could be sung.

"It's Carrie, right?" Jackal asked as he turned off communications with their sister plane.

The mention of her name caused Fletcher to almost jump out of his flight suit. He turned in his seat to get a firm look at the captain as he tried to conceal his shock. "How did you know?"

"You mentioned her name back at the barracks," was the smug reply. "I do have ears, you know."

A strange sense of relief crept through him as he turned back to the flight controls. "Oh yeah...right."

"Sandy has been nagging me about why you aren't married," his co-pilot said with a grin. "It bugs the hell out of me."

"What's your point," Fletcher responded, falling into the trap too easily.

"The point is that we'd both think it would be great if you actually found a woman who could stand to be around you for more than a week."

He had no answer, as he tried to picture Carrie hanging at the officers' club with Conrad and Sandy back at McGuire Air Base in the States. Somehow he could only see her in her scarlet and ebony Skimmer's uniform, a vision that was already becoming unclear, forced out by his own tolerance level for pain. His entire body ached with fatigue, and he realized that even though it was dawn here, it had been quite late at night back in *Twilight*.

"So who is she?" came the inevitable question. "When will I get to meet her?"

Despite his struggle for control, his eyes began to sting. "Never," he whispered.

"Hmmm," came the slow reply from behind. "Maybe it's something we can talk about?"

"No," Fletcher snapped back. "It just didn't work out."

Before his friend could come back with another question, he pushed down on the flight stick, causing the sleek jet to slip through the clouds and skim towards the ground.

"Hey, Phantom, Jackal," came the surprised voice over the communications unit that Con had just reactivated. "Where are you guys going without us? It's not like you're our wingleader or anything important like that."

"Just follow my lead," Fletcher ordered. "We're dropping to forty-five hundred feet."

"Are you nuts?" Jackal asked from behind. "You trying to go crop dusting or something? At this speed that altitude isn't safe."

"It's a hell of a lot safer than the new missiles that the enemy has," the major stated briskly. "We're leaving Saudi air space now, and we'd be dead in another few moments."

"Whoa," came the response that was shared by all three pilots. "What's this about a new missile?"

Suddenly their questions were silenced by the warning alarm of the tracking units.

"We've got a missile lock on us," Warlock shouted. "Ready to drop defensive measures."

Fletcher felt his heart pounding, echoing the steady throb in his temples that seemed like a drum beating in his head. A thin trickle of perspiration flowed into his eyes, mixing sweat with tears as his vision blurred out. His teeth clenched together as he forced his hands to stop shaking, the thought of what he was doing threatening to tear him apart.

"Negative," he finally yelled, "dive to under five thousand quickly, the tracking system will lose you there."

"I hope you're right," came Con's voice form behind, "because here it comes."

The two white hot trails of death closed in on the plummeting fighter craft, threatening to tear the silver plane apart with explosive ferocity. No thoughts entered Fletcher's mind as the constant wail of the alert continued to scream in his ears save one; get my men to safety.

The missiles streaked overhead, curving to readjust themselves to their target's new trajectory. They formed a perfect ellipse as they banked back towards the jets, closing in to complete their mission of destruction.

Fletcher's eyes never left the altimeter as it displayed the swiftly lowering altitude of the plane. Seventy-five hundred. Seven thousand. Sixty-five hundred. He knew the missiles were closing even without seeing them. The thought that at this altitude a Skimmer wouldn't even have time to save him never entered his mind, as he pushed his throttle harder, struggling for that curtain of safety.

"I can see them," Jackal yelled over the roar of the twin General Electric engines. "Two points of light closing in fast. I don't think we're going to make it."

"Yes, we are," came the firm response, as he maxed out the throttle, struggling to maintain control over the wildly bucking aircraft.

Suddenly the wailing stopped, as Fletcher looked back at his altimeter at the reading in disbelief. Forty-two hundred was firmly displayed, and dropping fast.

"Level it off," he ordered into his mike, "before we become a permanent fixture in the desert floor." He listened to the silence for a moment, as the fear that the other craft hadn't been fast enough dominated his mind.

"We're with you," came Warlock's response as both pilots breathed a sigh of relief. "Cruising at forty-one hundred."

Fletcher felt a pat on his back as his co-pilot let out a nervous laugh. "I don't know how you did it, Phantom, but both bogeys are toast. They lost our signal and hit the sands behind us."

"Good call, Major," Ranger signaled with a thumbs up gesture. "That's definitely one we owe you."

"It's like you knew the future," Warlock laughed. "Maybe you're the one I should call Warlock."

Fletcher let out a deep breath and smiled, feeling his friend's firm grip on his shoulder. "Let's keep it at forty-five hundred and cut the chatter," he ordered. "We want to be back before lunch."

## Chapter 17
# Ramifications

Sleep hadn't come easily to Fletcher, despite the fact that he had been up over twenty-four hours straight, been shot, flown a combat mission, and managed to make it through the little party the other three pilots had thrown for him back in the officers' club. Now that his eyes were finally shut, and his body relaxed, his subconscious continued to harass his conscious with the question of his actions.

What he had done had not been done lightly. His duty as an Air Force major was to protect the men in his flight, his oath to Justin was never to violate the sanctity of the time stream, but all his instincts were to protect the people closest to him.

In the end, he felt betrayed. How could any one man have such responsibility of life and death, *should* any one man have such responsibility at all? When it came down to it, he didn't want any of it. The choice between going back to save Carrie and try to get back their life together, versus letting three friends die was completely overwhelming. It was only the realization that Carrie would continue safely without him that offered any salvation, but it did little to fill the widening void that he felt in his heart. He wondered how Justin could handle running such a place all the time without the burden of what he was doing coming down on him, and he only hoped that this realization wasn't really a rationalization in disguise.

When his body finally gave into the sleep it so desperately needed, his subconscious made him wish he had stayed awake.

Twilight space was all around him, he didn't know how he had ended up here, weightlessly floating, but somehow his Skimmer armor was protecting him. Yet from the onset, he knew he wasn't out here alone. Below him he could see the vast *Twilight* complex. Workers were all around it, but they were taking it apart, piece by piece...no, not taking it apart, he realized, building it in reverse; as if time were unraveling. He struggled to drift towards the vast center, but there was someone in the distance, coming in closer. At first he thought it was Carrie, and his heart warmed at the thought of seeing her again, but as the figure closed in, he saw that he had totally black armor, without the usual scarlet highlights.

His eyes narrowed as he searched for a weapon to use against the assassin. Reaching for his belt, he felt a Plasma gun sitting in a holster and he quickly pulled it out.

"Who are you?" Fletcher yelled as the ebony figure drifted in closer.

"Damn it," he yelled again, "answer me."

But no sound came from the intruder as the distance closed to less than twenty feet. Suddenly Fletcher saw the Plasma gun that was in the intruder's hands and he raised his own weapon. Without waiting another moment, he fired the pistol.

The searing blast caught the assassin in the chest, charring through armor and skin. The intruder started to tumble head over heels in place, as smoke poured out of the hole in both sides of the body.

Fletcher managed to close in on the spinning figure, sheer anger propelling him onward. He grabbed the body and brought its head up to face him, so he could look at the armored helmet.

"Why did you do this?" he yelled at the lifeless form, as he shook the body from side to side. He felt hot tears starting to flow down his face, as he thought of the woman that this man had ripped from his life. Finally his anger boiled to a breaking point and he ripped the helmet off the assassin to finally reveal just who he had gunned down—

It was Carrie.

He awoke screaming.

The next three months did little to improve Fletcher's general outlook. He ran numerous missions, all of which ran smoothly and without incident, or emotion. As time went on, he found it more and more difficult to remember *Twilight* as anything other than a vague dream. If it wasn't for the steel case full of his burned-out armor, that explanation probably would have settled into a fact for him. He rarely looked at it, and almost threw it away more than once. But something kept him clinging to it, as if it were a last link to a lost life.

There were many times, like this one, in which he would simply stare out his window into the night. Sometimes it was as if he could almost catch a distant azure flash, but then it vanished, and he had to question whether or not it had ever been there to begin with.

The door opened quietly, as his co-pilot and friend stared into the room. Phantom's attitude bothered Conrad greatly, and he had hoped that he wouldn't find his friend where he had left him.

"Still at that window," he finally said with a sigh. Then he forced a laugh as he threw his duffle bag onto his bunk. "Man, you've *got* to get a life."

Fletcher turned from the window and gave his friend a short glare. "So you're back from leave, huh? How's Sandy?"

"Taking this wife thing all too seriously," he responded with a grin. "One month with her and I'm glad to get back to the front lines."

Despite his mood, Fletcher found it hard not to smile. Conrad seemed to shroud himself in this image that precluded a settled down life, but he knew that the captain was head over heels for his wife, just as he had felt about—

Conrad watched his co-pilot's face fall into shadow again and he gritted his teeth in determination. "You, my friend, have got to get out of this room."

"You think I never go out?" the major asked with a slight hint of annoyance. "You still think you're mister barhop, but I'll bet you and Sandy stayed in practically the whole month."

Conrad flashed a wicked grin as he jumped into a sitting position on his bunk, legs crossed. "So sue me, I love my wife."

"Then bug off."

"Actually," the captain said with a slower tone, "we spent the last week celebrating."

"Let me guess," Fletcher answered with a short laugh, "she was glad you were leaving."

"You kidding me? She always puts on a big production on my last day about me staying home," he explained with a sigh. "No, I was talking about us being parents."

Fletcher's mouth parted slightly as his lower lip dropped. "You serious?"

Conrad's smile broadened until it practically stretched from ear to ear. "Yup, I'm going to be a dad...can you believe it?"

For a long moment Fletcher wasn't sure he could. All the turbulent emotions of the last three months had drained him to the breaking point. He felt that he had made his decision quickly, because he had had too. But now, Conrad and Sandy's dream had come to pass, something that had never been possible in the life that had come before: the life he had sacrificed when he saved his fellow pilots' lives. A rush of warmth came over him, almost as if it was he who was going to be a father, but when the rush faded down, all he felt was empty blackness.

"About time," he finally said, making sure his smile never faded. "How about a drink? I'm buying."

"My two favorite words," Jackal said as he jumped back off the bed. "You know, Fletcher," he said with a sudden half serious tone, "maybe you should take some time off. Hell, you have over three months of leave built up. If you don't take some of it, you'll lose it."

"I'm fine here."

"Sure…" Conrad said sardonically as he put his hand on his friend's shoulder. "Heaven forbid you miss a night of sulking."

Fletcher flashed him a warning glare.

"Hey, I don't want to piss you off," the captain pursued, despite the implied warning, "but I know you're still in deep with this Carrie girl. I've never seen you so worked up over someone…someone that I can't figure out when you met…since you never go anywhere."

"I told you before," he responded softly, his words sifting like an echo through a ghost town. "It was something that just didn't work out."

"So you said," Conrad agreed as he eyed his friend carefully for hidden signs. "That seems to happen to you a lot, Phantom. That old demon of yours still watching your shoulder, huh?"

"You know," Fletcher said with a low sigh, "that demon is getting pretty old. I think I'm going to fire him."

"Well, if that's the case, why don't you take some leave? Go to Paris…or Rome, meet some anonymous woman and have a meaningful affair. I'm telling you, two weeks in the arm of some sultry French woman and you'll forget all about what's her name."

Fletcher's first instinct was to get angry, to lash back out at his insensitive remarks. But in an instant his anger faded, as he realized that his friend simply didn't know the situation—how could he possibly? Suddenly his suggestion held a level of desirability that grew quickly in his mind—almost at an inexplicable rate.

"Perhaps you're right," he finally agreed. "Months in this cramped base can get anyone down." Fletcher let out a laugh and patted his co-pilot on the back. "Now there's at least five drinks down in the officers' club with your name on it…Daddy."

Conrad did a theatrical flinch at the title, as if struck in the gut. Then his laughter joined Fletcher's, as the two of them left the room.

## Chapter 18
# Hyde Park

Getting leave time hadn't been difficult for Fletcher. As Conrad had pointed out, he had over three months in accrued time owed him. The difficulty was when he had told his commanding officer he wanted all three months together.

Even Conrad had been surprised, asking him if he was bailing out on him.

"This from a guy who just came back from a month's leave," was his weak defense. In truth, he didn't know why he had asked for all three months, or why the time frame had seemed so vital to him. But as he sat in the Cairo airport two days later, staring at his ticket to London, the answer slowly formulated in his mind: Kim Lee—Tsunami.

A smile came to his lips at the thought of the spunky Asian Skimmer that he had trained with. He remembered the first time that they had really talked, only to find out that they were from the same time frame as each other. Or almost, he reminded himself again as he looked at the date on the electronic calendar in a cigarette ad on the far wall. August fifth. Kim had been whisked away from a near death accident only a few months later than he had been, and he was sure she had said August sixth, at the lower corner of Hyde Park.

He picked up his silver briefcase as the announcement that his flight was boarding came over the loud speaker. His muscles creaked with a stiffness that made him feel as if planks had been inserted between the joints in his body. The MAC flight here from the Saudi Air Base had been cramped and bumpy, and he realized that it had probably been over twenty hours since he had had any sleep.

The moisture saturated air that hung in the airport dampened Fletcher's dress military blues as he boarded the small jet. His fingers, slippery with perspiration, tightened protectively around the handle of the metal case as he pushed through the crowded aisle, found his seat by a window, and sat down.

A soft groan of exhaustion escaped his lips as he slid the seat back a small bit, finding out quickly that it wouldn't go any further. Despite the uncomfortable situation, he felt lucky that he had made the flight at all, after all the arguing over the contents of the briefcase. Perhaps it had been foolish to bring his old armor along; he realized that the odds of him finding her were one in ten thousand. However, the simple fact remained that sometime tomorrow, Skimmers from *Twilight* would be popping in at Hyde Park to save the life of Kim Lee, future Skimmer Tsunami. If he could possibly be there at that moment, that ever so brief flash when they came in and out—then maybe—

*Maybe what?* he questioned himself as he felt the old DC-10 lift off the ground with almost a groan of exhaustion that mirrored his own. *Go back to Twilight? By changing history,* he realized, *I never went there in the first place, so they would have no cause to know or trust me.* The thought of all his new friends at *Twilight* not even knowing him sent a sudden pang of sadness through his tired body, especially when he thought of Justin. For some reason he found he missed the *Twilight* leader, as if never meeting him had opened up another hole in his life that couldn't be filled. *And then what? Even if I do get back, Carrie won't know me either.*

His thoughts continued to torture him, as he finally succumbed to sleep, falling into an almost mind-numbing state.

Despite his earlier trepidation, and a most unsettling flight, he felt renewed as he left the Heathrow airport behind and greeted the new day that had dawned in London. He ignored his strong desire to find a hotel and a hot shower, for it was now the morning of the sixth, and he had no idea when Kim was even going to be in the accident. It was barely past first light in the foggy city, so he doubted he missed it already, as he got in a taxi and let the driver know where he wanted to go.

The driver had given him a strange look at the request, but quickly shrugged it off after the stern glare that had greeted him in his rearview mirror.

Hyde Park was practically deserted at the hour that Fletcher arrived in his taxi. After paying the cab driver and dumping his bags by a park bench, he started glancing around the park, hoping for some sign that he was in the right time and place.

It felt as if an angel had come down and blown him a kiss when he spotted her less than two hours later. She was in grey workout sweats that read Oxford across the front, as she jogged down the path that led to the intersection at the south side of the park.

Quickly opening his metal case, he removed the charred left gauntlet that contained the remains of his WCD, realizing that it could be his only method of identification to the Skimmer who came in to rescue her. A sudden smile flowed across his face when he remembered who her savior would be. Kim had told him that it was Checkmate who had brought her to *Twilight,* and what a close call it had been. The thought of seeing the Brit again filled him with renewed energy, as he pushed the rest of his bags under the bench and began to walk quickly towards the corner that she was heading to. *This has to be it,* he concluded, as he searched for the cause of the near tragedy that was soon to happen. Then he slowed his pace as another realization dawned on him. He still had no time frame to go upon. *If she was out jogging, it may not be until later on, when she comes back this way that the accident happens. Or maybe she will be in a car later and drive by this way.* He shook his head and gritted his teeth in determination. Considering that the sudden desire to come here had happened just in time to be here for Kim's extrication could only tell him that it was another case of the time streams leading him along. He had to believe that, or there was no hope.

A squeal of tire upon asphalt snapped his head away from the jogger as he saw a black Rolls Royce careen around the distant corner and head this way at a speed far too fast for the narrow street. His heart started pounding as the rush of adrenaline surged through his body like an electrical flash. His eyes snapped back to Kim, who was taking her pulse as she jogged along. As she approached the intersection she glanced up and down the street, and he suddenly saw that a parked truck totally blocked her view of the speeding limousine.

Instinct took over as he started to run forward, every fiber in his body telling him to reach the young woman first, to stop what was going to happen. Then he froze, realizing that he was about to unwittingly change history again, destroying all hopes of getting back to *Twilight*. *She was rescued by Checkmate,* he assured himself as he struggled to suppress the desire to call out and warn her, *I have to trust in that.*

She slowed to a fast walk as she hit the street, then began to cross as the Rolls erupted from behind the truck like death upon his pale apocalypse steed. A look of sheer terror overshadowed her face as she realized a split second too late what was happening.

The world seemed to fall to slow motion for Fletcher as he started to run again, knowing that the moment would come and go with blinding speed.

The high pitched sound of braking tires screeched through the air as the driver desperately tried to avoid the jogger, as her scream echoed the car's wail.

Fletcher stopped short as the car struck her square on, his heart leaping into his throat as her frail body was flung into the air some twenty feet to crash into a trash can. Blood mixed with oil as the crushed front end of the Rolls slammed to a halt, the driver mimicking his stare of shocked horror.

Dumbfounded dismay streaked through Fletcher's mind as he stared at the bloody pile of broken bones and torn flesh that only moments ago had been a beautiful young woman. No azure flash of light, no last minute rescue by the resolute Skimmers who were to risk their lives to save her, nothing but the harsh reality that there was no way she could have survived the hit.

This simply wasn't possible, his thoughts yelled as he raced to her side and knelt down by her body. She had been saved right before being hit, he knew this to be true. He stared at her gentle face that still held the last moments of horror in her open eyes. Then he reached over and closed them, as he heard the driver sobbing in sporadic gasps.

"I n-never even saw her, govn'r," the driver said through heaving breaths. "H-honestly, s-she just bloody jumped out of nowhere."

Fletcher numbly stared up at the driver, his chauffeur's uniform firmly pressed. He heard the doors of the limousine opening, as the two passengers got out to stare at the spectacle.

"My lord," said one without the slightest trace of honest feeling.

"Poor child," echoed a second with even less emotion.

Running his hand through his dampened hair, Fletcher stood up and backed away from the scene of the accident, as the wail of a police car began to sound in the distance. *Something is horribly wrong,* his thoughts concluded as he numbly walked back to the park bench and sat down. He watched with detached interest as first the police, then the ambulance arrived to the scene of the tragedy. One cop came over to him and asked him what he had seen, and he told him that she never had a chance to even see the speeding car. The police officer went on to tell him something else, but his words fell on deaf ears as Fletcher's clear blue eyes only saw the medics as they zipped the body bag over her face.

An hour went slowly by as police sectioned off the area and chased all the on-lookers and accident hounds away.

*Something's horribly wrong,* echoed in his mind again as he watched the last of the officials depart, leaving the scene as if nothing had ever happened.

He had waited and stared, half expecting a Skimmer to pop in during the whole hour and whisk her away, somehow bringing her back. But in his heart he knew it would never happen, because somehow the fabric of time was out of whack.

*Maybe I wasn't the only target,* he wondered as he sat there into the early afternoon, *maybe Justin had been a target as well.* Who knows who else the assassin killed after shooting Carrie and himself. He had simply assumed that if he had never went to *Twilight,* then there would have been no cause for the attack. What if his decision to save his friends here, had condemned all of *Twilight* back there? His face fell into his hands at the realization of what he must have done by disobeying Justin's warnings about saving people that were supposed to die. Con was alive because of him—but Kim was dead.

He lost track of time as he sat there in the park, his only thoughts of the impossible task of finding some way to fix what he had done, and the woman he felt he would never see again.

"You all right, sir?" came the young voice that barely registered on his self-absorbed mind. Then he felt a light tug at his shirt. "Sir?"

Slowly he raised his face out of his hands to look at the girl of five or six that was standing in front of him. The innocent curiosity in her oval face made him momentarily forget his depression as he realized that she must have been wondering why he looked so sad.

"You don't look very happy," she said as she jumped up to sit on the bench next to him. "Are you a soldier?"

Her hair fell in silken russet waves that settled on her sky blue dress as she sat into place on the bench, and the light twinkle in her green eyes made him almost forget the situation he was in.

"As a matter of fact, I am," he told her as he glanced around for her parents, which he assumed couldn't be far away. "Do you always go talking to strangers?"

Her tiny face creased in thought as she shook her head defiantly. "No, sir," her soft British voice affirmed in delicate tones. "But you looked sad."

He nodded thoughtfully as he gazed back at her and froze, suddenly sinking into the gentle depths of her jade eyes. He felt a constricting in his chest which he almost feared could be a heart attack as he looked at the young girl, really looked at her and realized.

"Carridan," came her mother's stern voice across the park. "You leave that gentleman alone."

"Yes, Mother," she replied dutifully and hopped off the bench, breaking the spell. "Sorry you don't feel well, sir." Then she flashed him a smile and started to leave.

"Carrie," he heard himself calling to her before he even realized what he would say.

She turned back to him, her eyes opening wide at the sound of her familiar name. "Nobody calls me Carrie except my father," she informed him as if scolding a child.

He blanched at her sudden harsh tone, but smiled at her anyway. "I apologize," he told her. "I was wondering what your last name is."

She smiled back, then shook her head as a devilish twinkle came to her eyes. "I can't tell you. You're a stranger." Then she ran off to the tall, red-haired lady that waited for her with arms full of shopping bags.

As they started to walk off, Carrie turned back and waved at him and he found himself waving back, a warm feeling filling his heart with the simple but undeniable fact: she's alive.

But this simple revelation only posed even more unanswerable questions. He knew that Carrie grew up at *Twilight*, she had told him that, but here she was in London, and only a child. *However, the fact that she is only a child means that whatever happened to her to make her come to Twilight was still in the future, and perhaps not far away.* His thoughts reeled at the conclusions it was drawing. *What if the disaster strikes and no Skimmer comes to save her, just like with Kim?* The possibility of watching Carrie die again sent a shudder though his body and he suddenly realized that he had to make sure she stayed safe.

The thought of the infinite odds against this chance meeting boggled his mind, leaving him with the only conclusion that the time streams were once again responsible. However, this time they had played him a cruel twist, delivering to him the woman that he cared for, but only as a child.

Carrie and her mother were almost out of sight as he picked up his bags and started to follow. He wasn't sure what his next course of action would be, but he knew he couldn't afford to let her out of sight for even a few minutes.

It was just drifting into twilight when the two of them entered their house on the far side of Hyde Park. Fletcher watched from a distance for a while, then approached the house cautiously. He scanned over the front door, looking for any sign of the owners and noted a paper on the window that read, "Room for Rent." Then he spotted the metal crest over the mail slot that proudly displayed the family name, *Whitney*.

Fletcher let out a breath as this final confirmation came to his theories. Not wishing to be spotted lurking outside their home, he quickly backed off and returned to the park to try and reason through this new development.

First and utmost, he was worried about the fabric of time. Originally, he had not met her in her childhood; therefore, he was worried that his very presence would foul up time. But then he thought, *what could be the harm of that?* If time was altered she might live a long and happy life here in London; a life that he could never share in the way he had once before, but a life none the less. Then a memory struck him as her face filled his mind on that first day of Skimmer training. She had told him that he had looked familiar to her, despite the fact that she had never met him before. His head turned back towards the Whitney house in wonder. Perhaps his being here wasn't such a shift in history after all. He sincerely doubted that a casual meeting in the park would stay memorable enough to a young girl that she would remember some Air Force major some twenty years later, so his contact with her must have been more prolonged than that. With a smile of grim determination, he stared at the "room for rent" sign once more, then walked off to find a hotel for the night.

## Chapter 19
# Carrie

As the first rays of morning light filtered through the thin London fog, Fletcher found himself in the park once again. He had left his bags in the hotel, but he still wore his dress blues, hoping to appear familiar to the young girl should she return to the park again. A chill ran through his body at the thought of Carrie, but he shrugged it off to the cool mist that hung in the air.

A low growl emanated from within, and he realized that it had been over two days since he had eaten. He searched through his pockets and came up with the only food he had on him, an old candy bar. His stomach accepted the stale food with grudging resignation, but it enabled him to return to the task at hand. He checked his watch again, and realized that it could be hours before she made an appearance, if at all.

Raising his hands to his face, he tried to rub the exhaustion out of his eyes without success. Little to no sleep had come to him during the night at the hotel, as the image of what had happened to Kim replayed itself over and over in his mind like an old broken record. The only change to his dreams were that as the evening progressed, Kim's face was slowly replaced by Carrie's, as he stood helplessly by and watched her die again and again. In the end, black oblivion had seemed like a welcome relief. A soft groan escaped his parched lips as he leaned his head back on the tree that soared up from behind the bench and closed his eyes for what he promised himself would only be five minutes.

A soft, yet insistent tug on his coat sleeve tried over a few times to rob him of what he was sure was at least two of his five minutes.

"Sir?" came the haunting voice that pierced into his consciousness, jolting him awake.

His lips parted slightly as he took in the stark change to his surroundings. The empty post-dawn park was now bustling with people as they scurried back and forth. Parents with their children, children playing with dogs, lovers strolling arm in arm, all a picture of a park on a Saturday. The sun burned hot overhead, and the realization came to him that he must have slept for hours. It was the insistent tug on his sleeve again that brought him out of his wonderment. He gazed back down and fell back into those wide green eyes, a grin of relief spreading across his face.

"Morning, sir," she said with the same melting smile that had ingrained itself into his memory yesterday. "You were sleeping."

His own smile broadened, reflecting hers. "Indeed I was." Suddenly his plan of action that he had formulated last night jumped back into his thoughts, as he forced the smile on his face to fade away. He leaned back against the tree again, his eyes wandering to her mother who was some twenty yards away, talking with some other women. He shook his head with almost undetectable motion as he watched her, realizing that she didn't even know that her daughter was over here, talking with a stranger. The distance in his eyes grew as he sought to make his misery known to the young girl, hoping that she was as empathic in youth as she was as a woman.

Her reaction was instantaneous as her small hand touched his with an angelic softness.

"You look sad again," she almost whispered. "What's wrong?"

His heart ached with the deception he knew he was playing, but he could think of no other way to insure her safety. He gazed back into those pools of jade, but then looked down, unable to stare honesty straight on. "I'm going to be in England for some time," he began softly, as he continued to stare at his feet, "and I can't find any place that will let me stay for more than a few days."

She seemed to gauge to impact of his words for a moment, while absently chewing on her bottom lip, then her eyes lit up like two green stars. "My father is looking for a boarder," she said. "Maybe you can stay with us."

Fletcher shook his head doubtfully as he internally leaped for joy, his plan couldn't have gone better; now if he could only persuade the parents. "I don't know," he finally said, letting the doubt saturate his words. "They don't even know me."

"That's no reason not to try," she chimed with her perfect British accent. She tugged on his hand, persuading him with her exuberance to rise off the bench and follow her. Quickly pulling him along, she brought him over to her russet-haired mother, who was still absorbed in her conversation.

Hazel eyes darkened with suspicion as Carrie's mother turned to see the

Air Force major that her daughter had brought over. "Carridan," her lilting voice warned, "why are you bothering the gentleman?"

Fletcher smiled meekly, as if to translate to the mother that he had been forced against his will to be brought over. He glanced at the other two women, who he found appraising him with a connoisseur's eye.

"Mother," Carrie said, standing her ground and never taking her hand from Fletcher's, "this man needs a place to live."

"Taking in strays now, Bridget?" one of the women asked with a smirk.

Carrie's mother flashed a warning glare at the other woman, then turned back to smile at the Air Force major. "I'm *Mrs*. Bridget Whitney," she said, stressing the Mrs. as well as she could without being blatant. "And you?"

"Major Fletcher Taylor," he said with what he called his best political smile as he put out a hand, "United States Air Force."

She accepted the gesture and lightly took his hand, then reached out and took Carrie's other hand and moved her to her side. Fletcher pulled his hand back that had been in Carrie's and quickly put it in his pocket.

"So Major Taylor..." she began.

"Fletcher," he cut in gently, "please. Major makes me feel like I'm back at the Air Base."

Her smile broadened and she nodded. "Of course, Fletcher. So why do you need a flat? Don't the Yanks provide places for you soldiers to sleep in England?"

His mind churned through the fabrication that he had formulated last night, making sure it all sounded plausible. "I'm here doing a favor for a colonel friend of mine, helping him with a project, but the temporary lodgings that he had arranged for me fell through. So I'm sort of out on my own."

"How long of a project?"

"Through the summer and into the early fall," he told her. "Probably three months. But it's just a lot of paper work, so I'd be in a lot, but quiet and out of the way."

Bridget studied the major for a few moments and Fletcher had to keep from smiling as he saw the reflection of Carrie's expressions in her face.

"Can he live with us, Mother?" Carrie asked as she tugged at her mother's arm.

"She seems to like you," Bridget said with a guarded smile.

"I've always gotten along well with children," he fabricated, since he had actually known few.

"Well," she said, considering, "three months is a little short for a tenant, but we were also looking for a summer nanny."

"Excuse me?"

"Well, you said that you would be in a lot, and that you like children."

"Yeah," he said warily.

"And our regular nanny is away for a few months on vacation."

"Hmmm."

"If you could watch over Carrie while we're at work, we could let you stay for only three hundred pounds sterling."

Fletcher stared at her in shock for a moment, embarrassment giving way to annoyance at the position he was being thrust into—then he mentally slapped himself in the face, what was being offered was nothing less than a miracle. If he had the job of watching over her, he would be there when the accident would occur. He licked his lips nervously and he forced himself to stay calm and not scare her away.

"I have to pay you three hundred pounds to watch over your daughter while living there. Don't you pay your live-in nanny to do just that?"

Bridget's face went beet red as she realized that he was right. "True," she admitted, "but a regular nanny is putting all her attention to the job, where as you would just be child sitting while working on your project."

"Two hundred pounds a month and it's a deal," Fletcher bargained. He had made his point and didn't want to push too far.

"Say yes, Mother," Carrie implored.

"Well," Bridget said with a light laugh that set them all at ease, "as long as your father says it's fine, then yes."

Carrie grinned up at Fletcher, warming his heart with her open joy. Then she took his hand again, as the three of them walked off towards her house, leaving the other two women to gape with wonder.

Mr. Herbert Whitney was stiff and impersonal as he greeted the major, but a few moments alone with his wife had him quickly agreeing to the summer arrangement. The butler, Carl, showed Fletcher around the three story town home making sure to point out all the extremely expensive items that were worth more than the major could ever hope to earn in his entire military career. Fletcher accepted the tour with a soldier's eye, watching all the nooks and crannies, sharp stairs and tall balconies that could result in the accident that he would have to watch for. Carrie had never really explained the circumstances surrounding her arrival to *Twilight,* and that lack of knowledge weighed heavily on him as he tried to memorize the layout. But ever diligent at his side was the smiling young girl, who took time to point out any part of the grand home that he missed, especially if it belonged to her.

The Whitneys treated him to dinner that night, and Bridget apologized for how overly attentive Carrie was towards him.

"I've never seen her like this with a stranger before," she admitted.

Fletcher tried to shrug it off, confessing that most children didn't take to him like this, but that he truly enjoyed her company.

The evening ended with him back in his richly decorated guest room, lying on his four post bed as he listened to the wind whistle against the French windows in his room. As he drifted to sleep he contemplated just what he had gotten himself into, and how he could pull it all together to make it work out.

The next few weeks went by quickly for Fletcher—much too quickly for his liking. His daily routine was becoming easy enough to follow. It had been simple to fabricate the project that he was working on, as he spent leisurely hours working on papers that were actually nothing more than a journal tracking the events that led him to this time and place.

When he wasn't "working," he was watching over young Carrie: taking her to the park, to the zoo, to a movie, and generally enjoying being around her. Even when he was at work she was there. She'd sit and watch him scribbling at his notepad for hours on end, as if waiting for him to say or do something special. Sometimes she would draw or color while in the room with him, but she rarely left him for any length of time, and he never objected to her presence. It occurred to him what a sheltered life she led, and how lonely it must be to grow up in the Whitney household.

At first he convinced himself that her being around him all the time was simply a fantastic convenience, so that he could watch over her almost every minute. But as time went on, he started to realize that her company was growing more and more pleasurable. He had never fancied himself a father figure, but now he wasn't sure. When he had first arrived, all he could see in her was the vague shadow of the woman that he loved, but the child in her grew on him, endearing him to her vibrant personality.

The first week had been a week of maximum stress for him, as he watched and waited for the "accident" that never happened, and each movement that the young girl made reminded him of the woman he was trying to save. But as the weeks melted away, he felt the connection between the two people, girl and woman, fading as well, changing the feelings he had for the child. His diligence was also slipping, as he convinced himself that his simple presence would be sufficient to get her through whatever lay in store. It got to the point that almost every waking moment was spent in the company of the young girl, and he found that his only solitude was at night, when he locked himself into his room and fought for the sleep that was held at bay by the violent images that still plagued his thoughts.

It was on the morning of the first day of the second month that the reality struck him that early autumn might not be long enough for this accident to even happen. The thought of leaving the Whitney home at the end of his leave without being here when the accident happened sent shivers of dread though his body.

He sat in his bed for almost an hour as he stared blankly at the far wall, then he reached under his bed for the metal case that hadn't been touched since the day he moved in here.

Slowly he brought it up onto the bed, then opened it, letting his eyes sift over the torn scarlet suit and charred black armor that denoted a station he could barely remember filling. His fingers leisurely caressed the hard plastic of his left gauntlet, then he lifted it out of the case and stared at the blackened readout screen of the WCD. Flipping a switch, he opened the device and studied the burned out power crystal.

"All the secrets in the universe," he whispered bitterly to himself, "entombed inside a broken WCD."

"What's a WCD?"

Fletcher's mouth hung open as he quickly glanced up at his doorway to find young Carrie standing there in her night robe, her wide eyes open with unabashed curiosity as she gazed at the gauntlet in his hands.

"WCD?" he mumbled frantically as he searched through his mind for some answer that was plausible. "Um...I didn't hear you knock," he finally settled for.

Carrie wandered into his room, a look of apology crossing her soft features. "I forgot to knock," she admitted, glancing down at her feet. Then her embarrassment was quickly forgotten as she moved to get a look at the ebony armor in the case.

"Are those clothes?"

The major quickly closed the case, then realized that the gauntlet with the WCD was still in his hand. He closed his eyes for a moment to reassemble his thoughts, then a smile came to his lips as he put the device on top of the case.

"Now, Carrie," he began, firming his voice into the best disciplinary tone he could muster, "you know that coming into my room without knocking was rude, don't you?"

She nodded again as her wide eyes fell to her pink-slippered feet.

"Well," he sighed, as he allowed his frown to fade back into a smile, "no harm done. You want to know what this is, hmmm?"

Her face lit up as she gazed back up at him and the metal case.

"As you know," he said as he lowered his voice, "I'm in the military. This is a special uniform that I have to wear for secret missions." He paused for a moment as he read the wonder in her eyes. "You understand secrets, right?"

"Yes, of course," she agreed quickly.

"This WCD is a special device that helps me do my missions," he explained as he held out the gauntlet for her to see.

"But it looks broken," she said as her small face creased in concern.

"Actually, you're quite right," he admitted. "But I'm working on trying to fix it."

"Can I help?"

His smile broadened as he opened the case again and put the device away, firmly locking it closed.

"You're sweet for asking, but I'm afraid that it's beyond repair for the moment; however, you must keep this a secret between just the two of us. I'm entrusting you with secret military knowledge here, do you understand?"

She nodded again and stared at the case.

"I hear the circus is going to be in London today," he said, hoping to divert her attention. "Want to go?"

Her eyes lit back up as she suddenly hugged him tightly, squeezing his chest with her tiny arms. "I'm so glad you came to live with us," she said happily. Then she turned and ran out of the room. "See you at breakfast," she called behind her as she disappeared down the stairs.

For a moment he sat there, stunned by her gesture. He had known how much she meant to him, but didn't realize that she had felt anything in return. He glanced down at the case again, and hoped that his explanation had been sufficient. Then a shadow came over his face as he considered what a large part of her life he had become. Back in *Twilight*, Carrie had said that he seemed familiar, not that she recognized him instantly. But then he reconsidered. The odds that one summer of her life as a five-year-old would be well remembered was slim at best. He leaned back and let out a groan;

second guessing himself constantly was getting to be a strain and he wondered how long he could keep it up.

Two more weeks sped on by without mention of what she had seen in his room, allowing him to begin to relax again—when the bottom fell out of his plan to be with her constantly.

"We leave in the morning," Mr. Whitney announced happily at dinner time as he patted his wife's hand.

"Where were you going again?" Fletcher asked, hoping that he had heard wrong.

"To our yacht," Bridget explained. "We spend one week at the end of each summer on it, enjoying the channel and the local waters."

"You all go?" he asked, hoping that Carrie would be left with him.

"Well," she said, "the three of us will go. You should enjoy a week alone here, Major. It will give you a chance to get some work accomplished without Carridan getting in your way."

Fletcher felt his mouth dry out at the thought of losing her for a week; what if this was *the* week.

"Can't he come with us, Mother?" Carrie's high voice rang out with hope.

"I hardly think the major would enjoy being crammed on that small ship with the three of us for a week," Bridget tried to explain.

"Actually it would be no bother," Fletcher said, trying not to seem anxious.

Mr. Whitney's left eyebrow lifted in surprise at the major's comment. "Are you daft?" he asked. "You really wouldn't mind hopping along with the family for a whole week at sea?"

"Herbert?" Bridget questioned, openly shocked at the idea. "This has always been a time for just us. Don't you feel the major would…not *quite* fit in?"

Fletcher felt his throat tightening at the situation he suddenly felt that he was in the middle of. He tried to come up with some argument to make his tagging along seem logical, but he quickly realized that he didn't need to.

"*Dear,*" Mr. Whitney explained in a hushed tone through his teeth, which was their obvious way of talking in front of their child about something they didn't want her to hear, despite the fact that she could. "If the *major* was there with Carridan, then *we* could spend more time alone."

"Could he please come, Mother?" Carrie added in, then sucked in her bottom lip in anticipation of the answer.

Bridget took in a deep breath as she glanced back and forth between her husband and her daughter. Then she glared at Fletcher.

"If this is in *any* way the *slightest* inconvenience to you," her voice rang in sharp British tones, "you will please let us know, Major."

Fletcher felt the adrenaline flush out of his system, the same as it did when he knew a mission had gone over well. "Not a problem at all," he said with a polite smile. "I think I would miss Carrie if she was gone for a week. I've kind of grown used to her."

"Then whatever will you do at the end of next month when you *have* to leave," Bridget asked, her face hard and emotionless.

Warning bells went off in Fletcher's mind as he realized that the mother was feeling that he was coming between her and her daughter. He cleared his throat, then forced another smile. "My work is very important to me, Ms. Whitney. I'll miss Carrie, but I'm sure I'll get along just fine."

Carrie's lip stuck out at his statement, but it was quickly replaced with a wide smile when her mother spoke again.

"Then I guess the major will be coming with us," Bridget said without feeling.

"Good show, darling," Mr. Whitney exclaimed with a grin. "You'd better pack up, Major," he instructed, "we leave at first light."

The next morning the four of them piled into the Whitney limousine, as the chauffeur drove them from London to the marina where the yacht was docked.

As they got out of the car, Fletcher walked around back and helped the chauffeur pull out all the bags, making sure that his metal case was safely in his custody. He had considered leaving it behind at the town home, but he had never been far from it since arriving back in this time, and he was simply afraid something would happen to it.

Carrie was running with excitement, back and forth between the docks and the limo, as she called for the major to come and see the ship.

Fletcher looked up at the ships in the marina and took in a breath of wonder. All the ships here were full sized yachts with brightly polished trim and colorful flags. His eye caught the stern of the ship directly ahead, which had the name *Carridan II* written in big gold letters.

"I guess that's their boat," he commented to the driver with a grin.

The chauffeur let out a short laugh. "How ever did you guess? And it's *ship* with the Whitneys, sir, never *boat*."

Fletcher let out a laugh himself. "Thanks for the warning." Then he picked up the bags and headed for the yacht that must have been well over forty feet long and two decks high.

"It's named after me," Carrie said with a smile that stretched from ear to ear as she followed him up onto the deck.

"No kidding?" he asked as he followed the driver down the narrow steps that led to the cabins.

"One day it will be all mine," she continued. "My mother told me so."

For a moment Fletcher's good mood faltered, as he wondered if Carrie ever regretted growing up at *Twilight,* missing out on all the wonderful things that life in a wealthy London family afforded. He threw his bags on the bunk in his small cabin and sat down for a moment. But a moment was all that was allowed him, as Carrie came running in and pulled him to the deck, insisting that he not miss the launching. Seeing her shining face as she grabbed both his hand and her mother's, made him realize that no matter what the consequences, if he could prevent her "accident," he would; even if it meant never returning to *Twilight* again.

When nighttime finally came he was glad to retire to his bunk. Carrie had kept him going at full tilt as the ship had sailed out deep into the channel. He had taken some time to talk with the captain of the *Carridan II,* who seemed amiable enough, but Carrie had quickly found him there and insisted that he come and watch the fish that were jumping in and out of the water.

He pulled off his shoes gratefully and allowed himself to fall back on the bunk, as the gentle swaying of the ship began to lull him to sleep. The only other ship that he had ever been on was an aircraft carrier, and that was like a far off memory as his thoughts turned to dreams.

Although it only felt like a few minutes, Fletcher realized that it must have been hours later when he suddenly came awake and realized that he had never undressed. He reluctantly pulled himself to a sitting position as he tried to rub the grainy feeling out of his eyes. Then it struck him again, a strange sensation that had been the culprit for jarring him awake.

For a moment he sat there silently, listening for any strange noises, but all he heard were the waves pushing up against the sides of the ship. He shook his head, wondering if he had imagined the feeling, but he still couldn't shake the sensation. Reaching under his bunk, he pulled out the metal case and took out the left gauntlet. The dull WCD screen lay flat and lifeless as it sat there in his hands. He stared intently at it for a moment, as if almost expecting something to happen, then he let out a sigh as he realized that it was most likely just another bad dream that had woken him up. Not really knowing why, he absently pulled on his shoes and headed up to the deck, the gauntlet still in his hand.

The stars shone like a myriad of lights, illuminating the ship along with the bright full moon. He could feel the wind slipping along the deck, stronger than it was before as he leaned against the rail and enjoyed the breeze in his hair. Glancing up at the clock in the empty control cabin, he saw that it was just past three in the morning. He wondered who controlled the ship at night, then realized that it must have been anchored, since he could see the lights of the shore not more than half a mile in the distance.

He gazed up at the stars for a few minutes, as he silently chastised himself for not getting more sleep.

"She'll keep you going all day again," he half whispered with a laugh as he slipped the burned gauntlet on to his left hand, unsure as to why he did it. The cool plastic felt almost unnatural at first as his hand filled the glove. Then he clenched his fingers into a fist as the gauntlet settled into place. A smile came to his lips at the feel, but vanished instantly as his senses went on red alert.

For an instant he was unsure of what exactly it was, but at his next breath it became crystal clear—diesel fuel—the air was full of the fumes emanating up from below. His heart leaped into his throat as he turned to run down the stairs—when the explosion engulfed the lower deck.

The ship rocked violently to one side as a second explosion sounded below, knocking Fletcher to his knees.

"Carrie," he called out desperately as he forced himself back up to his feet and began jumping down the stairs. Instantly the intense heat assaulted him as he came down to the cabin deck. Flames were all along the walls and ceiling, and two of the cabin doors were already totally engulfed. His eyes flicked back and forth as he ascertained that it was the captain's and the master cabin that were consumed in the flames. He ran down the hallway to the door to the parents' room and called to them twice, but there was no response.

"Mommy?" came the frail voice behind him that was shaking with coughs.

Fletcher turned to see Carrie standing there, her blanket in her hand and a look of confused fear on her face.

"Stay right there," he ordered her, as relief came to him that she was still alive. Then he turned to the master cabin door again and kicked it in. The flaming door collapsed easily, sending out a tongue of flame that encircled him as he fell back. Carrie screamed as he quickly took off his burning windbreaker and beat the flames off his pants.

"*Mommy,*" Carrie called again as she tried to run past him into what was left of her parents' room.

"No, Carrie!" Fletcher called out as he grabbed her and picked her up, struggling against her flailing hands. "You've got to stay put," he pleaded with her as he hugged her tight until she stopped moving. Then she buried her face in his shoulder, whimpering softly.

Pulling himself to his feet, he glanced back into the master cabin, unable to see more than a few shadows among the flames, but that was more than enough to let him know Herbert's and Bridget's grizzly fate. Glancing back towards the captain's cabin, the hallway outside it was now totally consumed and he grimly realized there was nothing he could do for that man either.

Letting out a soft curse, he tightened his grip on the crying child and started to run back towards the stairs, as he silently prayed that what had happened to Kim wasn't about to happen to Carrie and him as well. He had almost made it back to the foot of the stairs when the floor suddenly gave way under his feet. Carrie rolled out of his arms as he grabbed on to the deck fragments around him. His arm hooked onto a jutting plank as he felt the fire licking at his dangling feet. Glancing quickly down, he saw the engines ablaze beneath him, the flames dancing up towards him like devils' forks. Then his heat seared eyes fixed on the one part of the engine room that wasn't in flames, the fuel storage barrels. Flames crept ever nearer towards the lethal containers, as Fletcher struggled to pull himself up from the hole. Tiny hands grabbed at his arm as Carrie tugged with what strength she had.

Suddenly the next section of the flooring gave way to the flames as well, causing Fletcher to start to tumble back in, as Carrie let out a shriek and followed him down.

Grasping frantically out with his gauntleted hand, he held on to a searing metal pipe that ran the length of the engine room's ceiling as his other hand shot out like a rocket, desperately grabbing at the girl who was falling into the conflagration.

His fingers sunk into the soft folds of her nightshirt as he pulled her back up to him, internally cringing at every ripping sound her flannel sleepwear made. Her blanket fell to the molten engines, disintegrating instantly in the flames.

"*Grab onto me,*" he yelled into the thick smoke as he looked back up at his armored hand that was sizzling against the red hot steel pipe.

Her small arms wrapped around his neck, half cutting off his windpipe, but he ignored it, putting all efforts into his left arm, as he pulled the two of them up enough to get a grip back on the deck above with his right hand. Already he could feel the deck section near the stairs giving way, so he wasted no time. Pushing his muscles past the levels of endurance, he shifted his weight to his right arm, and heaved the two of them up to the hanging bottom step.

"Run up the stairs, Carrie," he called out through hacking coughs. But no response came from her as she lay on the stairs, her tiny frame having finally succumbed to the blinding smoke.

Holding in his breath, he pulled her back into his arms and began forcing himself up the stairs. He could see the stars above again, and distant sirens called in response to the disaster. He just reached the top stair when the wood above him collapsed, striking him with a flaming beam. The weight of the wood stunned him, as Carrie's limp form rolled out of his hands along the top deck. Blackness clouded his vision in waves of pain, as he fell down and struggled to retain consciousness.

"Carrie," his burned larynx tried to call out, but all that came was a harsh whisper.

His vision began to go as he saw two blurred azure lights form on the deck above Carrie, and he shook his head to clear what he thought was his imagination.

The lights solidified into the two Time Skimmers, the taller of the two bending down swiftly to scoop up the young girl.

"Jesus," the other one said, "what a mess."

"Got her," said the first, whose British accent rang on Fletcher's ears with distant familiarity.

Suddenly Carrie's eyes opened wide, as she saw the men who were holding her. She tried to struggle free, to run to Fletcher, but he held her fast. Then she grabbed the brightly-lit control device on the Skimmer's arm and pointed to the fallen major, who seemed all but dead.

"WCD," she coughed, "WCD."

"What is she saying?" the second Skimmer asked.

"She knows about my Wrist Control Device," he answered, "I think." Then his eyes followed the girl's pointing finger and saw Fletcher, but it was the burned out Skimmer's gauntlet on the fallen man's hand that caused him to catch his breath. "My Lord," he said in a half whisper, "is he a Skimmer?"

He handed Carrie to the other Skimmer and ran over to the major, who

# TWILIGHT

lay in a dazed state.

"We only have a few seconds left, Checkmate," the other Skimmer warned as he set his WCD for the return trip.

Checkmate pulled Fletcher out of the burning rubble and rolled him over, pulling in a sharp breath at the seared gash on his forehead. Then he knelt down next to him and tried to shake him awake.

"Where did you get this from?" he demanded while lifting the major's gauntleted arm.

Fletcher forced his drifting mind to focus through the pain, struggling to get his burned larynx to function. "I'm...I'm *Twilight* Skimmer, Phantom," he managed as the blackness finally consumed him.

The two Skimmers looked at each other in wonder for a brief moment, then Checkmate started to activate his WCD. "Let's get the bloody hell out of here!"

The azure glow enveloped the Skimmers and the two survivors of the *Carridan II,* as the fuel dump finally ignited, erupting the ship into a hellish fireball of destruction.

## Chapter 20
# *Twilight's* Heart

Light cut brutally into Fletcher's world as he first started to open his eyes again. His muscles felt drained beyond exhaustion, but the pain held a familiar tone to it. As his vision started to clear, the face of Paula Kesseler came into focus.

"He's awake, Doctor," a woman's voice announced.

"Prepare twelve CCs of stimulant," Dr. Kesseler answered in an even tone.

"Paula," Fletcher tried to say, though only a slight rasp came out.

"What's he trying to say?" the disembodied woman's voice asked.

"I'm not sure," the doctor admitted. "His vocal chords were burned a bit. It's going to be a bit painful to speak for a while," she informed him. "You're lucky to be alive."

For an instant this all seemed like deja-vu to him, waking up to all of this after his first arrival at *Twilight*, but the memory of the flaming ship, and all he had been through still rang in his thoughts.

He cleared his throat, swallowing the pain that shot through him at the movement of his vocal chords. "Paula," he finally managed to get out, "is Carrie all right?"

The doctor's forehead creased in confusion for a moment. "How do you know my name?"

Fletcher forced himself up to a sitting position as he took another look at the doctor and realized his mistake. The Paula Kesseler that he knew was clearly almost twenty years older than this younger woman. "Of course," he cleared his thoughts aloud, "I'm still not in my own time here, this is Carrie's arrival time, not mine."

"Carrie?" asked the young woman who stood to the doctor's left, obviously her med tech.

"The young red-haired girl that arrived with this man," the doctor explained. "To answer your question, she'll be just fine, though she was asking about you."

"Let me see her," the major asked.

"That's quite impossible," a clear voice cut in from behind him.

Fletcher turned to find himself looking at a Justin who was a young man, who couldn't have been older than his mid-twenties. The major's face went blank for a moment, then constricted in anger. "She needs me."

"She needs to forget you, Major," Justin said in a firm tone that left no room for argument. "When she meets you again, twenty years from now, you can't be more than a slightly familiar face to her."

"Twenty years from now?"

"When you will arrive at *Twilight* for your first time, brought here by her."

Fletcher forced himself to stand up, and noticed that a good deal of his body was still wrapped in gauze. "I always knew it was her that saved me," he finally said with a half smile of satisfaction.

"But it's a Carrie of some years later that saves you," the young leader clarified, "after you have known her for quite awhile."

Suddenly the situation broke into the major's smug feeling like a lightning bolt. "But she couldn't have, Justin…Carrie died not long after we became partners."

Justin's thin lips went rigid and Fletcher realized that for the first time since he had met him, the *Twilight* leader seemed surprised by something.

"Let's talk," Justin said in an even voice, and led him out of the medical wing.

Fletcher's story hadn't been long, but Justin had asked him to repeat it over and over again, seeming to make many different mental notes each time. Finally the *Twilight* leader got up from his office chair and leaned against the far wall.

"I don't understand why," he asked, "when you first found yourself back in your own time, you didn't just go through with the mission again so that you would end up back here."

Fletcher knew this question was coming long before the words were issued; it had been a question he had asked himself many times since that night. It had gone against all of Justin's training, but he had done it anyway. But the same answer came to him that had come to him that night. "I just couldn't let

Con die again," he admitted. "I knew it was wrong, but he's my friend, and he had always been there for me."

Justin remained silent for a few minutes, then slowly nodded. "I understand, maybe more than you will ever know. But the damage has been done, none the less. You're very lucky to have found a way back here."

"There's something I don't understand," Fletcher asked as he eyed the young man suspiciously. "You told me during my training that time here in *Twilight* is linear, since we are protected from the time streams by shielding."

"Yes, I suppose I would have told you that."

"Then how do you know that I'm supposed to arrive in twenty years from now? I can understand how a future Carrie could bring me to a past place in *Twilight* because that is simply reading *Twilight's* history and finding out when I was supposed to arrive here. But knowing that I'll be here in the future is fortune telling...how do you do it?"

A slow smile crept over Justin's face that suddenly brought out all his boyish charm. "I wish I could tell you that, but suffice it to say that someone from *Twilight's* future told me most of this place's history when I was younger."

"How convenient," Fletcher snapped back sardonically. "Let me guess, it was me."

Genuine surprise flushed over Justin's face, then he let out a bright laugh. "I can see that you're getting the hang of this place, aren't you?"

"I was joking."

"Of course you were," the young leader said with another chuckle. Then his face grew serious. "If this rogue Skimmer killed Carrie and I didn't know about it, then this could represent a fracture in the whole *Twilight* time matrix. But at least that would explain the anomaly."

"I don't get it," Fletcher responded, annoyed that he never seemed to understand anything the *Twilight* leader ever said.

"Then let me show you how I really run *Twilight*," Justin offered. "I'll show you the Omni computer."

The computer was as symmetrical and flawless in appearance as any part of *Twilight's* structure. It was contained in a sub-level that Fletcher had never seen before, and as he gazed at the simple magnificence of the machine he marveled at how primitive it made the defensive system that ran the United State's military structure seem in comparison.

Justin watched the major for a moment, his eyes shimmering with prideful delight at the open amazement he saw in the older man.

"Not bad, huh?" he asked with a grin.

Fletcher glanced over at him in wonder. "Not bad? You must be kidding? Who built this?"

"I did," Justin answered matter-of-factly, then hesitated at the skepticism that was plain on Fletcher's face. "Well, me and a large team of computer engineers."

"From what time?"

"Twenty-fourth century Earth."

"Is that when we discovered time travel?"

"No," the young *Twilight* leader laughed, "that's when *I* discovered time travel, I suppose. I pretty much kept it to myself and the team I worked with." He hesitated and then cocked his head slightly. "Didn't I cover all this in your Skimmer training?"

"I suppose so," Fletcher said thoughtfully, as he tried to ignore the jibe from the *Twilight* leader. "So, then you really come from the twenty-fourth century, right?"

A shadow passed over the young man's face for a moment as he grew thoughtful, as if guarding his words. "Actually I was born here in *Twilight*."

Fletcher laughed. "How's that possible? You just said that you created *Twilight*."

"I didn't live here always. Right before I went to high school, my parents sent me to live in the twenty-fourth century so I could experience the real world. It was there that I built the Omni computer and created *Twilight*."

"But you knew of its existence from living here. So you were really only building something that you had already seen in existence."

"That's the very nature of a time paradox," Justin said with a shrug. "Which came first, the chicken or the egg?"

"So," Fletcher said trying to get off a subject that was making his head hurt when he tried to reason it out, "you had a team help you. How do you know they won't leak out the secret?" he asked with a sly smile.

"Because everyone who worked on *Twilight*: the computer engineers, the construction engineers, the lab specialists, they're all here with me, and sworn to stay here for the rest of their lives."

Fletcher stared at him blankly for a moment. "That's pretty impressive, how'd you accomplish that?"

"I would think after your recent experiences you would know the answer to that," Justin replied with a slight tone of annoyance. "Time travel in the wrong hands is very deadly. Not only to one or two people, but to the very fabric of time itself."

"And who entrusted *you* to this great responsibility?" the major snapped back, somewhat angered at the young man's tone, but more angered that he knew that he was right.

Justin's frown dissipated instantly as that boyish twinkle returned to his eyes. "I wish I could tell you."

Fletcher studied the young man for a moment as he tried to fathom who could have made Justin who he was; who would have taught him all he knew, then left him on Earth in the twenty-fourth century just so that he could fulfill his destiny; and why that subject seemed to trouble the *Twilight* leader whenever asked. Then his eyes narrowed again and he crossed his arms in indignation, his brow creasing in growing annoyance as he considered just how full of temporal paradoxes his life seemed to have become. "I'm working blind here," he finally said with short stubbornness, "and that isn't going to help me figure this out. I can never get a straight answer from you, but you expect total trust from me in what you do. Do you have any idea how frustrating that is?"

Justin let out a laugh and patted the major's arm. "I've accepted that I'm somewhat annoying at times, it's a trait I inherited from my father."

"So you're not going to answer my question?"

"I'd hoped that you understood that if I'm secretive it's for a purpose," the *Twilight* leader tried to explain. "Giving you too much information could alter my future, and therefore harm the future of *Twilight*." He read the exasperation on Fletcher's face and sighed. "Very well, *I'm* the one that gave me that responsibility."

"You?" he asked with surprise.

Justin nodded thoughtfully. "You have to realize that I grew up here with an older me keeping a watchful eye, constantly coaching my parents to lead me in the right direction."

"I see," the major said as he tried to understand what he was being told. "So, are you running around here as a kid somewhere?"

"Oh, no," the young leader said with a chuckle, "I won't be born here for quite some time yet." Then he became serious again as he turned to what seemed to be the vast computer's control center, totally dropping the subject at hand. "Anyway, let's get on to business. This is the Omni computer. From here, I can monitor everything that happens in *Twilight*. The Omni computer has vast sensors and memory banks that watch over all the time streams that flow outside the complex. This way it judges all the histories of the known worlds in the universe and lets us know when things are happening that deserve our attention."

"You told us all of this in Skimmer training," Fletcher reminded him, grateful to have the topic changed.

"Right," the leader agreed, "but you said that Tsunami was not picked up by Skimmers as she originally was, but Carrie still was."

The major nodded.

"This coincides with a temporal anomaly I noticed in the Omni computer just a few days ago. Although the computer can't tell the future, it still monitors its own existence up and down the timeline—"

"How is that possible?" Fletcher cut in.

"To tell you the truth," Justin admitted, "I'm not sure. There are a number of things that the Omni computer can do that I didn't program into it. I can only conclude that it's somewhat self teaching. However, what I was going to say was that a few days ago I noticed that the computer was suddenly unable to see its own existence past two decades from now."

"Right after I arrived here for the first time," Fletcher observed, then his face lit up. "I get it. Carrie was still rescued by the Skimmers because she arrived here in *Twilight* before I did, but Kim arrived *after* I did, so something happened after I arrived that stopped the Skimmers from saving her."

"*You* are what happened, Fletcher," Justin said solemnly. "You chose not to come back here like you were supposed to and instead changed history."

"But that makes no sense," Fletcher snapped back. "How could my actions have such an impact on *Twilight's* history?"

Justin stared at him for what seemed a long time as he internally gauged his next words, and their repercussions, but he knew he had no choice. "You are the key to *Twilight's* existence…you and Carrie."

Fletcher stared at him blankly again, then shook his head in disbelief. "*Twilight* was here long before either of us arrived. Even now, I'm here before I arrived the first time and *Twilight* is going strong. It's simply not possible."

"Why isn't it possible?" Justin challenged. "*Twilight* was here before I was born, but you accepted that I created *Twilight*. Even you, yourself, have begun to understand your significance here." He paused at the hard look that was fastened on the major's face like it was carved in marble. "When you arrived the first time, twenty years from now, I expected you, didn't I?"

Fletcher nodded slowly, never losing his stoic expression.

"And when you arrived just now with Carrie, I was there waiting for the two of you, right?"

Again Fletcher nodded.

"I don't do this for all Skimmers that come in."

Fletcher's glare wavered a bit.

"I was there both times because I knew about both times. I knew that I had to be there to help both of you arrive safely, or else *Twilight* would never exist."

"But you didn't know about Carrie's death," the major came back with as if it would blow a hole in the *Twilight* leader's theory.

Justin took a deep breath and glared at him. "No, I didn't. I wish that this information had been passed on to me, but I obviously left that out of my own education."

"So, you're not infallible," Fletcher stated plainly.

"Of course not," Justin replied in anger. "I'm not God here. I'm just someone trying to make a difference, like I was taught to."

"By you—"

"No," the young leader shot back as he stared deeply into the major's eyes, almost as if seeking reassurance, "by my father."

Both lapsed into silence for a few moments as what had transpired started to sink in. Somehow, Fletcher knew in his heart what all the implications that had been told to him really meant, but self denial kept his thoughts on the here and now. His mind ignored the incredible and stayed with what really mattered.

"I have to stop the killer," he stated flatly, his blue eyes darkening like the night sky at the thought of her death. "I need you to send me to save Carrie."

Justin nodded. "Yes, but more than that, you also have to go back to the twentieth century and stop yourself from changing history."

A pained look flushed over Fletcher's face. He had hoped that if he could stop the killer, then he could leave the past as it was and Con would stay alive.

"You can't let it be that way, Fletcher," the young leader said as if he was reading his thoughts. "We don't know where this rogue Skimmer came from, but his existence was never reported before Carrie's death so we can take no chances. What if your changing of history is somehow responsible for him?"

Fletcher started to protest, but Justin just shook his head.

"By saving your friend's past, you could have very well destroyed all of our futures."

## Chapter 21
# Race Against Time

Fletcher paced back and forth in the Departure Nucleus as he flexed the stiff joints of his new Skimmer armor. His mind was a turmoil as he tried to focus on his immediate goal: save Carrie. The thought of seeing her alive again, as an adult, filled him with elation and fear. What if he wasn't in time? Justin was unable to pinpoint the exact moment of her death due to the increasing anomalies and errors that the Omni computer was exhibiting. The best he could do was find the day and rough time that it happened.

"Why not just send me back a day early?" the major asked as he turned again in his pacing. "Save the trouble of maybe being too late."

"We can't risk it," Justin said with a sigh. "I told you already that we know nothing about this rouge Skimmer. The Omni computer can't tell me anything about him at all. That tells me that he might have some ability to pick the time and place that he appears. If this is so, and he finds that there are two of you in a place and time, he might choose some other time to do his killing. If I send you as close to the time of her death as possible, he might already be on his way and won't be able to change his time of arrival."

Fletcher glared at him skeptically.

"Look," Justin argued, "you're just going to have to do your best. You won't get another chance at this. Stop the rouge and give him to the me of the future. Then immediately Skim out to your past and stop yourself from stopping yourself from going on the mission where your jet was destroyed."

The major rubbed his temples for a moment as he felt the adrenaline build up in his system. "What are we waiting for?"

"Nothing," Justin admitted. "I'm going to control the Skim for you personally. I want no mistakes."

Fletcher activated his WCD, adding his glow to the iridescent blue light on the floor beneath him.

"Please be careful," the *Twilight* leader warned, suddenly seeming like a little boy to the lone Skimmer on the pad.

Fletcher nodded as he pushed the button, filling the room with a flash of azure light.

The Departure Nucleus came back into view, and for a moment Fletcher thought he hadn't gone anywhere, but then he quickly realized that it wasn't Justin at the controls.

"Phantom," Sender greeted him with a confused smile. "I didn't know you had skimmed out. Where are you coming from?"

"You wouldn't believe me if I told you," he answered with a grin, happy to see his friend. "What time is it?"

Sender checked his controls. "Almost twenty-two hundred hours."

"Thanks," he hastily answered as he quickly left the chamber and entered the circular curved hallway. His mind tried to calculate the exact time that Carrie had been shot, but he could only guess that it was close to ten at night, mere moments from now. He glanced up and down the hallway, knowing that both ways would get him to the observation hall where the fight happened, but to the right was definitely the shorter route. He turned down the hallway in a sprint and ran right into Paula Kesseler.

The doctor fell backwards from the blow and he was barely able to catch her before she hit the ground.

"D-Doctor," he stammered as he pulled her back up. "I didn't see you."

"I kind of guessed that," she said with a smile.

"Um," he continued, frantically glancing past her, "if you'll excuse me, I've got to see Carrie."

"Oh," Paula said with a knowing smile in her mahogany eyes. "I guess then that congratulations are in order."

Fletcher stared at her in confusion, the rush momentarily taken out of his pace. "Congratulations?"

"On your child," she answered with a grin. "Or are you trying to keep this a secret?"

"What child are you talking about?" Fletcher demanded, as a knot started to form in his stomach.

The doctor took a sharp breath, realizing her mistake. "I'm sorry, Phantom. I thought Carrie was going to tell you this morning."

"My God," Fletcher whispered, then he turned back the way he was going and ran, leaving a stunned doctor to watch him rapidly disappear down the curved corridor.

His heart beat like repeating thunder in his ears as he pushed to make himself run faster. Finally reaching the access way to the observation hall, he paused as the door slowly opened; then he bolted through it like he was running for his life—as the plasma shot rang through the long corridor like a herald signaling the arrival of the apocalypse.

He couldn't think, couldn't reason—he just ran—ran down the observation hall as if he could break the time barrier with his sheer speed and still arrive in time to save her.

Frantically he rounded the curve of the hall only to see himself holding her in his arms, black smoke rising from what was left of her head—and the assassin—ebony and cruel, as he raised his weapon again. Fletcher stopped dead in his tracks, the unbearable realization that he was too late tearing him apart at the seams.

"Vengeance is sweet, Phantom," came those same words from the figure in the distance which drove into his soul like hot coals. "I hope you rot in your hell." Then the assassin fired.

"No!" Fletcher screamed as he watched the plasma beam strike his alter self, sending the stricken *Twilight* Skimmer back to his destiny with his past. Then he broke into a run again, grief fading to anger as all his attention fixated on the source of his misery. His fingers clenched into rock hard fists, causing the knuckles to crack as he swiftly closed the distance between himself and his nemesis.

The rogue Skimmer turned at the sound of the yell and took a step back. His surprise was concealed by the mirrored helmet, but betrayed by the shake in his body. The assassin frantically fumbled with his WCD, as he set in his next destination. Then he struck the sending button, flooding the observation hall with brilliant azure light.

Fletcher's jaw clenched so tightly that he could taste the salty blood flowing from his gums as his eyes drove spears of hatred towards his fading quarry.

"You're-not-getting-away!" he yelled as the ebony Skimmer faded into the flash of azure light, mere yards from his outstretched grasp. Letting out a guttural scream, Fletcher vaulted himself at the heart of the blinding glow, feeling the temporal energies rip at his system as he struggled to grasp his enemy that was no longer there.

The light slowly faded a moment later, leaving only Carrie's still form in the silent hall.

Fletcher felt himself hit the ground, his head reeling as if it had been struck. His gauntlets scrapped across crusted asphalt as his eyes finally opened to take in his dank surroundings. He was in a darkened alley of a Middle Eastern city; that much he could tell by the building styles around him. There was a young Arabic boy who appeared unkempt and unwashed who stood a few feet from him, staring at him in open wonder. The major closed his eyes again, fighting back the nausea that accompanied a hard Skim, and hoped when he opened them that his situation would have improved. A harsh stench assaulted his senses, forcing him to abandon that hope as he realized that he was on some sort of garbage heap at the back of the alley.

The boy asked him a question in Arabic, his soft tone displaying his curiosity.

Fletcher knew only a few odd words of this language, and the question was lost on him as he pulled himself up to his feet, his aching muscles protesting the whole way. Then he saw his left wrist and a groan escaped his dry lips. There was a crack across the smooth black surface of his new WCD control pad, and thin tendrils of deep grey smoke were seeping up from it, instantly answering his question on why the language translator didn't work. Then his eyes narrowed to slits as his desperation over his situation turned back to the fury he had felt, when near madness had forced him to dive into the azure glow.

He grabbed the young boy by what could only loosely be described as his shirt and lifted him off the ground.

"Where did he go?" he demanded harshly, sticking his face a few inches from the boy's.

The young Arabic's mouth hung open in shock as his small hands closed on Fletcher's armored ones, as he vainly tried to pry his grip open.

"Like me," the major tried again, speaking slower and enunciating each syllable. "But all in black...*aswad*—do you understand?"

The boy suddenly nodded furiously and pointed down the alley and to the right. Instantly Fletcher dropped the child and broke into a sluggish run, his muscles still not performing at their peak. Emerging out of the narrow alleyway into the dank city street, his eyes desperately searched down the street to his right, hoping for some sign of the assassin.

The city's lights shone with a bright haze on the small street, obscuring the desert night with their luminous glow. The sifting illumination cast him in dark shadows, as passersby stared at him in shock. Now there was no question in his mind; everything here pointed to the old section of some

Arabic city, perhaps Cairo or Amman. In this aged section of the city, life had been preserved here the way it was hundreds of years ago. Electric lamps were the only betrayer of technology on this narrow street whose cobblestone way was far too small for regular traffic, even if it had been allowed. Small shops lined both sides of the roadway, as store keepers peered from behind tables piled with merchandise, or from the relative safety of the burlap awnings. Out in the air away from the alley, new scents struck him. The aroma of exotic spices and sizzling meat drifted past him as he started forward down the street at a slow pace, hoping not to miss anything. Despite the charm of antiquity that the market street displayed, telltale signals quickly made him realize when he had arrived, if not precisely where.

"I'm back in my own time again," he whispered in amazement as his language drew more attention than he had ever wanted before, "or close to it."

Then his eyes lit as he spotted his nemesis, over a hundred yards away down the narrow street, as the ebony-armored rogue Skimmer happened to pass directly under a street lamp and pause there. For a moment the assassin glanced back and they locked glares, quarry and hunter as they silently made clear to each other the terms of what had become a personal battle of survival. Then Fletcher's eyes opened wide as he spotted a glimmer of hope. His nemesis' WCD seemed damaged also, as lines of smoke rose from his left wrist as well.

"*Gotcha*," the major hissed almost silently with a venomous breath. "We're both stuck here, aren't we?"

The assassin glanced down at his left wrist, as if he had understood the words that he could never have heard, then he turned and ran down the street, quickly vanishing into the throng of people.

As if attached to his nemesis by an unseen umbilical cord, Fletcher leaped forward and began the pursuit, darting through the thick crowd as he yelled for people to get out of his way.

With both his and his enemy's WCDs apparently damaged, Fletcher understood that he was most likely marooned in this time again, and the realization of the scope of his failure burned in him like molten lava. He knew that he had not only let down Carrie, again, and their unborn child, but he had let down Justin and *Twilight* as well. Though the thought of failing Carrie ached within him, somehow failing the young *Twilight* leader filled him with shame he couldn't explain. All that he could see was red, the red of raw hatred as his anger and shame began to fuse into obsession. He would catch this killer, he silently vowed, and make him pay for what he had done.

As he approached the end of the narrow street, he could see that he was leaving the old section of the city and entering the modern half. Sounds of traffic and other noises of technology permeated the air as he broke through the iron gates and onto the hard asphalt parking lot where small taxis lined the area like mosquitoes waiting in turn for the next victim.

A roar of a car engine gave him a last minute alert to his side as he yanked himself back to the gate, as a speeding taxi whizzed over the spot he had just been standing.

He let out a silent curse as he glared at the hurtling vehicle, then his eyes widened at the sight of the ebony-helmed passenger in the back seat.

Diving into the next taxi in line, he quickly ordered the driver to give pursuit to the vanishing taxi ahead; however, all the driver did was stare blankly in his rearview mirror at the scarlet and ebony-armored spectacle that had jumped into his car.

Fletcher let out an exasperated half snarl and reached over and grabbed the driver's face and pointed it forward again.

"That car," he yelled, pointing at the vehicle that was just disappearing around a corner ahead, "follow it, now!"

Whether it was the strength of his grip, or the vehemence in his tone that motivated the driver, the Arab suddenly slammed his foot on the accelerator and leaped the car forward as he gave pursuit of the other taxi.

The major fell back in his seat at the sudden acceleration, but quickly pulled himself back to the driver.

"Where is he heading?" he asked as the car headed out onto a larger road.

The driver swallowed the lump in his throat and then cleared it. "It would seem, Sahib, that they are heading out of the city," he said with a thick Arabic accent.

Fletcher nodded thoughtfully as he tried to gauge the rogue's next move. He knew they were both stranded here, but why had the assassin chosen this time and place to flee to?

As they emerged onto the highway, suddenly an eighteen wheeler veered into their lane from out of nowhere, slicing across their path.

The driver let out a scream of horror as he pulled frantically at his wheel, trying to avert what seemed their inevitable destruction. Steel ground on rubber and steel as the mid wheels of the semi plowed over the front of the small taxi with a deafening squeal. Fletcher felt his Skimmer armor collide with the front seat, knocking the wind out of him, as the driver disappeared through the windshield with a shattering crunch. Then his world turned upside down as the crippled taxi's rear wheels lifted off the ground, turning the small vehicle end over end into the side of the truck.

The semi's brakes screeched as it skidded to the side, turning a full one-hundred and eighty degrees before stopping on the dune shoulder. The remains of the taxi bounced off its side and tumbled into the ravine on the far side, flinging its dazed passenger out the missing rear window. The small craft came to rest on the rocks below with a thundering crash, as the sparks caught the gas tank, erupting what was left of the car into a hellish fireball.

Fletcher lay on the side of the highway for a few moments, staring up at the night sky, which was alight with the flames from the demolished taxi. Then he shook his head, forcing awareness back into it as he sat up and glanced at himself to make sure he was alive. His armor was scratched in a number of places, and the chest plate had a crack in it, but what caught his attention was the dagger sharp splinter of glass that stuck straight out from the armor on his abdomen.

Letting out the breath that he had been holding in, he gripped the glass shard with his gauntleted hand and pulled it out, bringing out the half inch that had been imbedded there. Then he stood up and stared at the road. All traffic was blocked by the semi that covered half the highway, and the cars that had stopped to help. A smile came to Fletcher's lips as he saw a crowd around the taxi driver, who was covered in blood from a gash in his forehead, but was still very much alive. Then his smile vanished as he glanced down the highway for any sign of the other taxi, knowing that he'd see nothing, but hoping none the less. The empty stretch of asphalt lay like a barren wilderness now that the accident blocked all passage, and a tightening sensation pulled in his chest as he felt his quarry fade further and further away.

In the distance, a siren sounded the approach of the local authorities and he realized that he should get away from here before questions that he couldn't answer would be asked. He glanced at the accident scene once more, studying all the cars, then gazed back at the empty stretch ahead, knowing without a doubt that his enemy had really escaped, and he didn't have the faintest idea of where to search for him.

## Chapter 22
# Rogue Skimmer

    Deciding where to go next hadn't been Fletcher's biggest problem, getting away from the local military became a far more immediate threat. He had been searching among the abandoned cars whose drivers were over at the accident scene, when two old Jeeps pulled up out of nowhere. Suddenly a bright spotlight struck him full as the soldiers started to yell at him to stay where he was in four different languages.
    He knew he didn't have much time, and could only guess what the military would do to him and his equipment if he was caught. Then a feeble hope struck him and he looked back at his cracked WCD. Perhaps it wasn't completely disabled. The Jeeps closed swiftly in as he activated the hazing effect of his armor and prayed. The world shimmied slightly as the Jeeps sped by him, frantically searching for the person that they could no longer see.
    A wide grin flashed on Fletcher's face with the confirmation that the hazing mode still worked, but he knew he only had thirty seconds. Glancing around desperately, he spotted an abandoned car that a driver had left running. It was a small red Italian car that was far too conspicuous for his tastes, but he had no choice. Diving into the Alpha Romeo, he fastened his seat belt and pushed the accelerator to the floor. The car's wheels spun for a moment as they sought traction, then the car flew forward. He pulled around the accident on the shoulder and sped off down the empty highway.
    The instant that the Alpha Romeo had began to move, twin spotlights had flashed on it from both military Jeeps, but the drivers hesitated, as they stared blankly at the vehicle that was driving off with no one inside. However, diligence and duty outweighed superstition and they quickly gave chase.
    The major eyed his pursuers in his rearview mirror as the hazing effect finally wore off. He easily recognized the vehicles as American military

leftovers from the fifties, and smiled as he mentally gauged their top speed verses the Alpha Romeo—then put the pedal to the floor and cut off his headlights.

The empty highway was brilliantly lit by the full moon above, and he had no trouble navigating the speeding vehicle that was quickly leaving the military craft behind. However, he kept the lights off for some time, knowing full well that the soldiers would call air support to search for him, and he still had the hopeless task of finding the assassin before they found him.

"Air support..." he repeated his thoughts aloud as if they suddenly rang a bell. "If I needed to get to somewhere fast, how would I do it?"

As if to answer his query, his eyes caught a highway sign in the distance. He quickly flicked the headlights off and on, and though the words were in Arabic, the symbols next to the words were unmistakable. They clearly indicated that the airport was the next exit.

Moving to the right lane, he exited the highway at the next ramp and turned on his lights as his car blended into the regular traffic that was entering the airport.

Once in the parking lot, he stopped the car and considered his situation. He wasn't sure if the assassin had come here or not, but his gut feeling was that this was his best shot. However, the commotion that he caused at the accident made him want to rethink his garb. He didn't want to take off the armor. Aside from protecting him, he somehow wasn't quite ready to give up on getting back. But he took off the helmet, realizing that even if found, would only seem like a fancy motorcycle or pilot's helmet. He got out of the car and opened the trunk, hoping for an answer there. Inside were a number of pieces of road side hazard equipment which he shifted through with disinterest. Then he found a khaki rain poncho made of a thin canvas material.

"Perfect," he whispered as he pulled it out of the trunk and put it on over his armor. The poncho was long and thick, leaving only his ebony armored boots to be seen below the khaki cloth. Taking his helmet, he stuffed it under his poncho and prepared to close the trunk when his eyes caught something that he had disregarded before. A two shot hand flare gun was wedged under the spare tire, which he grabbed and stuffed into his armored belt. Then he slammed the trunk closed and started towards the terminal entrance. He knew it might not be long before the car was discovered, but he had purposefully parked far away from lights, in the hope that it would be obscured until much later, in case he needed it again.

The warm night air comforted him as he crossed the parking lot at a brisk pace. A million different concerns flashed through his head; what if he was questioned by security and he had no passport, what if the police found the car he stole, what if he were stranded here always? But all fell as a pale shadow to the real question in his mind—would he find the assassin here?

The harsh air conditioning struck him in the face as he entered the airport terminal. It was busy at this time of night, with both tourists and natives as they rushed back and forth trying to get to their destinations. At first the soldier at the door gave him a suspicious glare, but then turned from him as some punked out teenagers came in right after him. With his back turned, Fletcher risked a second glance at the soldier now that he could take the time to study the uniform in the light; he smiled as his suspicions were confirmed. The soldier was definitely Jordanian, which meant that he was in the Queen Alia International Airport. He glanced at the tourists as they milled about, a few of them speaking in English. It was almost like being home again, and for a moment he almost forgot his purpose as he meandered through the terminal, listening to the people he could understand. He got a few more glares from security, but every time he did he moved on to the next airline. His feelings that he was close to his own time were substantiated by the idle chatter of presidents and world events, but still there was no sign of the assassin.

Realizing that it had been hours since he had eaten, he wandered over to a restaurant, but let out a grumble when he remembered that he had no money. He turned back towards the first airline to do one more sweep of the terminal when something on a tourist counter caught his attention, and almost blew out his mind. There was a desk calendar set for each day, and it was there plain to see. Today was the day before his fateful mission in Saudi Arabia that led to him arriving at *Twilight*. For a moment he forgot his anger as the hope of getting back to *Twilight* again surfaced in his mind—then went cold with suspicion.

*Why now?* he wondered. *Why had the rogue Skimmer escaped to his time in the late twentieth century, and why the night before his 'mission'?*

As if in response to his demands, his nemesis walked out of the men's room some two hundred feet from the tourist counter, directly into Fletcher's point of view.

The major's mouth went dry as he eyed the ebony-garbed assassin. He had removed his helmet, but was still too far away to identify, other than being a dark-haired Caucasian. As if spurred by some unseen force, and against all his better judgment, Fletcher broke into a run as he swiftly tried to close the gap that separated him from his nemesis, and bumped into a French tourist on her way to the airline counter.

The annoyed French woman screamed a barrage of insults his way as he ignored her and kept on running. But his hand had been tipped. The rogue Skimmer saw him approaching and quickly turned and ran, snapping on his helmet again to conceal his identity.

In his peripheral vision, Fletcher caught the sight of two members of the Jordan military police, as they also broke into a run to try and catch the two people who were disturbing the peace.

Vaulting over velvet line ropes like a track star over hurtles, he closed in on the assassin whom had become entangled in a throng of students. A third police officer arrived at the rogue's side and grabbed at him while yelling at him in Arabic.

Without warning the assassin attacked the soldier, pulling him off guard as he drove his armored fist into his face. The Jordanian soldier went down hard, leaving the rogue Skimmer holding his Uzi sub-machine gun.

Fletcher only had a second to re-gauge his actions as the small gun leveled at him and spewed forth a flow of bullets. He dodged to the left, as the hail of deadly projectiles screamed past him, one skimming off his breast plate as he dove behind the protective covering of another courtesy counter. The police officer directly behind him didn't fare as well, brought down by a deadly blow meant for another.

Immediately chaos broke out in the terminal as passengers started screaming and running about, as the remaining police officer quickly found cover from which to return gunfire.

Fletcher suddenly realized he was in a no-win situation, as he huddled behind the counter for protection. If the police killed his nemesis here, they would get their hands on technology that he knew they couldn't be allowed to have. Somehow he had to get them both out of here, so that he could deal with this murderer on his own. He glanced around desperately for some aid, as both assassin and soldier continually exchanged gunfire. Then his hand came to his belt where the flare gun was. Quickly pulling it out, he looked above until he found what he was searching for and fired the gun. The flare streaked upward like a miniature comet, striking the ceiling in an explosion of ruby sparks, mere inches from the sprinkler system. Immediately he was rewarded as fire alarms went off and a sheen of water erupted from the ceiling all over the terminal.

Now the terrified tourists were not only running about and screaming, but they were slipping and sliding into each other and the police as the reinforcements entered the building.

As he hoped, Fletcher watched as the assassin used the newfound pandemonium to fire the Uzi at the picture window next to him, shattering it in a thousand pieces. In a second, he was through the window, diving out into the night air.

The moment that his nemesis turned and ran, the major was up again, hurtling himself over the counter to avoid the hail of bullets from the police that considered him just as great a threat as his dark enemy. He hit the ground doing a somersault and came up running, diving through the shattered window mere seconds after the assassin had gone through.

There was a full story drop to the ground from the window, which took Fletcher by surprise as he jumped into the night. Twisting in mid-air to keep from falling face first, he managed to land on his feet and roll with the drop, feeling the armor crack in his side as he struck the hard asphalt of the landing field. He quickly shook the daze from his mind and stood back up, wincing as a flash of pain shot through his ankle. Hoping it was simply a bad sprain instead of a fracture, he ran as fast as he could in the direction of his still fleeing nemesis.

The assassin sent one more hail of bullets back at him which fell short of their target, then he threw the empty weapon aside, useless. Quickly climbing into one of three airport pickup trucks that were parked by a hanger, the rogue Skimmer started across the field, his tires squealing as he gained speed.

Fletcher had just reached the second of these pickups when a hail of bullets from above riddled the top of the vehicle with holes and blew out the rear widow. Without taking the time to look at the military police who he knew must be at the shattered terminal window, he dove into the damaged pickup and gunned the push button starter. As the engine came alive, his foot was already pushing the accelerator pad to the floor when another volley of bullets came from above, heralding him on his way.

The speedometer rose quickly past fifty as he sped across the flat landing field after the other pickup which couldn't have been more than a hundred yards away. Down one of the runways they sped, hunter and hunted, both pushing their vehicles past performance maximums.

Suddenly a bright light ahead blinded Fletcher as if a midnight sun had suddenly appeared before him. The thunderous roar of jet engines screamed in the small cabin of his pickup, as he realized with horror that they had chosen a poor runway for their chase.

Lifting a hand to stop the glare of the plane's front lights, his eyes narrowed to hardened slits as he willed the truck to go faster, as the 757 descended in front of him, seeming to hover just over the lead pickup.

The lowered rear wheels of the gigantic passenger jet barely missed the assassin's pickup as they struck ground with a high pitched squeal, placing the jet between both vehicles. Yanking the steering wheel hard, Fletcher forced the small pickup to skim just to the right of plane's huge landing gear as he temporarily lost control of the vehicle and spun on the asphalt, completing three 360-degree turns before coming to a stop, as the jet continued on its way down the runway.

For a moment Fletcher sat there, watching the jet diminish further away as he let out a slow breath. Then he jammed the pedal down again and swerved the pickup back into relentless pursuit.

His mind set in determination as he watched his nemesis plow through the fencing that separated the landing field from the highway, sending up a flurry of sparks as he started down the almost empty road.

Gunning the engine, Fletcher pushed the small pickup truck to its limits as he flew through the new opening, vaulting over the dune that separated the field from the highway and striking the roadway with a short skid. Despite the extremely light traffic at this late hour, the small cars seemed to Fletcher to be doing their best to get in the way of the chase. Two station wagons immediately cut him off, almost forcing him off the highway, and then an eighteen wheeler practically turned his pickup into a hood ornament when it bumped him from behind as he swerved back onto the road.

Hours passed by as the two combatants maintained their distance from each other. At times, the traffic seemed to hinder the assassin, letting Fletcher close the gap, but then someone would get in his way, letting the lead pickup pull away again as they sped along the highway deeper into the desert.

As night started to turn into the early hours past midnight, the major saw signs that indicated that the Jordan border was coming up as they headed south towards Saudi Arabia. His engine sputtered a few times as he tried to coax more speed out of it, but it seemed that the two vehicles were equally matched.

He took a deep breath as he evaluated the upcoming situation. His knowledge of the military gave him no false illusions of what they would face at the border. Without passports they would simply not get through, though he doubted that his nemesis would even slow down long enough for them to ask him for one. Such a break in the lines would alert the military of both countries as they crashed through the border. He gripped the wheel harder as he determined that there had to be a way to stop him before that point. A*nd where is he going, anyway?* he continued to wonder. Then a thought struck him that was so obvious he marveled that he hadn't realized it before. He could think of no other reason that the assassin had chosen this time and place other than to somehow effect him on the day of his fateful mission—but how?

Before he could continue his internal detective work, the opportunity that he had been waiting for occurred. A large truck cut off the assassin's pickup, causing him to swerve into another car, bouncing off of it and forcing the other car off the highway. The accident didn't stop the lead pickup, but did force him into a place behind the truck, slowing him down considerably.

Keeping his numbed foot to the floor, Fletcher rapidly closed the distance between the two vehicles until he was just pulling parallel to it. He could see the rogue Skimmer turn towards him, his ebony-mirrored face plate staring at him with blank vehemence. Then the assassin pulled sharply to the left, slamming his pickup into the major's. Both vehicles rocked as Fletcher's veered off to the left barely missing another car. Quickly the major pulled his pickup back again, this time ramming into his nemesis as he tried to force him off the road. The two vehicles locked together as vibrating metal ground on metal. For a few moments the two pickups stayed together as the two drivers stared at each other in hatred. Then Fletcher reached across his seat as if he could grab the other car out the window. Seeing him do this, the rogue Skimmer pulled his pickup to the right again, shearing it away from the other car, pulling the major's passenger door off as they separated.

Fletcher fought for control as the pickup flew to the left again, this time hitting the far left railing. More sparks shot along the damaged metal frame as the small truck threatened to tip over. He slammed on his brakes, finally jarring the pickup away from the steel railings that had ripped up the side of the vehicle. Once free again, he hit the accelerator as he pulled back onto the highway, but the assassin had already gained another lead over him.

Then his spirits sank as he saw the traffic slowing down ahead for the border—he'd run out of time and he knew it. The rogue Skimmer veered around the eight cars that were waiting in line as he raced along the shoulder. Fletcher's lips tightened into two thin lines as he watched his nemesis close on the gate that was set up to only allow one car through at a time.

Soldiers on both sides of the border began to raise their weapons as they realized that the pickup showed no signs of slowing down at all. Shouts and orders flashed back and forth as they formed a line directly in the path of the two pickups and yelled for them to stop.

The major's heart began to ache as he realized that he was not breathing as the rogue Skimmer continued on at full speed, heading right for the chain link fencing that blocked off the shoulder pass.

The staccato rapping of machine-gun fire sounded as the soldiers fired into the air above the car, warning it off one last time. However, the pickup paid it no heed, as it bore down on the soldiers, now only a few feet away. This time the gunfire wasn't into the air as they fired into the front of the pickup, turning the windshield into a spider web of cracks. Then the assassin plowed through them and struck the fencing, barely giving them a chance to dive for cover before mowing them over. He careened through the chain link fence as if it wasn't there and bore down on the soldiers on the other side, who were already backing up to save their lives. Hails of bullets rained across both sides of the pickup as it flew across the border and out of Jordan, heading on down the highway.

So engrossed were they in trying to stop the first pickup, the soldiers barely had time to turn and face Fletcher as he screamed past them. More bullets rained on his truck, shattering the rear lights and destroying what little was left of the rear window.

Then the two pickups were free on the highway again, though both full of many holes from the vicious onslaught. Exhaustion threatened to take its toll on the major as he realized that they were getting further into the night, and that time could be running out. He glanced behind, spotting the two military police cars that were slowly gaining on them. Both pickups had no lights now, since they had been totally destroyed by the border gunfire, so he doubted that they could be easily seen. However, he knew it would only be a matter of time before they would be caught. One simply did not burst through the Jordan-Saudi Arabia border and get away with it.

Another long hour went by as they raced through the desert night; assassin, Time Skimmer, and the diligent military police. Suddenly smoke began to erupt out of the front of the rogue Skimmer's engine in thick billowing clouds.

A wry grin formed on Fletcher's lips as he began to close the distance between the two of them. "At last," he whispered, as his pickup came to only one car length behind the assassin's. So intent on catching up to his nemesis was he, that he was totally unprepared when the lead pickup's engine exploded in a shower of metal and flames. The fatally crippled pickup fell onto its side and struck another semi-truck on the highway, causing both to skid as the flaming vehicle pushed into it.

Cars struck other cars as the accident quickly escalated in the denser traffic that they had encountered. Fletcher tried desperately to pull his truck out in time, but he was going far too fast. The front of his pickup collapsed upon itself as he struck the back of the other truck, as flames began to engulf his vehicle as well.

Quickly grabbing his helmet off the seat, he dove out the open passenger side where the door had been destroyed, as his pickup practically evaporated in a deafening eruption that sent him spinning head over heels onto the sandy dunes that bordered the highway.

Fletcher lay there in the sand for a moment as he wondered how many times he would have died in this chase if he wasn't wearing the Skimmer armor. Then he took in a deep breath and forced his aching muscles to work to get him up again, realizing that if he had survived, then his nemesis could have as well.

He could see over eight vehicles involved in the crash, though none as seriously as he had been. The military police were closing in fast, and he hoped that they would find the accident consuming enough to ignore him long enough to get away. Quickly he scanned the wreckage for some sign of the rogue Skimmer, but he was nowhere to be seen. Fighting the intense blaze, he managed to get right up to what was left of the lead pickup, but the flames were so dense and burning that he couldn't be sure if anyone had made it out in time.

Seeing the police and military closing in, he backed away from the wreckage and slipped to the far side of the semi to take cover, then sank to his knees with utter fatigue. Whether or not it was broken, his ankle now ached with a numbing sting that felt like a hot coal was under his armored boot.

Another engine starting up behind him caught his attention as he glanced over his shoulder at yet another eighteen wheeler that had narrowly missed the accident but had stopped anyway. Fletcher could see the driver taking one last look at the accident and then pulling back onto the highway.

He almost gave it no notice when he caught movement out of the corner of his eye. The semi rig was hauling a flatbed, piled high with some boxed material under a loose grey tarp, and he thought something had moved on top of the tarp. Then he saw the movement again and there was no mistaking it—a black-garbed person was on the huge flatbed, climbing between the mammoth boxes that obscured him from the truck driver.

Fletcher broke into a run, as shearing agony shot up his injured leg. The semi had pulled fully back onto the highway now and was starting to pick up speed. For an instant he was sure that he wouldn't get there in time, then he leaped at the back of the truck, barely grabbing onto the rear edge of the flatbed. He legs dragged along the asphalt as he fought the muscle strain and pulled himself up onto the grey tarp. Once safely on the truck, he let out a sigh of relief and glanced back at the multi-car accident that was quickly fading back. More soldiers and air support had arrived on the scene, but none were giving the truck any notice as it slipped away. A moment passed as he marveled at his luck, then his jaw tightened as he turned to the rest of the flatbed and began moving along the sides of the huge boxes, looking for his target that had never seemed nearer.

The truck had picked up considerable speed as he clung to the ropes that lashed the heavy tarp down. There were barely a few inches to stand on past the edges of the boxes, and the tarp which over hung the edges was slippery and loose. Wind sliced into his face as the truck exceeded fifty miles per hour barreling along the quiet pre-dawn highway. The lights and sirens of the accident diminished to nothingness far behind them as Fletcher passed the first of the four six-foot square crates that took up all but a little of the flatbed space. He didn't know exactly where the rogue Skimmer had chosen to hide up here. For all he knew, his nemesis was in the front with the driver now.

Deciding that getting the upper hand was what he needed, he started to pull himself up on top of the box, using the binding ropes for traction. Almost immediately he regretted his decision as his level of exhaustion peaked. Taking in a deep breath of determination, and biting on his tongue to hold in the groan that threatened to escape his lips, he managed to get on top of the crate. Once there, he had to hold on to the rope to prevent being flung from the truck like a rag doll.

After he made sure that he wasn't about to fall off, he pulled himself to his knees, squinting against the fierce grainy wind that buffeted against him like a sand blaster, blurring his vision. It was getting hard to breathe as airborne sand started to get in his nose and mouth, but he tilted his head down and crawled forward, pulling himself to the edge of the second crate. He quickly glanced down at the narrow space between the crates but it was empty. As tempting as it was to seek refuge down there, he pulled himself across the two foot gap, almost losing his grip again as the truck rounded a bend, now well over seventy miles per hour.

Fletcher wondered just how fast the driver intended on going as he pulled himself forward to the edge of the third crate. The harsh wind continued to slam against him, trying to pry him off the back of the crate like a pancake from a griddle. Placing his hands on the edge of the crate, he peered over the edge, careful to keep himself as concealed as possible—and caught his breath. Crouched below him, in the two foot gap between the third and last crate, knelt the rogue Skimmer, gazing out the side of the flatbed.

Fletcher froze—his emotions in a turmoil as he realized that his nemesis was not only within arms' reach, but unaware that he was being watched. Numbers of possibilities flashed in his mind; from waiting in secrecy to find out what the assassin's plans where, to ringing his neck. It took only a second for the later idea to win out and he shot his hand down the gap and grabbed the ebony Skimmer by the neck ring that fastened his helmet to his armor. Suddenly finding strength that he had long felt lost, he pulled his enemy upward, grabbing him with the other hand as he hauled his flailing form up on top of the crate with him.

However, despite his surprise, the assassin was not totally caught off guard and lashed out at the major with his gauntleted fist, striking him hard on the jaw. Fletcher fell backwards, losing his grip on his enemy as he fought to keep from sliding off the crate. He grabbed onto the loose tarp as the other Skimmer came over him and laughed.

"How pathetic, old man," he scoffed as he hovered over the prone major, as the wind caused him to continually shift his footing to stay steady. "You chase me across time and deserts only to fail at our first face to face." Then he raised one armored boot and sent it directly at Fletcher's head.

The major pulled his body to the left as the boot came crashing down, then he reached out and grabbed the assassin's other leg and pulled it forward, sending the rogue reeling backwards to fall on the crate. Without hesitating a second, Fletcher pulled himself over the assassin, grabbing at his neck as he struggled to force him back into the space between the crates.

The truck rounded another bend, sending them both scrambling for a hold on the tarp as the major lashed out with his fist, striking the mirrored black helmet with a loud thud. A large bump in the highway jumped them both into the air as they fought once again to keep from falling off to certain death. Rogue and major rose up together to face each other in the wind, as the crate, now loose from their struggling, shifted slightly under their feet.

"Who the hell are you?" Fletcher demanded, yelling to be heard over the wind.

"I'd like to say your worst nightmare," the assassin laughed boyishly, "but that would be too cliché."

"Why me, why Carrie?"

"It's a secret," he chucked again. "One that I'm afraid you'll die not knowing."

Fletcher let out a scream of anger as he lost all sense of self preservation and launched himself at his nemesis, catching him in his grapple as both tumbled backwards towards the driver's cab. Together they struggled in a life or death match for the upper hand, rolling over each other as their hands locked on the other's neck.

Suddenly the truck hit another bump, sending the loose crate forward to crash into the crate in front of it, catching the assassin between them as Fletcher stayed on top and was forcing him down. A loud crack sounded as the rogue Skimmer's helmet took the brunt of the blow, splintering in half. Then the crate shifted back and they both fell down to the flatbed between the crates, the major still on top.

Before the assassin could recover from the blow, Fletcher grabbed what little was left of the locking mechanism of the helmet and gave it a hard pull. It tumbled off the truck and he prepared to drive his fist into the revealed young face that couldn't have been more than twenty, when he stopped—the dark brown hair, the stern grey eyes—the resemblance was unmistakable.

"You—you look like Con," he half stammered in the wind. "What the hell is going on?"

Despite the trickle of blood that smeared the youth's mouth, he smiled a devilish smile that was all too familiar.

"Can't you figure it out, Uncle Fletcher?" he laughed. "I'm Kyle Stryker, Con's son. Certainly the last time he saw you he told you my mother was pregnant?" He laughed at the blank look on the major's face. "No? He made sure to tell me all about you."

Fletcher's head began to reel as the weight of this news struck home. How could his best friend, the man he saved, have had a son that would do this to him, or *could* do this to him?

"Why the pained face, Uncle Fletcher?" Kyle said with a bloody grin.

"Stop calling me uncle, you little punk," the major spat angrily.

"*Phantom*, then," he said as his eyes did a dark dance of triumph. "And you can call me Jackal...that's my Skimmer name...I took it from Dad."

"I know where the name came from, but how could you have ever become a *Twilight* Skimmer?"

"Same way as you," he laughed, "wrong time, wrong place…you know."

Fletcher shook his head in confusion as he continued to hold his best friend's son by the neck. "This makes no sense. Even if it's true, why kill Carrie? Why attack me?"

"Easy enough," Kyle explained with an almost jubilant glee. "I became a Skimmer when my Jag went off a cliff side…I guess the car was harder to control than I thought with the police in close chase. But then some guy in armor pops in out of nowhere and saves me right before I hit the canyon floor. Next thing I know I'm at *Twilight* and I meet this old man named Justin. He tells me about you and then goes and offers me a second chance at life…the fool…I think because of you and your friendship with my dad. I grabbed it and became a Skimmer."

All Fletcher could do is stare at him in shock as he told this story that was so incredible it had to be true.

"But I always knew something was wrong," Kyle continued. "I could feel it in my guts, so I snuck into the computer room one night and asked the Omni computer about my history, and was able to dredge up an anomaly…you. I found that for me to exist, my father had to survive—for my father to survive, I had to shoot you and send you back to save my father."

"The computer told you all this?" Fletcher asked, incredulous over the scope of what he had drawn himself into.

"Sure," Kyle laughed. "It seems this computer is a lot smarter than Justin realizes. It doesn't just watch time waves, it watches *multidimensional* waves as well, and it was able to warn me that if I never did what I had already done, I would never exist…go figure."

Fletcher's head hurt, his ankle ached, and all he could do was think about the punk that his best friend had fathered.

"I can't let you do it," Kyle whispered, suddenly serious.

"Do what?"

"Stop yourself from saving my dad. That's what you're trying to do, isn't it?"

Suddenly Fletcher realized he was right. It was all his fault. When he interfered with history, like Justin told him not too, he created the monster that killed Carrie and destroyed *Twilight*.

"It's impossible," he spat at the pinned youth, as he tried to absorb it all. "How can you have gone to *Twilight* after I saved your father? It makes no sense."

"You're thinking is limited, Uncle," the rogue laughed. "You're only thinking of one dimension. Do try to broaden your mind."

Fletcher pushed down hard on his prisoner, causing him to cough once, as if the pain that he inflicted could somehow ease the pain in his own soul.

"But why kill Carrie if all you had to do was send me back to save your father?"

"That's easy to explain also," Kyle said as a wicked grin returned to his bloody lips, "she simply got in the way."

Blind rage swelled within Fletcher as his thoughts returned to pummeling Kyle's face into an unrecognizable pulp. Just as he was raising his fist, the third crate shifted again, knocking both of them over. Fletcher quickly struggled to get back up but Kyle was on top of him, grabbing at his belt. They struggled for a moment then separated, leaving the assassin holding the flare gun in his hand, leveled directly at Fletcher.

"You had your chance, Uncle," Kyle scoffed, raising his voice above the deafening wind, "but instead you wanted to talk, to understand why I'm the way I am." He raised the gun a bit to aim it directly at the major's head. "So you lose. Vengeance is sweet."

"Why do you keep saying that?" Fletcher asked, hoping to keep him talking while he thought of a way out of this. He had no illusions that his armor would save him from a hot flare at point blank range. "Vengeance for what?"

"Why, for killing me."

"Killing you?"

"You let my father die in that jet while you survived," Kyle's voice took on an almost child-like whine. "You should have died, not him. Killing you is the only way to make it right."

Fletcher felt a pain in his chest at the memory of Con dying the first time, knowing that it was something he had to let happen again somehow. "You don't understand," he tried to explain. "I was miserable when your father died. I would have traded places with him in a moment. That's why I couldn't let him die when I went back."

"Then why kill him now?" the boy assassin protested vehemently.

"Because of what you are…what you've done, Kyle. You personify everything that Justin warned us about."

Both were caught off guard as the truck began to curve to the left as it closed in on a bridge that traversed a wide crevice. The crate closed in on them again and they both turned instinctively to block it by pressing their backs against one crate and pushing against the moving one. They strained together as they kept from being crushed; and as the truck stabilized again and the crate stopped moving, they both let out a long breath, then stared at each other.

"Too bad, huh?" Kyle asked, for a moment losing his sneer as he wiped some blood from his mouth with the back of his hand.

Fletcher nodded.

"But not bad enough," Kyle said as he started to lift the gun again.

Instantly the major was in motion as he dove at the assassin, bringing him down as they struggled for control of the flare gun. They fell to the flatbed, all their hands on the gun, as they pushed and pulled at the weapon. Then a divot in the road bumped them to the right, as they half slid off the truck, their torsos hanging off the edge of the flatbed.

Self preservation instincts took over as Fletcher let go with one hand and grabbed the rope that kept the tarp down. "Give it up or we'll both fall," he yelled over the thunder of the engine and the scream of the wind.

Kyle pushed back at the major, causing him to scramble for a better grip. Then he forced the flare down to Fletcher's head and pulled the trigger—firing nothing.

The assassin let out a frustrated yell as Fletcher jumped back at him, pushing the gun away as he saw the spark within that indicated that the weapon was only delayed somehow. The gun went off an instant later, sending the flare streaking along the side of the truck where it struck a side mirror and exploded the glass window on the driver's side. The semi veered sharply to the right, just as it began to cross the bridge.

Both combatants stared in shock as the truck plowed through the side railing and launched itself into the air some hundred feet above the river below. The last thing Fletcher was able to do was pull himself off the flatbed, as the eighteen wheeler struck the shallow water in a roaring explosion of water, metal, and rock.

There were a few moments of watery blackness that Fletcher thought he had finally died, then his head broke the water and he quickly engulfed a lung full of sweet air. The truck was less than fifty feet away, twisted and destroyed with more than half of it still above the water. A body lay on the far shore, and the major quickly waded over to it to get a better look. It was the truck driver, who lay face down in the muddy bank.

Fletcher's lips tightened at the thought of another death that shouldn't have happened in the past, when he heard a soft groan from the body below him. Careful not to move him too fast, the major gently rolled the driver over. The older Arab was badly hurt, but still alive. Fletcher quickly took a piece of the driver's shirt and ripped it off, tying it around his head to stop the deep gash that was there. Once he felt that the driver was stable for the moment he began the task of searching for Kyle.

The wreckage of the truck had burst into flames, leaving no point of looking near it. He then searched both banks up and down the river for a hundred feet, but there was no sign of the young rogue Skimmer. Suddenly Fletcher realized he hadn't really wanted it to end this way and he searched once more for Con's son.

The voice from above caught him totally off guard.

"You all right down there," came a strong Texas accent.

Fletcher looked up into the bright night and saw an American HMMWV, High Mobility Multipurpose Wheeled Vehicle on the bridge, with two men in desert camouflage staring down at him.

"Air Force or Army?" he called up to the soldiers in the Hummer.

"Air Force," the Texan answered with pride.

"I'm Major Fletcher Taylor, USAF," he called back up, deepening his tone with authority. "I've got an injured man down here, I need your help at once."

"Yes, sir," they responded together as they rushed down the embankment.

Within fifteen minutes they had the truck driver on a makeshift stretcher on the back of their Hummer. It turned out that the two young airmen were stationed at the same airbase he had been, and didn't question his authority, or strange dress at all as they jumped in the vehicle.

"What's the time, Airman?" Fletcher asked the Texan, remembering that his mission had taken place just past dawn.

"Oh-five hundred hours, sir. The sun should rise in the next half hour or so."

The major's eyes went wide at the lateness of the hour. "How far are we from base?"

"Three quarters of an hour."

"I have to be at the airbase for a mission within the next half hour, Airman."

"Sir?" the Texan questioned.

"Punch it, Airman," he ordered.

The young Texan put the pedal to the floor as the Hummer quickly pulled back onto the highway and sped towards the airbase, as the first hint of sunlight began to stretch its fingers across the desert sands.

Fletcher made it his personal responsibility to watch over the injured truck driver as the Hummer flew along the desert roadway at speeds which pushed the outer envelope of the vehicle specifications. There were times that he was fearful that they would arrive too late, as he had with Carrie, but as the airbase came into view the Texan proudly informed the major that they had made it in just under twenty-five minutes.

The Air Force special security at the gate had glared at the mud-covered, scarlet and black armored officer with a suspecting eye. However, the shift leader was a friend of Fletcher's and waved them through at the sight of him, but not before landing a crack at the "Halloween" costume, which the major informed him was a test flight suit.

Once inside the base, Fletcher quickly jumped off the Hummer.

"Take this man to the base hospital immediately," he ordered the airmen.

"Yes, sir," the Texan responded, but then gave the major a concerned glance. "Sir, you might want to report there yourself. You were in the accident also, and y'all do look like you lost an argument with an angry alligator."

Despite his exhaustion, Fletcher let out a small laugh, not doubting for a moment how terrible his bruised and battered appearance must seem to the young soldier. "You're quite right, Airman. I'll head there as soon as I check in with my flight commander."

Seemingly satisfied with that answer, the airmen drove off with the wounded driver, leaving Fletcher to his own agenda. Instantly the major went on alert, he knew that he had to be careful not to run into himself at the wrong moment. Slinking into the shadows behind the hangar, he ran over what had happened the last time he was here and tried to figure out the best way to handle the situation. The answer was simple—intercept himself when he had first came here from *Twilight* after Carrie's death and stop himself from ever running into the Fletcher who was about to go on his mission with Con. Taking a deep breath, he started to head around the hangar to where he remembered Skimming in the first time.

Almost instantly, his ankle began to throb again with almost blinding pain, making him wonder just how badly it was broken. He kept close to the wall, which was just shy of pitch black under the shadows of the large building. Inside, he could hear the engines of the F-15Es warming up, giving him warm assurance that he hadn't arrived too late.

The sky was beginning to slowly dissolve from inky black to subtle tones of violet and ruby as the sun began its daily journey, and Fletcher forced himself to limp faster to make sure he would arrive in time.

He was just rounding the first corner of the hanger, when he caught the glint of light on metal as the iron pipe swung out and connected with the lower part of his wounded leg with a crash. Letting out a muffled yell, Fletcher fell to the ground, holding his shattered shin with both hands in shock and agony. Then he glanced up at the disheveled figure in black that loomed above him like an angel of death.

"Game's over, Phantom…" came from a bloodied and burnt Kyle who held his makeshift weapon in fists clenched with malice, "you lose."

Before the major could even ask how he had survived the crash and gotten here at the same time, the pipe came down like a headman's ax. Fletcher pulled himself to the side but the iron bar still skimmed off his head with a loud crack, sending him reeling to the left. For a moment he lay there as dizzying bright lights swam in his mind and nausea wracked his body. Then the salty flavor of his own blood that flowed down his face trickled into his mouth, bringing him back with its stark taste. He could hear the grunted laughs between gulps of air that came from the wounded assassin.

"You thought it would be that easy," Kyle scoffed as he wiped some of his own blood off his face, "didn't you?"

Fletcher didn't answer as he built his strength up for a final assault, fearful that he wouldn't last much longer than that. He knew he now had a concussion to add to his list of injuries, and his head was still bleeding badly; he was running out of time. Taking in a deep breath, he swung out his good leg, catching the rogue Skimmer off guard as the iron pipe rose in the air again for what was to be a death blow.

As the young assassin fell backwards, the metal pipe flew out of Kyle's hands, firmly imbedding itself in the ground next to the hangar's steel wall. Springing instantly back, the rogue Skimmer was up and ready for action, just as Fletcher pushed himself to his feet with his good leg.

"Still a little spunk left, old man?" came the hateful stab as he took a swing with his gauntlet hand, which Fletcher just barely managed to block with his arm.

"You haven't won yet, Kyle."

The major feigned with his left hand and swung out with his right, landing his fist firmly on the assassin's jaw. The blow staggered the young Skimmer as a tooth came flying out of his mouth along with blood-laced saliva. Not giving him a chance to recover, Fletcher tried to advance to strike him again, but his crippled leg gave out as the fracture grew, throwing him to the ground in blinding pain.

For a moment Kyle stared at the older Skimmer with a deep satisfaction as a cruel smile came to his cracked lips. Then he kicked out with his boot, slamming it into Fletcher's abdomen. Armor struck armor as the major felt the wind knocked out of him as he lay there, trying to muster the strength to get back up. Again the young assassin kicked the major, and again, and again, until he wasn't moving anymore. The rogue assassin let out a hollow laugh as he pushed his enemy with his foot to verify his status. The major let out a soft groan, almost inaudibly.

"Don't you know when to die, old man?" Kyle sneered.

Fletcher forced himself to swim through the blackness that threatened to envelope him, focusing with the anger that was still vibrant within him.

"Don't you know when to shut up?" he managed to retort, then pushed himself up with his arms and struck out and up with his good leg, putting in every bit of strength he still possessed, catching the assassin in the chest with the surprise blow. The impact knocked the young man off his feet from the force of it, to fall back into the hangar wall, where the iron pipe stood upright in patient silence. The sharpened metal bar caught Kyle between the joints of his armor, piercing his back as he tried to stop his fall. With a sickening crack the crimson slicked iron pipe burst through his check plate, as the young man finally fell to the ground, the bar sticking straight up through him.

Kyle's eyes opened wide with shock as the realization of what had happened struck home. Then they narrowed with concentrated hatred as he stared up at the major.

"You haven't won," the dying youth sputtered through the dark blood that was flowing out of his mouth. "I'll still win in the end."

Fletcher pulled himself back to his feet as he stared at his nemesis blankly, no emotional signs giving hints to his inner mood, as a pool of blood spread out from under the assassin. Kyle gave two more short gasps, then his eyes fixed open like two lifeless grey marbles as his body stopped moving. The major leaned over and closed the youth's eyes and stared at him for a moment in silence, when the unmistakable static burst of a person Skimming in drew his attention like a shot fired.

Biting down the white hot pain, he began limping around the side of the hangar, trying to get to the place where he remembered Skimming in the first time. As he came around to the front of the hangar, he caught his breath as the early dawn shone brightly off the two F-15Es that stood ready, their twin

# TWILIGHT

engines humming brightly—

Then he saw him, the he who had been sent back the first time. He was obviously dazed and confused, as he walked towards the jet as if it held his salvation. Then a voice just to his right sent off warning alarms as he heard himself talking with Con as the two Air Force officers emerged from the hanger. Fletcher quickly flattened himself against the outside wall of the building as panic started to rush through him like a tidal wave. *Not again*, his mind screamed as he frantically looked around for an idea to hit him. Then he saw a Coke can on the gravel next to his foot as an old memory jumped his mind into action. Quickly picking it up, he threw the can at himself, the major on his way to his mission. The can struck Major Taylor in the back, causing him to glance around.

"What's up?" Con asked him as he caught up to his friend, wondering why he had stopped.

Major Taylor glanced down at the can as a curt smile came to his lips. "I think our friend Warlock is up to his old games again. Let's check it out."

The two Air Force pilots walked back into the dark hangar bay, calling out to their wingmen. As they passed within a few feet of the disheveled major hidden in the shadows, he held his breath, half expecting the younger version of himself to vanish as he had once before. But when they passed safely into the building and out of sight he let out a sigh of relief, realizing that the phenomena that would only allow one of them to exist in a time frame must have something to do with eye contact.

Fletcher knew he had only bought himself a few seconds at best. Biting down hard to endure the pain, he swiftly hobbled across the field to the waiting jets, to where the other him—the stunned Skimmer who had just arrived—was reading the name on the side of the F-15E in wonder.

Without hesitation, he put his hand on the shoulder of the other him and spun him around to face him. For a brief moment he could read the utter pain and torment in this Fletcher's eyes, eyes that had just watched Carrie die for the first time. Then that Fletcher faded away into a blurred non-existence, leaving the older Fletcher wiping away the blood that dripped into his eyes, to be sure of what he had done. Without hesitating a second, he limped back to the side of the hangar, just as the younger him walked back out with Con, a scowl on his face.

"Don't sweat it, Phantom," Con laughed.

Major Taylor let out a sigh, as he patted his friend on the shoulder and walked out to his F-15E.

The rising sun began to diminish the shadows around the hangar, but Fletcher stayed and watched the younger him climb into the jet with his co-pilot, as their two wingmen climbed into theirs. It was only after both fighters had taken off and were diminishing into the distance that he finally struggled to move.

"Good-bye, Con," he whispered, then began to limp back to where Kyle still lay in the dark shadows of the other side of the hanger. As he struggled along an itch of a thought began to gnaw at the back of his mind as it slowly scratched to the surface. It was only when he had reached the dead assassin, and gazed at his lifeless body, that the thought coalesced into something tangible. *Why haven't I vanished as well?* he silently challenged. *By stopping myself from stopping myself from going on my mission, I've eliminated the cause that created Kyle and eventually sent me back.* He continued to stare at the dead youth, feeling that both of them should have vanished into the time stream when the F-15s took off. Then he recalled his Skimmer training, and Justin telling him that the *Twilight* complex was shielded from temporal paradoxes. Since the original event—Kyle killing Carrie and sending him back—occurred in the complex, that's why nothing seemed to have changed, even though everything was fixed.

Or was it? Fletcher's mind continued to rationale out the scenario as all the possibilities played out in his mind. Kyle had said that the Omni computer was watching multiple dimensions as well as time streams. If he fixed his own dimension by stopping himself from stopping himself, then Kyle was never born—*except* for the fact that Kyle had appeared in *Twilight before* he had the chance to stop himself and change history. *What if Kyle could somehow start it all over again?* Feeling his fear rise and his head pound he quickly scanned both his own cracked WCD and that of the dead youth. His LCD screen was cracked, but the power crystal was obviously still working since he was able to haze earlier. The smoke he saw earlier from Kyle's WCD may have come from the power crystal, which meant his screen was still working. Kneeling over the body, he quickly opened up the burned out WCD of the dead youth and felt a rush of hope flood his body. The screen seemed intact. With the care a father holds his newborn infant, Fletcher removed the working WCD screen from Kyle's wrist unit and replaced his own cracked one with it—instantly he was rewarded with bright colors as the unit came back to life. The return circuits were still fused; however, and the only point of re-entry to *Twilight* would be the same moment that he had arrived the last time, which had gotten him to the scene too late to stop the shooting.

Gritting his teeth in determination, he pulled the bloody iron bar from Kyle's body and pressed the flashing return button, flooding the shadows with azure light.

The Departure Nucleus came back into view, disorienting him for a moment. At the doorway, he saw his own back as he turned to the right and ran into Doctor Kesseler. For the briefest of seconds this confused him, then he realized that the Nucleus' own safety devices had delayed him a few seconds to prevent two people from Skimming in at the same time.

Sender was standing behind the control console, as he had been the last time he arrived, but the expression of total confusion on his face almost made the major smile. Before the older Skimmer could even try to ask why two Fletchers had appeared within seconds of each other, the major put up a hand.

"Don't ask," Fletcher said with a forced smile, "I'll explain later."

As he limped off the departure pad he almost fell and Sender came over to him immediately.

"I'll be fine."

"You need a med tech right away," Sender observed as he noted the bloody footprints that the major was leaving behind.

"No time," Fletcher explained as he quickly moved towards the door, leaving the stunned Skimmer behind.

As he reached the doorway he could hear the other him talking with the doctor, as the shocking news of Carrie's pregnancy came back to him in a rush.

*Why didn't she tell me?* echoed in his mind, but he forced it quickly out, realizing that it was this conversation that had slowed him the last time. Turning to the left to avoid the other him and the doctor, he shut his mind off to the pain as he began to half run, half limp towards the observation hall. Although he realized that this way was longer, it would enter the observation hall at the other end, much closer to where the battle had taken place. His head throbbed to the brink of dizziness as he raised a hand to where he was struck, bringing it back down covered in matted blood. He realized that he must have lost a lot of it by now, and for a moment all threatened to go black as he staggered against the wall close to the observation hall and closed his eyes.

They opened again with a start and he quickly wondered if he had lost consciousness temporarily. A desperate panic ran through him as he realized that he would be arriving too late once again. Letting out a scream of rage mixed with pain, he forced himself forward at his best speed, entering the hall and rounding the curve that led to where the battle had happened.

He saw a clean but confused Fletcher and Carrie, staring in bewilderment at the ebony assassin who was just raising his gun as the last traces of azure light faded away.

"Carrie," he called out as he limped out into the open where they could all see him.

She turned and took a half step towards the almost dead Skimmer just as the assassin's gun went off—sending a lethal beam of energy forward that barely slipped past her head, only a few inches off mark from her sudden movement. Fletcher's weary body filled with both elation and trepidation as he realized this was his one chance. Taking in a sharp breath for support, he brought up the bloodied iron bar and hurled it with all his strength at the rogue Skimmer.

The metal spear struck the shocked assassin right below the chin of the black helmet, penetrating the thinner latex armor covering and skewering through his neck. Kyle's body stood still for a moment, as blood poured out of both sides of his neck, then he fell forward with an almost silent motion. The three of them stared at his still form for a second, then he vanished in an azure flash.

Fletcher gazed at the spot that Kyle had been then glanced up to find himself facing the other him and Carrie, as well as the third him that came running from the other direction at the sound of the shot. For a moment the three Fletchers stared at each other, one understanding, and the other two only guessing what was in each of their minds. As if in answer to a silent unasked question, slowly the youngest disappeared, as if blown away by a gentle breeze; then the second one, who had arrived too late, vanished like smoke in the air; leaving only the third, who was barely able to stand.

Carrie let out a soft gasp as the Fletcher next to her evaporated, then she looked over to the one that was left, the tale of his unknown odyssey written over his body in burns and blood.

"Fletcher," she called out as she ran over to him and pulled him into her arms, her eyes swelling with tears over the hurt in his body. "Please," she pleaded softly into his bruised ear, "I don't understand what's happened here."

He smiled weakly as he put his arms around her and brought her in close. "Neither do I, and I was there." Then he sank to his knees, as his body finally lost the ongoing battle it had been fighting, and sweet darkness came to engulf him.

*Epilogue*
# Twilight

There are different pivotal moments in a person's life that will always be remembered. For Fletcher Taylor, AKA Phantom, one of the high ones was when despite all that had happened, he realized he was still alive.

"He's awake," announced a relieved Paula Kesseler, as he opened his eyes to the soft lights of the med lab.

"Thank God," came a voice to his right, which with its very sound filled his heart, making it a second pivotal point happening right after the first.

"Carrie," he whispered as he gazed over at her and took her soft hand in his. There were tears in her eyes as she pulled his arm against her chest and cradled it there, then flashed her quirky smile at him.

"I told her most of what happened," Justin explained as he emerged from behind Carrie to stand next to her.

"Then I did it?" Fletcher asked, half knowing the answer. "All is set back to the way it was."

The *Twilight* leader nodded with a warm twinkle in his hazel eyes. "You did it, Phantom."

Suddenly that last confrontation flooded back into the major's mind, raising questions that had no answers. "Why did the other two Fletchers disappear? I thought *Twilight* was protected from that."

"It is," Justin confirmed with a smile. "But I was watching the whole scene on my viewer, and when I realized that you'd won, I shut down the temporal shielding in the observation hall for five seconds. Not long enough to damage the section, but long enough for the other two to vanish."

Fletcher's brow creased in confusion. "But how did you know to watch that specific area at that specific time? The whole thing couldn't have lasted more than half a minute."

The *Twilight* leader put his hand on the major's shoulder and let out a soft chuckle. "You warned me all about it…twenty years ago…remember?"

Fletcher let out a short laugh and squeezed Carrie's hand in his, reveling in the vibrant warmth. "I suppose I did." He gazed up into her sea of jade and almost melted, then he lifted his other hand and gently wiped away her tears.

"I can see you two have much to talk about," Justin said after subtly clearing his throat. "Doctor, why don't we get some breakfast."

"Why not," Paula said with a smile as she ushered Eric out of the med room, followed by the *Twilight* leader. Kim moved out of the shadows where she had been waiting and gave Fletcher's shoulder a caring squeeze. Then she flashed the two of them a grin, and left as well.

Once alone, they held each other for a few minutes, and then Fletcher sat up and pulled her next to him on the bed, his face growing serious. "Why didn't you tell me about the child?"

Carrie's face went blank for a moment. "How did you know?"

He let out a short laugh and put his hand on hers. "Jumping through the same moment in time over and over has some advantages. But you didn't answer my question."

She hesitated a moment longer, her eyes searching his for the answer to her soul. "I was afraid…" was what finally came out.

"Afraid?"

"I was going to tell you," she admitted, "but I didn't want you loving me for that, and you seemed distant, as if you didn't want to commit."

He nodded, remembering his emotions before the incident. "You were absolutely right, but that's always been my problem. Sometimes you have to lose something to understand just how much it means to you."

"And now?" she asked, her eyes seeming to shimmer with each word he said.

He smiled and pulled her hand to his lips, lightly brushing them against her silken skin. Then he gazed directly into her jade pools and softly squeezed her hand. "Would you believe me, if I told you that I've loved you since you were five years old?"

She slowly bit her bottom lip as she tried to understand what his words were supposed to mean, then her face lit up as a realization struck her. "Oh my God…it was you on the yacht who saved me…wasn't it?"

His smile spread from ear to ear as he turned a light shade of pink, confirming her revelation. She threw her arms around him and pressed her lips to his, as he returned the embrace with fiery passion. Briefly raising her mouth from his she looked into his deep blue eyes.

"I love you too," she whispered as she reclaimed his mouth, smothering any possible response with her kisses.

Neither noticed the thin frame of the *Twilight* leader as he hovered in the shadow of the doorway. He allowed himself a small grin of self pride, then turned and disappeared down the corridor.

"So," Fletcher said with a smile as they eventually pulled apart, "we're going to be parents, aren't we?"

Carrie laughed in return. "I guess we are."

He hugged her tightly again, his eyes flashing over to where Justin had been, as the obviousness of all that he had learned in his journey finally, really, sank in. "And you want to know what," he said with a wide grin as he gazed back at her, "I know just what to name him."

"Him?" she asked playfully. "How do you know it's a him?"

"It's a long story," he said with a warm twinkle in his blue eyes. "One that started on the day you Skimmed into my life."

"But I haven't done that yet…"

"You know what?" he said as he lifted his lips to hers and gave her a light kiss. "Sometimes stories begin at the end."

Printed in the United States
26111LVS00004B/258